Death at a Dumpster:
The Stabbing, The Sex
& The Sequel

Jan 27 2010

Death at a Dumpster:
The Stabbing, The Sex
& The Sequel

A crime novel
Based on a murder at the Jersey Shore

Best wishes —

Linda Ellis

Linda Ellis

A Crime Time publication

ISBN: 0-75960-363-4

This book is printed on acid free paper.

1stBooks - rev. 1/18/01

And this is the story we will share...

People would converge on a spring night, a Saturday night in 1982 at the Jersey shore.

One of them wouldn't be going home.

It was a cold-blooded murder spurred by the heat of lust and greed. Mistakes were made.

Nevertheless, it could quite easily have been a perfect crime.

It is only because one of the players was rendered stone stupid by an insatiable appetite for sex – a special kind of nothing-to-do-with-love sex – that this case ever reached a courtroom.

Eighteen years later, the family of the victim is able to shed the black of mourning and don the blood red of retaliation. Enraged by what they saw as inadequate punishment meted out by a court, the grieving family has a new opportunity for dark justice.

More than one family seeks closure. Another victim has been mourned all these years.

It's a race for revenge. Who will win?

vi

In memory of my mother
Who left me books and baseball
And of Grace and John's mother
Who left too soon

Author's note

This crime novel is a fictional nugget culled from extensive interviews, original research and a review of the police files and medical records attached to several homicide investigations.

Individual, municipal, corporate and place names are fictitious. Resemblance to people living or dead is coincidental. Situations are, in the main, picked from a pool of documented events.

Dumpster™ is a trademark of Dempster Brothers, Inc., Knoxville, TN

Acknowledgements

The unconditional love 24/7 of my officemate Guinness, a dog of amazing grace and unbounded joy.

The contribution of Gerry Campion, Newark NJ attorney, was the *sine qua non*. Of all the newsrooms in all the world we wandered into one of the best.

Dominick Dunne, who perfected this genre of reality based fiction.

I'm blessed to have people near and/or dear who are grounded in reality. For sharing their realities, I thank:

Dave, beloved husband and great teacher.

Margo and Ross. They make us proud to be parents.

Donna Jenkins Clapp, the wind beneath my wings.

The women of McMaster and Wilson courts.

The Nordonia Hills and Wrentham book clubs.

The Cleveland Indians radio broadcast team.

Above all, Godspeed to the child to whom I promised this story all those years ago.

Contents

Prologue

The call came in at 7:22 p.m. to Boothbay NJ police headquarters. The dispatcher at headquarters notified the patrol car in the area of First Avenue and Cable Court that a woman had been attacked in an alley.

When the first police officer arrived, he found Felicia Cusack, 44, lying in a pool of her own blood, the victim of 22 stab wounds to the neck, stomach, chest, arms and hands.

She was barely alive.

Her husband, a cop himself, stood by shaken and incoherent.

"The fucking maniac stabbed her," Larry Cusack, 43, repeated over and over.

An ambulance arrived; attendants lifted Felicia into it and sped off to Harbor Medical Center, two minutes away. She was slipping in and out of consciousness. One of the ambulance attendants noticed with pity that Felicia's large brown eyes were full of pain.

At the emergency room, medical staff people cut her chest wall for open heart massage, inserted tubes that pumped in blood plasma and linked her to a respirator. It was no use.

At 8:30 that evening, a priest and a physician were sent to tell her waiting husband that Felicia Girardi Cusack, hard-working and much-loved mother of two, devoted wife of Larry, daughter of Carmen and sister of 12 siblings was dead.

Introduction

The witnesses were finished. The evidence was in. The defense attorney and the prosecutor had given their summations. Now it was up to the judge to give the case to the jury and then for the jury to decide.

Maybe it would take hours, maybe days, but, unless the jury failed to decide, the case would be over - one way or another.

So many months had passed. So much had happened. Now the case would come to an end.

Sheriff's officers locked the courtroom doors. The spectators in the back of the court were free to stay and listen to the judge, but if they did stay, they couldn't leave until she was done. This was no time for the jury to be distracted by people coming and going in the court.

Proof, doubt, circumstantial evidence, common sense - those were the things the judge told the jury about.

Guilt, the judge said, had to be proved beyond a reasonable doubt. Reasonable doubt doesn't mean an imaginary doubt or a possible doubt, but something real, something probable. It was up to the prosecution to prove the case beyond a reasonable doubt. The defense didn't have to prove anything, but, as jurors, they should consider anything the defense had to say that disproved guilt.

Yes, you can use circumstantial evidence, the judge said, but you have to use it carefully. Here's a thought that will help:

Assume you go to bed at night and there is no snow on the ground. In the morning, you get up, look out your window and see snow on the ground. You didn't see it snow, but you have circumstantial evidence that proves it snowed.

How do you decide guilt or innocence? You use ordinary common sense, the judge told the jurors. You weigh everything you've heard. You decide who told the truth and who didn't.

Don't rely on what the lawyers said the evidence proves. Rely on what you think the important evidence is and what it proves. Listen to what the other jurors have to say. Don't be afraid to change your mind if you think they're right. Don't be afraid to try to convince them if you think they're wrong and you're right.

Reaching a unanimous decision is important, but it isn't so important that you should vote for a verdict you don't think is right.

A trial is supposed to be a search for the truth. The prosecution presents its version of the truth. The defense presents its version of the truth. In the end, the jury decides the truth.

Truth on that pleasant fall day was the answer to a simple question:

Who killed Felicia Cusack?

Mrs. Cusack was by most standards an average, even an ordinary woman - a middle-aged, middle-class housewife who had lived in a New Jersey suburb with a husband and two children. She was loved by many, disliked by few. Her life choices would be known in Germany as *kinder, kirche und kuchen*: children, church and kitchen.

What was extraordinary about Felicia Cusack was the vicious, gut-wrenching way that she died.

Discovering why she was killed and convicting the person responsible for her murder became an obsession for many people: lawyers, police and, above all, her family.

The prosecutor remembered going to the spot where she was attacked and seeing the pool of blood. He remembered going to the hospital and seeing her body.

These were images that stayed in his mind and still made him angry. He had known her alive; this case was tough for him.

The family of the victim - her husband, her children, her brothers, her sisters, her father - had been in the courtroom every day of the trial.

In the months before anyone was arrested, her relatives fought with police, trying to get them to arrest the person they were sure was guilty. Her family, hard working, mostly law abiding people, even considered taking the law into their own hands when they thought that the law would never reveal the truth.

When the judge was finished with her charge, the court clerk drew the names of two of the 14 jurors from a drum. Now the jury was down to the 12 men and women.

After the sheriff's officers took an oath to guard the jury and make sure no one interfered with their deliberations, the jury left the courtroom to do its work.

Now there was nothing left for everyone else in the courtroom to do but wait - wait and remember.

Part I

The Murder. 1982

Chapter 1

The Crime

At 6:30 a.m. on the morning of March 20, 1982, Larry Cusack took the 9 millimeter Walther PPK out of the kitchen cabinet where he always kept it.

He took a clip out of the cabinet and loaded the automatic. It was the weapon he carried to and from work as a cop in Webster. As he stepped out of the house, he found himself alone on the street at that hour on a Saturday morning. He was due at the station to start the 8 a.m. shift, and he had an almost phobic dread of being late for anything.

As he pulled out of the driveway, his wife Felicia, at 44 a year older than her husband, cleared the table of the dishes he had used for his light breakfast of coffee and toast. Their children, 11-year-old John and 13-year-old Grace, were still asleep.

Home for the Cusacks was a four-bedroom colonial in a place called Gullwing Cove. It's a small town in a part of New Jersey known as the Jersey Shore or just the Shore, about an hour south of New York City and 10 minutes from the Atlantic Ocean.

In 1954 the Garden State Parkway opened, and that made it easy to get from a home at the Shore to a job in New York or northern New Jersey in a reasonable time. The opening of the Parkway started a building boom that transformed Gullwing Cove and the bigger towns around it from summer resorts and farming towns into suburbs.

The Cove was a tight-knit bedroom community, population 5,500 in 1982. The median house price was $89,000. The schools produced students who

3

Linda Ellis

went on to do above-average work at the regional high school. The municipal facilities and services were viewed as superior and the streets were considered safe. Many surrounding communities admired the Cove's annual Memorial Day event. The main event was a parade that showcased the town and its veterans, its service and youth groups, school bands, ball teams, fire engines and police cars.

Felicia and Larry Cusack had spent time in the summer at the Shore and they decided it would be a great place to raise a family. Like many other men at the Shore, Larry became a commuter.

*   *   *

Larry's day at work was routine. Even police work could be boring at times. He and his partner, Joe Maloney, investigated two domestic disturbances and the theft of furniture from a cargo holding area at the port. The partners had had to break up a knife fight in one of the domestics but the guy, goofy on heroin, had collapsed like a house of cards.

"Heroin is a good drug if they're gonna do drugs," Maloney said as they left that scene. "They just sort of fold up, real quiet."

They spent more time on the paperwork than they had at the scene.

"If I didn't know better I'd nail Felicia for taking off with that furniture. She always wants more stuff," Cusack joked with Maloney as their Saturday was winding down towards 4 p.m. "What she needs is a treadmill, not a corner cupboard for the dining room. She looks at food, she gains."

4

Maloney had heard his partner complain about Felicia's weight several times. It made Maloney uncomfortable.

"Hey, she works hard, two jobs, the kids, all that crap that women have to do. She cooks meals all the time; she's not supposed to eat a meal? Give her a break," Larry's partner lectured. "If my ex had done all that she wouldn't be my ex."

On Saturdays, Felicia cleaned the house, picked up groceries at the supermarket or went to the mall to shop. People who knew Felicia well considered her meticulous about keeping her house clean. She held a part-time job as a secretary for an auto parts manufacturer in Lincoln Village, eight miles from home, and when she returned home at 4:30 she would clean or do laundry. The other two workdays she was the Cove's liaison to tenants of the senior citizens' apartment building.

On this Saturday, she took a half hour to run over to the beauty shop that Larry's sister owned. She had her thick wavy hair teased and sprayed. Then, back home, she turned the telephone ringer off so that she wouldn't be interrupted while she dusted and vacuumed.

Around 5:00, Felicia telephoned her sister, Gerry Bucci, who lived in Barrington, a town about 10 miles away from Gullwing Cove. Almost every day Felicia talked to her, often two or three times a day, and that afternoon she called to wish her a happy birthday and talk about plans for that night. Felicia had hoped to go to Gerry's to give her a card and have some birthday cake. Now, she told Gerry, she and Larry might do something else. The Cusacks had friends who were hosting an engagement party for a niece, and she told Gerry she wanted to go there.

"You won't be mad?" Felicia asked.

"No," Gerry assured her. "You planned it. You go."

"Can I come over tomorrow for dinner?"

"Sure, don't worry about it. I won't even touch the cake," Gerry said. Felicia worried about hurting her sister's feelings because the bonds between them were stronger than the bonds that normally tie two sisters nine years apart in age.

In 1964, when Felicia was 26, married and out of the house and Gerry was 17 and still in school, their mother died. Gerry needed someone to look to for the kind of help and advice a 17-year-old girl can't get from a father. So she had turned to Felicia and thought of her more as a second mother than as an older sister.

Before the conversation ended, Felicia said she still might have time to see Gerry that night. It all depended on whether Larry worked a double shift, something he often did for extra money.

"If Larry doesn't come home, I'll be over at 7:30 for cake and coffee."

Felicia, still worried about Gerry's feelings, told her several times how sorry she was about leaving her plans hanging in the air.

"Stay as sweet as you are. I love you," Felicia said and hung up.

Larry went off duty at 4 and got home shortly after 5. Earlier in the week he and Felicia had talked about seeing a movie, possibly with the children or possibly with some friends, Jeff and Jenny Russo. In any event, the Russos couldn't go, and, as Larry remembers it, the children didn't want to go. Felicia agreed to forget about the engagement party and seeing Gerry. Larry overruled her on most decisions and this was to be no exception. Because they were going to the movies alone, they decided to see the R-rated *Richard Pryor, Live on the Sunset Strip.* They left home at about 7 to make the 7:30 show at a movie theater in Boothbay, a town next to Gullwing Cove.

The signs of spring were in the air that night. It was still cool, but the winter chill was gone. It was warm enough that Felicia didn't have to wear a coat. She wanted instead to wear a leather jacket that was a twin to one she had bought for Larry several years ago.

As they were leaving the house, Larry saw the leather coat and had a fit. "Don't wear that coat. You don't need it. I told you to wear a sweater."

Felicia complied, as she always did, and wore a heavy sweater that Larry's mother had knit for her.

On their way to the movies, they stopped at a 7-Eleven and Larry bought Felicia a pack of Barclays. Felicia had smoked Carltons; she was switching brands thinking that would help her stop smoking.

The Cusacks were going to a part of Boothbay called the South Strip, an upper middle-class neighborhood with high-rise oceanfront condominiums and well-kept homes and garden apartments.

The Cusacks knew the South Strip well. They occasionally ate at Dublin, a popular restaurant at the corner of First Avenue and Cable Court and two blocks from the theater. Just the night before they had been to the restaurant for dinner with Larry's friends in the Gullwing Cove Lions Club.

That night, the Richard Pryor movie was at a theater on First Avenue, a main street that runs

7

parallel to the ocean. Two films were playing at the theater that night. The other movie was called *Amin* and dealt with former Ugandan dictator Big Daddy Amin.

Instead of parking in the lot behind the theater or on First Avenue near the theater, Larry parked in a lot off Cable Court across from Dublin because he wanted to go there for a drink after the movies.

There were about 300 people in Dublin that night. For the restaurant and other businesses along the beachfront, winter meant bad business. Many businesses closed for the winter but not the larger restaurants.

March is a time when the restaurant's bookings begin to pick up after the slow period. To boost business, Dublin holds a St. Patrick's festival. The mood inside the restaurant was festive that night. Waitresses were dressed in Irish costumes instead of uniforms. There was ample food and Irish brews flowed freely. A buffet was offered on a table that looked like a shamrock. Waitresses with good voices sang Irish ballads and sometimes customers, moved by the atmosphere or the Guinness, joined in.

There were two performances by Irish step dancers, one at 8 and another at 11.

By the time Larry and Felicia drove into the lot across from the restaurant, Grace Brown, a 64-year-old widow, had been sitting in her Cadillac in the lot for about five minutes. She was due at a dinner at Dublin but did not want to walk through the dark lot alone. She had decided to wait in her car, with the lights out, for someone to come by.

When Felicia and Larry were about 15 feet beyond her car, Mrs. Brown got out and started walking behind them toward the restaurant. They gave no indication that they saw or heard her as they headed toward First Avenue.

Instead of going all the way to First, Larry and Felicia turned into a 20-foot wide driveway parallel to First Avenue to take a shortcut to the theater. People who walked in that neighborhood often used the driveway for a short cut. Some customers at Dublin even parked in spots off it.

"I dropped my keys," Larry said to Felicia and they stopped in the driveway near some parked cars and an overflowing Dumpster. "I got to go find them. Wait right here. I'll be back."

"Make sure the doors are locked," Felicia said.

"Yeah, OK," Larry replied.

Mrs. Brown, not yet in the restaurant, saw Larry and Felicia stop in the driveway, and then she saw Larry head back toward the parking lot.

Felicia, thinking she was alone, stood facing the parking lot, watching her husband, waiting for him to come back. She didn't know - she couldn't have imagined – that someone was hiding behind one of the cars parked near her.

Suddenly, Felicia sensed a person behind her and felt almost immediately, a shocking, jolting pain below her right shoulder. She felt a hand trying to grip her.

"Larry! Larry!" Felicia screamed.

Larry, hearing his wife yell, stopped and turned around. Grace Brown heard a cry too and looked over toward the alley. She could no longer see Felicia.

The attacker stabbed Felicia in the back.

Linda Ellis

The knife was driven into her again and again. To keep her from screaming, the attacker reached around her and covered Felicia's mouth with one hand and continued to stab her with the other.

Ten times the knife went into Felicia's back. Five times it did damage that would not have been fatal. Five blows, however, went through her ribs and into her heart and lungs.

Felicia's tortured screams grew faint.

Felicia started to fall, and she and the attacker seemed to drift together to the ground, the attacker's arms slowly lowering her prey to the ground for the kill. Now Felicia was on her back on a patch of gravel, and the attacker, straddling her, continued the slaughter.

As the autopsy would reveal, Felicia's hands went up in self-defense in a pitiful but instinctive attempt to protect her face from the slashing knife. Desperately, Felicia tried to save herself. She grabbed for the knife with her right hand but the blade cut her palm and fingers. She raised her left hand to fend off the knife, but the blade sliced the back of that hand near the wrist.

The attacker stabbed her in the left side of the chest; another blow slashed her throat, and then the knife sliced through her left breast.

Felicia couldn't protect herself anymore. She couldn't resist anymore. Still, she was shown no mercy.

Blood began to fill her lungs and windpipe, and she made a gurgling sound as she tried to breathe. The attacker heard her struggle for breath and thought she must be close to death. Just to make sure, the assailant stabbed Felicia twice more.

About then, an ER surgeon would later tell a reporter, the shock would have begun to dull the victim's pain. Mercifully, Felicia would have begun to drift away from the horrid reality.

"Still, a horrible way to die," the physician would add.

"Make sure she's dead. Make sure she's dead," the attacker thought and brought the knife down again. "I have to leave her dead."

In less than two minutes, the attack was over. Felicia Cusack lay in the gravel bleeding to death, her freshly styled hair pushed into the side of the filthy garbage container.

The attacker rose to a crouch, grabbed Felicia's purse and ran off between two buildings toward First Avenue.

Larry, about halfway to the car, thought he heard Felicia yell a second time. He stopped and turned around. Everything became a blur, Larry said later. He wasn't sure whether he ran or yelled out something. When he got closer to Felicia, he saw someone on top of her, he said. Then he saw that person get up and run away between two buildings toward First Avenue.

Mrs. Brown saw a person get up from out of nowhere and run away between the two buildings. An awful fear settled on the widow as she saw the person flee. She would later say that the fear arose out of the way the person was dressed: all in tight dark clothing with something hiding the face.

When Larry got to Felicia, he saw her on the ground with blood on her mouth and hands. Her eyes were open, and she waved her hand at him, as if to say, "I'm here, I'm here."

11

Larry did not stop to help her.

He ran to Dublin to get help. Ann Padgett, whose family owned the restaurant, was inside by the front door when she saw Larry throw the door open and lean inside. She looked at his face and thought that something terrible must have happened.

"My wife's been stabbed," Larry yelled and ran outside.

Despite what she had just heard, Ann thought to herself maybe it's not that serious. Maybe they had a fight outside. Maybe his wife cut her arm on a tree branch. At that point, Ann thought that whatever had happened was on the restaurant property, and they could be held responsible. She told Patricia Cirrino, the hostess on duty by the front door, to call for an ambulance. The call to police headquarters was recorded at 7:26.

Phil DeVito, who was eating dinner with his wife in a booth near the entrance to Dublin, heard Larry yell and ran outside to see what had happened. Someone might have had a heart attack, or maybe there had been a car accident, he thought. He ran down Cable Court toward Second Avenue, away from the driveway, and saw nothing. At that point he thought it was a practical joke, all part of the St. Patrick's festival.

As DeVito walked back toward the restaurant, he saw Larry standing by a car and heard him crying. DeVito ran to him. It was dark and DeVito tried to open a door of the car because he thought whoever was hurt might be in it. Then Larry pointed to the ground, and DeVito saw Felicia for the first time.

She was covered with blood and wasn't breathing. DeVito, a marketing manager with no training in first aid, felt he had to do something. He knelt by Felicia

12

and started mouth-to-mouth resuscitation, just as he had seen it done on television.

It worked. Felicia started breathing again.

Ann Padgett grabbed some napkins and ran outside. A busboy, Juan Gonzalez, grabbed a linen tablecloth and followed her. Reaching Felicia, Ann saw she was covered with blood from the chin down.

"Oh my God, stabbed? This is slaughter," Ann cried out.

She saw blood, but no stab wounds. Ann remembered her children's bloody nosebleeds. Maybe the woman on the ground had been mugged, she thought. She knelt by Felicia's head and wiped the blood from her mouth. Juan, the busboy, checked Felicia for a heartbeat and pulse. She was breathing, but her pulse was weak. As Juan knelt there, Felicia stopped breathing. He started mouth-to-mouth resuscitation. Blood kept flowing from her mouth and nose, but she began to breathe again.

A woman in a fur coat came up to Larry and put her arms around him. Larry didn't know the woman, but he reached around her back and his hands felt the fur and the warmth. The soft texture of the fur comforted him. He never learned her identity. In later years, he could feel the comfort of the warm fur and he would think of her.

One of Ann Padgett's sons, Jeff, ran out of the restaurant and asked Larry where the attacker had gone. Larry let go of the woman, pointed between the buildings by First Avenue, and he and Jeff Padgett ran there. A young white man was standing by a car and Jeff asked Larry if that was the man. It couldn't be, Larry told him, because the attacker was black.

Meanwhile, the police dispatcher answering Patricia Cirrino's call radioed Patrolman Larry Dolan, who was driving Patrolman Neal Siegel to headquarters, and told him to go to the driveway. Dolan got there, parked his car and walked slowly to the crowd of people around Felicia.

"This woman is hurt very badly. She needs help immediately. Hurry!" Ann Padgett shouted at Dolan. As soon as Dolan saw Felicia, he ran back to his car, opened the trunk, got his first aid kit and ran toward the victim.

Ann knew she couldn't do anything else to help. She stood up and for the first time saw the pool of blood around Felicia. She walked over to her husband Dan, who was standing next to Larry. Another policeman walked over to them and told them they had to leave. Ann told the policeman who she was and that the man next to her – a man whose name she still didn't know - was the husband of the woman on the ground.

The policeman asked her to take Larry into the restaurant and wait. As they walked back to the restaurant, Ann noticed that both she and Larry were trembling. She brought him into a small room and asked a server to get him a brandy. He sat on a staircase and held his head in his hands and said over and over, "That fucking maniac. That fucking maniac".

"Did you see anything?" Ann asked.

"No, it was a dark figure. I just saw a dark figure bent over her," he said.

Dad. This is John! I know who it was! Help Mommy

As Larry drank the brandy, Ann noticed how neatly he was dressed in a short leather jacket over a silky shirt with gold chains around his neck. She was wearing a black print dress with long sleeves

14

that billowed at the wrists. She saw that the ends of her sleeves were stained with blood, and then she noticed Larry didn't have any blood on his clothes or hands.

In that moment, she found it curious. Later she found it profoundly disturbing that others, strangers, carried his wife's blood away from the killing ground but he, her husband, had not one drop on him. He had not even touched her.

Outside the Boothbay First Aid Squad arrived and lifted Felicia onto a stretcher and put her in the ambulance. The nearest hospital was Harbor Medical Center, only three-quarters of a mile from Dublin.

Felicia was brought into the ER at 7:36. Her pupils were fixed and dilated, and there was no sign of a pulse. Nurses stripped her clothes off, and the wounds in her chest and back became visible.

When the call came into Boothbay police headquarters, Detective Luke Weathers was meeting with police from Lincoln Village and the county prosecutor's office about another case. Sgt. Tim Hudson told Weathers about the attack, and both of them left for Dublin, Hudson in a marked police car with lights flashing and sirens screaming and Weathers in an unmarked car behind him.

Weathers reached the driveway moments after Felicia had been taken to the hospital. Patrolman Dolan told the detective that the victim was in very bad shape and might not live. Weathers told him to make sure no one disturbed the area where the body had lain. Hudson and Dolan talked to people standing around the area to see if they could learn anything. Dolan found Grace Brown, and she told him that she was on the street when the woman was attacked.

Weathers went inside Dublin, found Larry and told him Felicia was on her way to the hospital. As they walked outside, Larry asked how Felicia was. Larry was nervous and confused and apparently unaware of just how badly injured Felicia was, Weathers thought.

Larry wanted to go to the hospital, and Weathers, the only policeman not guarding the scene or talking to potential witnesses, drove him there. On the way to the hospital, Weathers tried to prepare Larry for the worst and told him Felicia might not live.

"Don't tell me that!" Larry shouted.

Considering everything that had happened, Larry had been relatively calm up to this point, Weathers thought. But now Felicia Cusack's husband was getting very upset.

He told Weathers how he and Felicia were going to the movies, how he found he didn't have his keys and headed back to the car. He thought he heard Felicia yell his name. He stopped, and then he was sure she yelled his name out again. Larry wasn't sure whether he walked or ran back to her. When he neared his wife, he saw someone squatting next to Felicia. As he approached, the person got up and ran toward First Avenue.

At the hospital, Larry described the attacker. He wore either a dark pea coat or bomber jacket and dark pants. Larry hadn't seen the attacker's face but what might have been the reflection off the attacker's skull indicating very short hair. He was probably black, but Larry could not rule out a white suspect. Larry never saw the man in the act of stabbing Felicia.

16

Weathers called Larry's brother, Jake, a police officer in Newark, and asked him to come to Boothbay. Jake Cusack was on duty, but he signed himself out for a family emergency.

Larry was given 5 milligrams of Valium in the emergency room to calm him down. While he was telling Weathers what had happened, doctors and nurses inside the emergency room were trying desperately to save Felicia's life.

ER surgeon Sinjai Bhashkar typed Felicia's blood (B-positive) and ordered a transfusion. An intravenous line was inserted in the left side of her chest just below the collarbone. A tube was snaked down her windpipe to help her breathe. An incision was made in the right side of her chest and another tube was inserted to suck out air and re-expand her punctured lungs. A tube was put into her groin to check for internal bleeding.

Despite what they were doing, nothing was working. There were too many wounds. Felicia was losing too much blood. Her heart stopped and Bhashkar decided on one last desperate measure. With a scalpel, he made a nine-inch incision in her chest to reach her heart and massage it with his hands to keep her alive.

Father Ed Nitkowski, a young priest from St. Mary's, the Catholic church closest to the hospital, was called to the emergency room. If the doctors couldn't do anything to save her at least the priest would make sure that she died with her sins forgiven. In a ritual that dates back centuries, Father Nitkowski put holy oil on his thumb and traced a small cross on Felicia's forehead with the oil. "Through this holy anointing, may the Lord in His love and mercy help you," the priest implored. "May the Lord who frees you from sin save you and raise you up."

Larry saw a priest enter the room, and a cold feeling came over him. What's the priest doing here, Larry wondered, trying to fight the obvious.

A man dressed in green surgical scrubs came up to Larry and spoke.

"We've lost her. She was stabbed in the . . " Those were the only words Larry remembered. His mind went blank. He punched a wall in anger and barely missed hitting the priest.

Less than an hour after she was attacked, Felicia Cusack was dead.

When it became apparent how serious the attack had been, police started calling in extra help. Boothbay Detective Sgt. John Peters, who was off duty, got a call at home about the stabbing at 7:45 and was told that he was needed at the hospital. The county prosecutor's office was called at 7:46.

At the emergency room, Peters heard Larry repeat the story of what had happened. Then the detective went to see Felicia's body. A hospital staff member asked him if the body could be moved because they needed the space in the ER that night. The body had to be treated as evidence and police had to make sure no one tampered with it. Peters followed the body out of the ER and had police headquarters send another officer to stay with it.

Murder investigations have rigid protocols. The body would have to be held at the hospital until the arrival there of investigators from the county medical examiner's office. A pathologist from that office would perform the autopsy.

Once another policeman arrived at the hospital, Peters and Weathers left with Larry and headed back to Dublin to have him re-enact what had happened. Larry was very upset, but he walked them through what he had told them before. He had been standing, he said, by the doorway to 3 Cable Court when he heard Felicia cry out his name. When investigators measured the distance, Larry had been 64 feet away from his wife. Just as he had done at the hospital, Larry broke down as he re-enacted the event. He was near hysteria now, Weathers thought. Peters told Weathers to take Larry back to police headquarters to make a statement.

Within a few minutes after Larry had left with Weathers, Kevin Glanville, a 37-year-old investigator in the homicide squad of the county prosecutor's office, arrived at Dublin. Glanville had been at his home in Gullwing Cove, just about to have dinner with his wife, children and brother, when he got a call saying that he was needed at a murder scene in Boothbay.

Outside Dublin, Glanville saw Peters and Greg Brocail, the first assistant prosecutor, the man second in command at the prosecutor's office. Like Glanville, Brocail lived in Gullwing Cove, Felicia's hometown.

"You know it's getting a little close to home," Brocail said to Glanville.

"Why?" Glanville asked. At that point all he knew was that there had been a murder. "The victim is from town," Brocail said.

"Oh, yeah? Who is it?" Glanville asked.

"It's Felicia Cusack."

"Oh my God. You got to be kidding me."

"Do you know her?"

"I've known her many years."

Then the shock hit Glanville. This was the first time he had ever known the victim in a murder.

Growing up, Glanville had been friendly with Larry's cousin, Pete Cimino, who lived in Hopeville, a town near Boothbay. He must have been 14 when he first met Larry through Pete, Glanville thought. He didn't consider himself a friend of Larry by any means. He was just an acquaintance - someone he would see from time to time because they both knew Pete and now both lived in Gullwing Cove.

Through Larry, Glanville had come to know Felicia, and he saw her occasionally in town. He grew to like Felicia much more than he liked Larry. On second thought, he didn't like Larry at all. He had heard rumors that Larry liked to rough up suspects just to show that he was tough. In Glanville's experience, a cop who had to show his toughness was both dangerous and stupid.

Felicia, though, was warm, open and seemed to sincerely love being a wife and mom. She always seemed to have a smile on her face. She was a fulltime worker out of necessity and out of devotion to her family. She wanted the best for Grace and John.

After Glanville found his bearings at the driveway across from Dublin, he went to the hospital to look at Felicia's body. Glanville considered looking at the body of a murder victim as part of his job. He knew that pathologists and forensic detectives were the experts on what evidence the body can give in a murder. However, whenever he was assigned a case, he looked at the body so that he could make his own judgments about what the evidence meant.

Felicia's body, still guarded by a policeman, lay under a sheet on the hospital gurney. The wounds

20

on her chest and neck were visible. There was blood on her face and hair. The tubes that doctors had inserted in her body were still in place. There was an incision in her chest from the open-heart massage.

If there is such a thing as a routine murder, this wasn't it, Glanville thought.

There was one wound to the neck, one wound to the right breast, one to the abdominal area, one to the right hand and one to the left, seven wounds to the left chest and ten in the upper back. He counted 22 in all. It wasn't the most violent murder he had ever seen, but it was extremely brutal. Glanville was taking it personally. He couldn't help it. He was only human, after all. He had been at children's birthday parties with this woman, to community parties after parades, at basketball games in the grade school gym.

In murders with no confession or clear evidence against someone, Glanville saw his job as calculating probability. He tried to use his experience from other cases and his common sense to decide what was probable so that he could figure out what had happened. As he looked at the body of Felicia Cusack and said a silent goodbye to the lady who smiled all the time, Glanville considered several alternatives.

He knew that her purse was missing, but he wondered whether this really was a purse snatching that turned violent. When a mugger kills someone, there are usually just one or two wounds. The idea is to grab the wallet or purse and to escape, not to kill.

If this was some new variation on a purse snatching, they had a big problem, perhaps a madman on the loose. On the other hand, maybe it was someone from Felicia's past - everyone had a

21

past - and this was a person who was extremely angry or vengeful.

Perhaps there was another explanation, Glanville thought, and maybe Larry knew it. Glanville knew he had to consider Larry a suspect. So far, there was no hard evidence pointing to him, but there was the simple circumstantial evidence. He was nearby when Felicia was killed. He was her husband. Statistically, the odds are that the murderer is a family member.

"One thing I've learned in my experience is that you don't jump the gun in things like this," Glanville said months later. "You have to keep an open mind. You don't close your mind in a homicide investigation - in any investigation, I suppose. I've seen some guys zero in on one theory. You're all right if your theory happens to be right, but if it isn't, you could have some major problems. You may form an opinion and you may lean toward one theory, but close your mind to any other possibilities and you're going to have problems," Glanville said from experience.

At Boothbay police headquarters, Weathers used a standardized police form in questioning Larry.

"What is your full name?"

"Lawrence Andrew Cusack."

"Do you use or are you known by any other names?"

"No."

"What is your address and telephone number?"

"545 Bay Boulevard, Gullwing Cove, 249-3911."

"What is your birth date and your age?"

"Sept 26, 1938. I'm 43."

"What is your educational background?"

"I graduated from North Side High School."

"Can you read and understand the English language?"

"Yes."

The next question Weathers decided not to ask, but filled in the answer himself.

What is your marital status?

Widowed.

Weathers asked Larry to say in his own words what had happened.

"We drove down to Dublin - to the parking lot for Dublin. I was going to surprise her after the movie and buy her a drink. We got out of the car and started walking towards First Avenue. We were going to take a short cut through the alley. At that point, I patted my pocket and I realized I didn't have my keys.

"I said, 'Hang on a minute, hon.' I started walking back to where I parked the car. I got about halfway past the office - whatever it is, that white building on the right hand side. Then I thought I heard a yell, like 'Larry, Larry!'

"Then I looked back and I didn't see Felicia standing there. At this point, everything was moving in slow motion I guess. I don't know. I started toward where I left Felicia. I don't know. I think I started to run. I'm not sure if I started to run. I think I hollered something. I think I hollered. I don't know what I hollered. Everything just seems to run together at this point now. As I got closer to the Dumpster it appeared as if someone was on top of Felicia ... humping her."

At this point Larry broke down and had to stop. He left the room for a minute to compose himself before he continued the story.

"I got to where Felicia was lying, and there was blood all over her. I don't know what I did. I started towards Dublin. Then I started back towards Felicia. Then I saw a silhouette dressed in dark clothing running between the buildings towards First Avenue. I blew my cool. I didn't know what to do. I panicked."

At 10 o'clock, while Larry was still giving his statement, Glanville and Larry's brother Jake arrived at police headquarters. Jake Cusack was still in his uniform as a Newark cop. When Larry saw them, he started to cry.

Weathers began to ask Larry specific questions.

"Were you going to the movies tonight?"

"Yes."

"Do you recall the film you intended to see?"

"The one with the guy who sets himself on fire - Richard Pryor."

"Do you know at this point what became of your keys?"

"You mean now. I don't know."

"Do you recall finding your keys at any point?"

"I don't have my keys."

Larry had conducted interviews like this himself; as a reflex he declined to answer a question with specifics. Weathers knew what Larry was doing but decided at this time to abandon that line of questioning. There would be better times to press Larry.

Larry told Weathers that Felicia was carrying a purse, a brown purse with small straps. Weathers asked him what was in it. Larry said "the usual stuff women carry plus some Barclays I bought for her on the way. Then tissues, comb, you know, makeup."

The description of the attacker Larry gave to Weathers was the same as the description he gave at the hospital earlier in the night: a man, probably a black man, with close-cropped hair and wearing a dark pea coat or a bomber jacket. At 10:43 Larry was given the statement to read and correct, if necessary. He read it, said it was true and then signed it at 10:55 p.m.

Weathers asked for Larry's leather jacket. Why, Larry wondered, did Weathers want his jacket? He looked at his brother, Jake, who nodded to go ahead and then Larry gave Weathers the jacket.

Larry appeared to have no blood on him and the detectives wanted the jacket examined in a laboratory for bloodstains. Evidence like that could help tell them whether Larry was telling the truth about what had happened.

In murder investigations in New Jersey, a detective from the county prosecutor's office usually works with a detective from the local police department. The idea is to have a detective who specializes in murder investigations working with a detective who knows the town where the murder took place.

Glanville and Peters teamed up that night but had little to go on in the first hours after the murder. The descriptions of the killer they got from Larry Cusack and Grace Brown didn't tell them enough to make a positive identification of anyone. They didn't have a murder weapon or the victim's purse.

Patrolmen and detectives searched the neighborhood around Dublin for clues. The killer might have dropped the knife after running away. Felicia's purse might have been discarded after money and credit cards were taken from it and there might be bloody fingerprints on it.

25

Linda Ellis

Police looked inside and under cars parked in the area. They walked down to the beach and looked around. They checked the drugstore and the movie theater - the only businesses open on First Avenue - to see if anyone suspicious had been seen in the area, but no one had seen anything useful.

When the movies ended, police went to the theater to get the names of the people who were leaving. Maybe one of them had seen something. Maybe one of them had seen the killer. Maybe one of them *was* the killer.

Police got the name of Donnie Bottalico, who lived in a garden apartment just across from Dublin. Bottalico had been seen in the area around the murder that night. Jim Whitney and Fred Tenney, detectives from Boothbay, went to Bottalico's apartment to ask him what he had been doing. Whitney noticed that Bottalico was wearing a black jacket.

Bottalico said that he had left his apartment about 6:30 to go to the apartment of a friend named Vic who lived on Penbrook Avenue. To reach Penbrook Avenue, Bottalico had to pass the area where Felicia had been attacked. Vic wasn't home, Bottalico said, so he returned home and saw police at Cable Court about 6:45. This made Whitney suspicious, because the call on the stabbing didn't come in until 7:26. It was a lead, something to follow up.

Police knew that after the attack, the killer had run toward First Avenue across a lawn between two buildings. Police couldn't follow the trail after that, but maybe a police dog could.

The police department in Sudbury, a neighboring town, had a bloodhound unit. Boothbay police called to ask Sudbury police if Jeter, the lead dog, were available. The bloodhound began his work at 9:40, picked up several scents, including Felicia's, and tracked them all for a block. Then Jeter picked up a scent at the Dumpster in the driveway and tracked it to First Avenue. The dog led police through the streets of the West End until it came to the back yards behind houses at 536 and 540 First Avenue, less than half a mile from Dublin. Jeter found a strong scent under a pickup truck parked there.

Junior, the Boothbay Police Department's German shepherd, searched for a weapon around the place Felicia had been attacked and behind 536 First Avenue, but couldn't find anything.

When Det. Weathers finished questioning Larry, he went to 536 First Avenue to see if he could learn anything. He saw four cars and the pickup truck behind them and looked through the windows for anything inside that might give them a clue. Investigators knocked on doors, and spoke to the one person home in the area, but didn't learn anything useful and left.

At 11:00, Glanville and Peters drove to Grace Brown's home in West Boothbay. At that point she was the only witness they had other than Larry. Yes, she said, she had seen the couple walking up Cable Court and stop in the driveway, she told them. She saw the man walk back to the parking lot. She heard a moan and didn't see the woman she had seen just a moment earlier. The man who had left the woman ran back toward the driveway. Another person, someone young, about 5' 7" with short, dark hair and with a thin build ran toward First Avenue

27

between the two buildings. Next Mrs. Brown remembered seeing the man, who had gone back to the woman, pounding on the hood of a car. She went over to see what the problem was.

The man pointed to the woman on the ground and said, "That's my wife over there."

Glanville and Peters drove Mrs. Brown back to Dublin, and with policemen playing the roles of Felicia, Larry and the attacker, she showed them what she had seen.

At 12:48 a.m., a station wagon from the medical examiner's office picked up Felicia's body at Harbor County Medical Center and took it to Crooked River Hospital for autopsy later that morning.

At around 9:30, Larry called Jeff and Jenny Russo from Harbor Medical. The Russos were the friends from the Cove who had been asked to go to the movies with him and Felicia that night. He asked them to go to his house and pick up the Cusack children, Grace and John. There "had been an accident" was all Larry told them. At about 11, Larry called Jeff again and told him Felicia was dead.

"Break the news to Grace and Johnny and keep them at your house for the night," Larry said.

"No way," Jeff said. "You should do it. The children shouldn't be at someone else's house on the night their mother died."

Larry got to the Russo home at about 11:30 with his brother Jake.

"Your mother is with the angels," Larry told the children. They walked away from the Russo home and to the family car and the Russos recall the scene as somewhat odd: Larry had his arm tightly around Grace and they both were sobbing. John pulled away from Larry's other arm and walked alone.

Felicia came from a big family and they had to be told the devastating news.

Her father, Carmen Girardi, still lived in the house where she grew up in Hilltown, a town just outside Newark. Her three brothers and nine sisters also lived in New Jersey.

The Girardis first got the word when Larry's sister, Dolores Cunningham, started making calls from the Cusack home before midnight. After the first few calls, there was still confusion about what happened. Felicia's sister, Joanne Quatraro, called her brother Carmen Girardi Jr. in Newark to tell him Felicia was hurt, but she didn't know how badly. Carmen Jr. called his father and told him what little he knew.

Carmen Jr., who always felt close to Felicia, could hardly believe what he had heard. This was the sort of thing you read about in the newspapers. It doesn't happen to you. It doesn't happen to someone in your family - someone you know and love. Carmen Jr. feared the worst and called the Cusack house in Gullwing Cove. But the line was busy, so Carmen Jr. called an operator to break into the call. This was an emergency. Jake Cusack, Larry's brother, answered the phone.

"What happened?" Carmen Jr. asked.

"Felicia was stabbed."

"How is she?"

"Dead."

Tony called his father and tried to break the news without being brutally direct. But his father wanted the truth quickly.

"Cut the shit!" shouted Carmen Girardi, who rarely cursed.

"Felicia's dead," Carmen Jr. said.

· At 11:45 p.m., another one of Felicia's sisters, Andorra, called Gerry who had talked to Felicia earlier that day.

"Where's Felicia?" Andy asked Gerry.

"She's at the party Denyce's relative is having, the engagement party. What are you talking about this for?"

"Are you sure?" Andy said angrily. "I heard she was stabbed, she was stabbed to death."

"That's crazy. Who would stab her at an engagement party?" Gerry shouted. "They all like her. Everybody in Gullwing Cove likes her."

Andy said she had been trying to call Felicia's house, but the line was busy. Gerry told her to calm down and said she would call their niece Grace's unlisted phone.

"Hello," Grace said.

"It's your Aunt Gerry. Put your mother on the phone."

"I can't, Aunt Gerry," Grace wailed.

"What do you mean you can't? Put your mother on the phone right now, dammit!"

"Aunt Gerry, I can't. Mommy's dead."

*   *   *

At 1 a.m. Sunday, Boothbay Patrolman John Marzano got a call to go to the rectory at St. Mary's Church, a little more than a mile from Dublin. Someone was ringing the doorbell at the rectory and the priests wanted the police to check. Marzano found Robert Rolf, a 17-year-old who lived in an apartment on First Avenue, not far from Dublin.

When Marzano came on duty, he and the other men on his shift had been briefed about the murder. What Rolf told Marzano made him suspicious. Rolf said he had a problem and wanted to talk to a priest about it. Marzano looked at Rolf under the light of his flashlight and noticed what he thought was a spot of blood on the heel of Rolf 's right boot.

"Were you in the West End tonight?" Marzano asked.

"Do you mean by the stabbing? Yes," Rolf said.

Marzano asked Rolf to come to police headquarters. Felicia had been murdered five and-a-half hours earlier. Now the actions of observant policeman had given detectives someone to question.

Before Glanville and Peters started to question Rolf, they called his father, Tom, and got him to come to headquarters. Because Rolf was under 18, he had to be advised of his right against self-incrimination and his right to counsel in front of one of his parents or a guardian. At l: 50 a.m. Sunday, Mar. 21, Rolf and his father signed a police department form saying that police had given the Miranda warnings.

Rolf agreed to talk. He said he didn't have anything to do with the murder. Yes, he had been in the West End, but he was with a friend, Eugene Brower. They saw the ambulance and the police and someone in the neighborhood told them there had been a murder. Rolf had wanted to talk to a priest earlier in the night about problems with his girl friend. Tom Rolf said his son often tried to speak with priests when he had problems. Yes, it was blood

31

on his boot, Rolf said, but that was from a cut he got on his arm a month earlier. Peters and Glanville asked Rolf to let them take his boots so the bloodstain could be analyzed. At 2:40 in the morning, Rolf and his father signed another police form, this one voluntarily consenting to let police have the boots.

Glanville considered Rolf a lead worth checking out, but he didn't think it was a lead that would take them anywhere. Rolf didn't seem like a murderer, just a mixed-up teenager.

At headquarters, Glanville got a call from Gullwing Cove Patrolman David Manning, who had learned about the murder and had another lead. On Oct. 3, 1980, Tony Giglio, the janitor in the apartment where Felicia worked at that time, had argued fiercely with her. Tony had shouted at Felicia and had threatened her. Manning had to call other policemen to back him up.

What made Tony angry had been the cancellation of a Tupperware party for the senior citizens in the building. Felicia said she had taken the sign for the party down, because the owner of the building had told her to do it. It was against company policy, Felicia reminded Tony. Tony was furious because Felicia, an ardent Democrat, allowed that party's political posters to be displayed but took down any Republican campaign posters, Tony said. Tupperware isn't something you vote for, Tony raged. Is Tupperware a Republican thing?

Felicia always tried to make him look bad in front of the owners of the building, he said. Manning could tell Tony had been drinking, but wasn't drunk. Police finally calmed him down and then left. No charge was ever filed, but now it provided another lead for police to follow.

Before Glanville left police headquarters that night, he got another lead. A few people called to say that Larry had a young girlfriend named Amy Lee Halford. It wasn't clear to Glanville from the information whether Larry was still seeing her. Glanville wasn't troubled or even surprised by this information.

The fact that a married man has or had a girl friend doesn't make him guilty of murder. It doesn't make the girlfriend guilty of murder. However, it was another lead that had to be checked.

Law enforcement personnel were more troubled by the fact that Cusack had done nothing at all to help his wife as she lay dying in the gravel and dirt of the alley, brutally pushed against an overfilled garbage trough. It was despicable, but it was impossible to make any assumptions from that failure to act other than that Cusack didn't care about his wife, alive or dead. Police couldn't invent a charge against a fellow cop because of something he did not do, but they would sure make him pay if they discovered any evidence against him.

At the very least, he was an embarrassment to his fellow officers.

From the interviews with Grace Brown, it was clear that Larry seemed confused for a time, going back and forth between the alley and his car. However, even when the attacker was out of the picture, even when there seemed to be no danger to others, this cop, this husband, never went near Felicia to help her, to learn if she were alive or dead.

It would be learned much later that the dying Felicia had motioned to her husband to come to her

33

and that he had not. He said he didn't see her do that.

No drop of her blood stained his immaculate clothes. Larry had had first aid training at the police academy and had just completed a course in cardiopulmonary resuscitation. Still, he did nothing to help Felicia, his own wife.

Our own MOM. You have to Help her Daddy. Love, Grace and John.

"As a cop, I have been able - on the streets, in the morgue - to look at bodies, murder victims, mutilations, accident victims and I'm OK. But it was like being paralyzed last night," Cusack said. "I couldn't, I really don't know why I couldn't help her, my wife. My own wife."

Chapter 2

The Mourning

Ann Padgett was still at her family's restaurant when she learned Felicia was dead. She wept at the reality of Felicia dying without hearing a word of comfort from her husband. Later when they were closing Dublin for the night, Ann talked to her husband Dan about it.

"Can you imagine any human being would be like that, on the dirty ground, in so much agony, dying with no one to say her name?" Ann said. "There was no one there to say 'I love you' or 'Everything's going to be all right.' Anything. But there was nothing for her."

"You were with her," Dan said.

"Yes, but me, I was a stranger. I didn't know what to say to her. I wish I had held her to comfort her. I didn't even know her name. I know it now. The police told me, Felicia, but when I was with her, I didn't."

"Poor woman," Dan said.

*   *   *

Death is a time when most families come together in grief. At the Cusack house in the early morning hours of Sunday, however, death brought division and dissension between families who had not been close under the best of circumstances.

The telephones in the houses of Felicia's father, brothers and sisters and friends were busy. The news was as bad as it gets: your daughter is dead.

35

Your sister is dead. Your Godmother is dead. Your aunt is dead.

Felicia's three brothers Joseph "Joey", Mario and Carmen, Jr., and Mario's son Tony, who lived in Sycamore Grove, a suburb near Newark, decided to meet in Bellaire, pick up Carmen, Sr., and drive to the Cove that night. When the brothers were together, Carmen, Jr., called Jake Cusack, Larry's cop brother, at the Cusack home to say they were leaving.

There was no sense coming down, Jake told Carmen, Jr., because there is nothing you can do.

"You got to be kidding. You don't know this family if you don't think we're coming down," Carmen, Jr., said and had to stop himself from slamming the phone in Jake's ear.

The drive from Bellaire to Gullwing Cove, most of it on the Garden State Parkway, usually takes 45 minutes to an hour but not that night.

Of all nights, this had to be one straight out of a *Saturday Night Live* skit. An ashtray on the passenger side had been pulled from the door and Mario didn't realize it. He kept putting out his cigarettes in the car door.

Half an hour into the drive the car door caught on fire and they had to stop on the parkway, pry the door panel off with a tire iron and put the fire out.

That added 30 minutes to the drive.

By the time Felicia's father and brothers reached the Cove, around 1:30 Sunday morning, the Cusack house was filled with family and some close friends. By that time, the sisters and their husbands were there as well.

Larry was having Scotch on the rocks and seemed nervous. He minced no words about what had happened.

In front of her father, his mother, the brothers and sisters Larry said again that he saw "a bald-headed nigger humping Felicia."

Why didn't he use his gun? Why didn't he do something, *anything* to protect her? a friend of Felicia's asked. Larry said he didn't have his gun, because he usually only carried it on duty or to and from work. He was a uniformed cop, he reminded the woman, not a detective. Detectives always had their guns, he said. That was different.

He said that he had panicked. He said that at the moment everything happened, he didn't know what to do.

When Mommy wakes up you're going to be sorry. We know what to do Dad

Rolling eyes and skeptical stares were directed at Larry, mainly from Felicia's family. Even Larry's partner, Joe Maloney, looked at him quizzically.

The 13 adults and five children representing Felicia's family felt out of place at her house that night.

"Leave me alone," Larry told Felicia's family. "I don't believe it happened. I don't want to hear about it, especially from you. All you ever do is yak, yak, yak and you're always YELLING LIKE THIS and you don't even realize you yell and it drives me nuts."

It is true that they yelled a lot and not in connection with anger or fear; it was a family habit and drove outsiders to distraction. Having a family of 17 probably made that level of communication a necessity. In any case, there was no excuse for Larry's words that night.

It was their child, their sister who had just been murdered a few hours before and the Girardis felt not only the absence of shared grief but also a total lack of consideration for their feelings. They felt unwelcome in the house that their Felicia had made a home.

They kept expecting her to return home and fuss that the kitchen floor didn't shine.

"I want to go to the hospital to see Felicia," Gerry insisted. "I want to go to wherever my sister is, to see her, to say goodbye to her."

No, she couldn't see the body, Larry said. There was no reason to see Felicia now.

"She's dead, woman," Larry said. "She's dead."

Larry's moods changed dramatically as the night passed. One minute he was depressed. The next minute he was angry. He drank steadily and said it was to calm his nerves. He cursed. He yelled. He threw a neighbor who had been close to Felicia out of the house. He said that the neighbor was hysterical and he couldn't stand it.

"I can't take any more hysterical women in my house!"

"Well, you're down one," Felicia's sister Christine shouted at Larry. "Feel better now?"

*   *   *

When Felicia's nephew Jack learned about the attack, he rushed directly to Harbor Medical; he lived not far away. Felicia's body was still there when a nurse who recognized that he needed help gave him directions. He didn't realize it was too late to ever see his aunt alive again. He didn't see Larry. What he did see was a note at the nurses' station: *Felicia Cusack d.o.b. 6/20/37/ pronounced 3/20/82 by Dr. Bhashkar/post to Dr. Morrill.*

"My aunt! That's my aunt!" Jack Girardi said. "I wanted to keep them from taking her away; I thought there must be something more they could do, something that could be fixed the way we did when we were kids and got hurt and went to the doctor."

Jack went to the Cusack home and found his uncle's family already there. Larry was at the Russos, telling the children their mother was dead.

The gathering at the Cusacks became more thick with tension as the night turned to morning.

"When the kids came home, they saw Larry's sister and his brother on the phone, notifying people," Felicia's brother Mario recalled. "But they didn't notify us, her family, until they'd called a lot of other people, even until five minutes to midnight in a few cases."

"Gerry said nothing was said on the phone that day about no movie. Felicia told Gerry that she'd either come to her house for birthday cake or she'd be at that relatives' engagement party, Denyce Buckley's relatives," Joey said. "So Gerry's waiting for her to come there, not one of Larry's people called her and she didn't even know Felicia was dead until nearly midnight."

By 3 a.m., civilization at the Cusacks was breaking down. Some buried their thoughts in booze, others cried, a few read from Bibles. It was eight hours since Felicia had died on a cold and alien ground and the people she had held most dear were close to civil war.

No one knew what to do to defuse the situation.

Mommy can make it OK. Where's Mommy?

39

Linda Ellis

Larry had ratcheted up the stress level by focusing on the coming burial. He ran upstairs to the master bedroom, opened her closet and looked at her clothes. "What am I going to put on her'? What's she going to wear?"

Gerry was furious. Just eight hours after her sister had been murdered, her brother-in-law seemed more concerned with what Felicia would wear in her coffin than with what had happened to put her there.

Then matters worsened from the Girardi family point of view.

Larry picked out a cranberry-colored velvet blazer, a white blouse with ruffles at the throat and cuffs, a black tie, a pleated plaid skirt and gray shoes. It was an outfit he had bought for Felicia as a Christmas present.

He knows she hated that outfit, Gerry said to Carmen Jr. Felicia had confided to her sisters that she was hurt that Larry made such a big deal of his present to her because she had told him pleats made her look fat and plaid made everyone look fat. He would yell at her to wear it and so she would.

So now, yet another insult from the Girardi's point of view. The last sight of her that anyone would have would be in this outfit. Felicia would be viewed and buried in clothes she hated.

She had lost 10 pounds in the past two months and the clothing Larry chose was not only ugly it was too big.

"It's too large for her now, Larry," Christine yelled at him, crying. "No, you won't put that on her!"

Several of the Girardi clan believed Larry made a point of disrespecting their sister and openly enjoyed humiliating her. The clothes, they said, were a good example. It's why Grace was snotty to her mother sometimes, Andy said. She just took that cue from Larry. John, on the other hand, tried to make up for it all.

Larry grew very quiet. He went toe-to-toe with Christine.

"I will decide what goes on my wife's body when she is put in her coffin. So shut your face. If you don't like it, get outta my house."

The ease with which Joe Maloney, Larry's partner in Webster, fit into the household bothered Felicia's brothers and sisters. He seemed to know who everyone was but no one had introduced them to him.

Felicia didn't suffer, she didn't bleed very much, the policeman told them. They could console themselves knowing she died peacefully, he said.

How did he come off saying all this, Carmen Jr. and Gerry wondered. We've been told different.

"The way we heard it, she was still alive even at the end of all that killing, those knife wounds and in terrible pain until she went unconscious," Mario, another of Felicia's brothers, said. "She did suffer and she bled a lot. So you're full of shit, Joe."

"Larry was very nervous," Carmen Jr., Felicia's oldest brother, recalled. "He used the words 'bald-headed nigger', saying that's who stabbed my sister to death, who was 'humping' her, he said. I don't think my father and sisters needed to hear that while we're all still in shock."

Maloney, who was still in his blues, pulled his partner aside and asked Larry why he didn't take action, why he didn't use his gun when he saw someone on top of his wife.

"I was too confused to do anything and I didn't have my gun with me. We're not supposed to carry

41

Linda Ellis

guns when we go out for the evening," Larry said. "You know that."

Joanne Quatraro, another of Felicia's sisters, called his bluff. "You always have your gun. You love to show it off," she said.

He would put it in plain sight, hitching around his body so that no one could fail to notice, she added.

"He went to our aunt's husband's funeral in street clothes, I remember, and he made sure we knew he had a gun on him. But his own wife, our sister...she's there, she called for him and he didn't do anything. It doesn't make sense," Joanne said.

"It's not like he had to prove his manhood by carrying a weapon," a former lover of Larry's commented. "He had one built in."

Maloney, who was meeting Felicia's family for the first time, tried repeatedly to get Maria, the "rich" sister who lived in an expensive suburb in a big house, to take a drink.

"Drink. It will calm your nerves down," he said.

"I don't want a drink. Leave me alone."

" Felicia, have a Scotch."

"I'm not Felicia."

Felicia was attacked in the few moments when her husband went back to the car to look for the keys he had dropped by the car. The keys were found in the parking lot and turned in at Dublin. Later the keys were returned to Larry at his home by police.

He sat at the kitchen table that night and looked at the keys in his hand. If he hadn't dropped them, his wife would be alive, he shouted. He stood up, threw the keys against the wall and ran out of the room.

The Monday after the murder, the Girardi family completely rejected Larry's description of the events of Saturday night. They didn't know how, but they suspected that Larry was involved in Felicia's death.

"For example," Vicki explained, "Larry would never lose or misplace his keys. He always had to have things where he knew where they were. He was obsessed like that. We know him all too well. When he threw the car keys against the wall in what was supposed to be a rage, then he looked around and he saw me and he gets even more upset. It's all a bunch of crap," Vicki concluded. "He was pretending."

In a murder investigation, detectives follow a set routine. When police don't have a suspect and/or enough evidence to charge anyone, automatic routines kick in. Put a lot of men on the case and follow every lead until it produces something or until it becomes clear it doesn't lead anywhere. Interview anyone who might know anything about the crime. Interview people who have already been interviewed to see if they forgot something important when they were first interviewed. See if there were any similar crimes recently. See if anyone was seen in the area around the time of the murder. Investigators did all this in the days after Felicia's murder.

A light rain fell Sunday morning when police returned to search the neighborhood by Dublin. Maybe in the daylight they would find something that they had missed in the dark the night before - a piece of hard evidence like the knife, Felicia's purse or bloodstained clothing that the killer might have discarded. On the roof of a nearby apartment building, detectives found two knives. This could be what they needed. They didn't move the knives until photos of their location were taken. After pictures were taken, the knives were put in evidence envelopes and sent to the state police laboratory to see if they would yield any clues.

Carl Hayden, an investigator in the prosecutor's office who had photographed and diagrammed the murder scene Saturday night, found blood on a car parked next to the spot where Felicia had been stabbed. The car was impounded so that the bloodstain could be analyzed.

Material was scraped from the side of the Dumpster. Two rookie investigators were assigned to isolate and examine every item from the odoriferous green container, the scene of the crime. The wish list of the authorities included the weapon and the victim's handbag; neither was disgorged.

A pair of gloves, stained red, was found on a concrete post on First Avenue, not far from where Felicia had been attacked. The police bloodhound, Jeter, was brought back to try to pick up a scent from the gloves. The dog headed toward the Beachside Manor Apartments, just across from Dublin, and went down to the beach but returned to the apartments.

Four detectives from Boothbay and the prosecutor's office canvassed the apartments to see if anyone had seen or heard anything the night before. Only half the people were home in the morning and early afternoon, and those who had been home Saturday night had little or nothing useful for the detectives.

Boothbay Detective Luke Weathers called the state prison unit for sex offenders at Ardenne for names of recently released prisoners capable of the murder.

The husband of the victim said the killer was attempting to have sexual intercourse with Felicia Cusack, was "humping her" in Larry's parlance at the same time the killer was stabbing the victim to death. Law enforcement officials know that some murderers reach orgasm at the moment of the victim's death; investigators in the Cusack case could not ignore what Larry had said.

On the other hand, Weathers and his partner did not believe this crime had anything to do with sex. No semen had been found in Felicia's vagina or rectum, in her mouth or on her underwear. Her panties had been slashed, allowing access to her internal passages, but the pathologist, at autopsy, found no bruising or abrasions in the vaginal area.

Sunday morning, Kevin Glanville, the homicide investigator from the county prosecutor's office, and John Peters, the detective from Boothbay, again interviewed Grace Brown, the woman who had been outside the restaurant when Felicia Cusack had been attacked and the only person to see Larry's movements in the critical moments of the murder. Most valuable was the fact that Larry had no idea he was being observed at the relevant time.

The widow, who had rarely ventured out at night since the death of her husband six months before, had not been able to sleep all night after the murder. It had been after 1 a.m. when she finished walking the detectives through what she had seen. Glanville called her at 9:30 Sunday morning, apologized for bothering her again and asked if he could send a car to bring her to headquarters to tell the story one more time. She was, so far, the closest the police had to an eyewitness aside from Larry.

She was a near-perfect witness, Glanville decided. She was calm, she had good vision, a retentive memory and she appeared to have no association or familiarity with anyone connected to the crime to date. Mrs. Brown again told about seeing how a couple walked from the lot, how the man headed back toward the lot and how far he was from the driveway where the woman, his wife, was being stabbed to death.

"When this gentleman (Cusack) turned around to run, that's when I was alerted and that's when I saw this figure running toward First Avenue. I heard a loud groan," Mrs. Brown told Glanville and Peters.

"At what point did you see this figure appear?"

"While he was running to his wife, to the woman I have since learned was his wife, I saw this different person flee through the buildings, run in the vacant lot."

"Can you describe this person?"

"Thin build, 5-foot-6 to 5-foot-7, dark clothing. I feel this person was young."

"When you saw the person running, where was the husband?"

"When he went to his wife and bent over her, this person ran off from between the cars. I heard another groan. That poor woman; she must have been in so much pain."

When the police were finished with her, Mrs. Brown called Larry. She worked as a volunteer at a social service agency that could help him out if he needed it, she said. She had learned of his daughter and son and wanted to know if she could find him some help. A temporary homemaker from her agency could take care of the children after school, Mrs. Brown said.

Larry told her he was grateful for her call. The children would be well cared for, he said, but he needed her help himself. Could she tell him everything he did last night? He was confused. Had he run or walked back to Felicia? Did he yell?

Mrs. Brown told him what he had done and said not to worry about it. Whatever he said or did was understandable under the circumstances.

The first friends began arriving at the Cusack house about 8 Sunday morning. They brought muffins, rolls and cake for breakfast. More friends bringing casseroles and cakes stopped in after church. Food began to pile up in the kitchen. A family friend, Jenny Russo, and Larry's brother Jake made telephone calls about funeral arrangements.

The local arrivals found a houseful of family, his and hers, and a degree of chaos, which was to be expected. Larry was not a good host, but then he had never been a person who concerned himself with making others comfortable.

Many of Felicia's friends learned of her death at Mass at St. Genevieve's, her parish church, or from the front page of the local paper, *The Coastal Call*. There was a short story on page one with sketchy details and a picture of Carl Hayden, an investigator in the prosecutor's office, photographing the bloodstains in the driveway.

In the same edition of *The Call*, there was another story about a series of attacks on women in the last two weeks.

"There is a maniac running loose on the streets of this county, attacking, savagely beating and

47

attempting to rape the women of the county," Glenn
G. Beatty, the county prosecutor, was quoted as
saying.

Just two weeks before Felicia's murder, a 22-
year-old woman named Debra Hamilton had been
murdered in Barrington, a town north of Boothbay.
The last time Hamilton was seen alive was Friday
night, Mar. 5, in a bar in Atlantic Beach, an
oceanfront town north of Boothbay. Her body was
found on the side of a road in Barrington early the
next morning. She had been stabbed once in the
heart. No one had yet been arrested.

*   *   *

At the moment Felicia was attacked, Weathers, a
Boothbay detective, was meeting with investigators to
talk about an assault four days earlier on a woman
in Lincoln Village. There had been several attacks on
women in nearby towns in recent weeks. This was a
matter of deep concern to law enforcement. There
were complaints from local politicians, who had been
bombarded with calls from constituents.

Nine investigators from the prosecutor's office
were assigned to help local police.

At the Cusack house Sunday afternoon, the
unsettled mood of the night before turned hostile.

The information for the obituary incorrectly said
that Felicia's 71-year-old father was dead and that
Felicia's mother, who had been dead 18 years, was
still alive.

You've got it wrong, Felicia's father, Carmen, told
Larry's mother, Gladys. Gladys Cusack had been
asked to give the funeral home the information for

the obituary. The funeral home then phoned the local papers.

Gladys didn't want to hear anything from Carmen. She had never thought much of this family anyway. She began screaming at him.

"I'm just telling you, you got it wrong," Carmen said. Felicia's sister, Gerry, told Mrs. Cusack to calm down. Gerry said it loudly because Mrs. Cusack was hard of hearing, but the older woman felt insulted and yelled louder. Then Larry stepped in.

"Everybody get the fuck out of my house except for my mother," Larry screamed. Carmen stared at him, open-mouthed in disbelief. "Larry, what did you say to my daughter? Did you say only your mother could stay in your house? If you had treated my daughter Felicia halfway decent, my daughter would not be dead now."

"Pop, shut up, just shut up," Larry shouted and started for Carmen. "I'll whip you with my bare hands, you piece of pus" Carmen yelled. "I'll rip you apart. No one talks to my daughters like that." The 71-year-old senior citizen stood his ground and got ready to hit his 44-year-old son-in-law.

Carmen had already lost his wife and two of his 15 children and now his daughter Felicia who was as precious as any of them. She was one of "his girls," one of the reasons he'd worked two jobs at a time to make sure they could have decent clothes for school and special dresses for Christmas and Easter and gloves and hats.

Felicia's sister Andy stepped in to hold back Larry who turned to Gerry.

"Gerry, you bitch, you get the fuck out of my house."

She went to the living room crying.

Larry followed her to apologize.

"Gerry, I lost control. Please forgive me."

She looked up and gave him the middle finger. *youknow about thisyou pile ofchickenshit and we'll get it out of you oneway ortheother. My precious sisterwouldbe aliveif she neverknew you bastard*

*   *   *

In New Jersey each county has a medical examiner responsible for giving the medical reasons for violent or unexplained deaths. Even in a case like this where the cause of death was apparent, an autopsy was required. At noon Sunday a pathologist named John Morrill performed the autopsy on Felicia in the medical examiner's office at the county hospital.

Carl Hayden, the investigator from the prosecutor's office, and John Romano, an investigator in the medical examiner's office, took pictures of the body to show where the wounds were and what they looked like.

Romano took Felicia's fingerprints. Fingernail clippings - still brushed with Purple Sage, her shade of nail polish - and a vial of her blood were taken and turned over to Hayden to send to the state police crime lab. The chain of evidence was preserved each step along the way. I

The external examination showed the signs of the attack - a concentration of stab wounds in the chest, blood dried on her hair, face and nose.

The clothing and jewelry Felicia had worn the night before were next to her body. There was a wrist watch with a black band, the simple gold wedding band she had worn for 22 years, a gold "mother's ring" with two green stones, a chain with a gold cross. One earring was in her left ear. The other was with her clothes.

Felicia's clothes also showed the signs of the attack and the attempts to save her life at Harbor Medical. Next to her body in the morgue were a pair of black high-heeled shoes that tied on the top and a pair of brown knee-high stockings. The gray pullover sweater was riddled with holes from the knife and had been cut open down the front by the medical team. It was heavily bloodstained in the back.

The heavy knit sweater Felicia had worn – the one knit for her by her mother-in-law – was stained with blood and had punctures that corresponded to the wounds on her body.

The bra Felicia had worn was shredded front and back by the murder weapon.

Both bra and panties were stained with blood, the bra particularly dense with it. The assailant had cut the designer jeans Felicia had worn open along the front and that front was soaked with blood. Her pockets were empty of anything but congealed blood.

All the clothing would be handed over to the county prosecutor's office as part of the chain of evidence.

The signs of the treatment at the emergency room were apparent. The lines and tubes that had been inserted into her body were left there. The incision in her chest that permitted the futile attempt at heart massage was visible.

Morrill, the pathologist, located, examined and described each wound. He measured the wounds to see how deep they were. He estimated the angle of the wound from the ground. He checked to see how the skin was torn.

Morrill found 10 stab wounds in her back and 10 stab wounds in the front of her chest and neck. Her right palm and two fingers had been cut, a defensive wound that showed she had reached for the blade. There was another wound on the back of her left hand. She had been stabbed 22 times. The wounds to her heart and lungs would have been enough to kill her.

He noted that the most distinguishing characteristics were the multiple stab wounds apparent and concentrated particularly in the chest region.

Eight of the 22 wounds penetrated Felicia's lungs and heart and Morrill did an internal examination on these. One of the three wounds in the front of the chest went three inches into the left lung. One of the wounds in her back went five inches into the chest and cut the aorta and pulmonary artery. In her chest cavity, Morrill found half a pint of blood.

The cause of death was what had been expected: massive internal hemorrhage, multiple stab wounds to the chest and neck and a defensive wound to the right hand.

By Monday, the plans for Felicia's wake and funeral were complete. The viewing was to be at the DeAngelis Funeral Home in Boothbay Tuesday and Wednesday. The funeral Mass was to be Thursday at St. Genevieve's, the Cusack's parish church.

Monday morning, Glanville and Peters drove to the senior citizens' apartment building where Felicia had once worked. They talked to Superintendent Steve Gagne about the arguments that Felicia had had with the previous superintendent, Tony Giglio.

Gagne called the owner of the building who said Tony held Felicia responsible for his being fired, but wouldn't have been angry enough to murder her.

On Monday afternoon Peters and Glanville went to Larry's house to ask the old questions and a few new ones. Larry said the picture he had in his mind by then of the murderer was of a figure kneeling over Felicia, rocking back and forth, hands clasped together. The head, he said, looked like a skull.

Glanville asked Larry about Amy Lee Halford, Larry's 21-year-old girlfriend. Larry acted as though he knew the question about her was inevitable, Glanville thought.

Yes, they had been lovers and had stayed together for a while, but they broke up two months ago, Larry said.

Why, Glanville asked.

I wanted to work with Felicia on our marriage, Larry said.

She knew about Amy, Larry told Glanville, but despite that affair and others he and Felicia were trying to put their marriage back together. Larry seemed forthright, Glanville thought. When asked, Larry gave them Amy's address and phone number.

Larry mentioned that the detectives might want to interview former tenants at the house he and Felicia owned in Boothbay. They had, from time to time, been forced to evict some of them and Larry had an idea that eviction could have been a motive for the murder.

Felicia's body was brought to DeAngelis' funeral home in Boothbay on Monday.

53

Linda Ellis

When Vida DeAngelis, the manager of the funeral home, prepared bodies for viewing, she liked to leave a pleasant look, even a slight smile on the faces of the dead. Nature seemed to do part of her work for her, Mrs. DeAngelis said, because the expression on the face often changes on its own before embalming. It may be hard to believe she said, but she has seen the expression on the face of a dead person change from fear to peace.

However, Mrs. DeAngelis felt that nothing she could do worked with Felicia. There was a look of pain and shock on Felicia's face that just wouldn't go away.

On Tuesday Glanville made an appointment with psychiatrist Mark Hawkins for the following Sunday. The detective wanted Hawkins, who had worked with police in other cases, to hypnotize Larry. Hypnosis is an investigative tool that Glanville used with witnesses to get more details of what they had seen. Maybe under hypnosis Larry could remember more things about Saturday night.

That same day, Tuesday, March 23, Felicia's body was laid out in an open casket.

Her face seemed bloated. Her sisters thought that her makeup and hair were wrong. Instead of being parted on the left with bangs that flipped over to the right, her hair was styled in a modified pageboy. All the ends were curled under, surrounding her face. Her hands were swollen and her wedding ring was perched on her left ring finger knuckle.

In her hands Felicia held a rosary with beads made from pressed white roses They were the roses that had been on her mother's coffin 18 years earlier.

For Felicia's father, Carmen, the scent from those roses seemed to fill the room. He had planned on being buried holding those rosary beads. *Now our Felicia will have them forever, Mama, Carmensaid tothe insideofhishead.*

At 3:42, Mrs. DeAngelis was called to the phone. The caller, who sounded like a young girl, asked "Is Mrs. Olivio there?"

"No, Mrs. Cunningham or Mrs. Cusack are here," the manager said (Larry's sister Dolores or his mother Gladys).

"That's it," the caller said. "I want you to know my boyfriend killed her. His name is Lloyd Wheeler." The caller hung up before Mrs. DeAngelis could say anything.

Glanville and Boothbay Detective John Fargo were at the funeral home that afternoon and Mrs. DeAngelis told them about the call.

In murder investigations Glanville usually went to the wake.

"You never know what's going to happen at a wake. You want to see who comes and who doesn't come. You always want a copy of the visitation list. In this case, particularly, I wanted to see how Larry was. He acted extremely emotional."

Larry wept openly and had to leave the room many times. He looked no one in the eye as he went in and out. Tears were pouring down his face, and he acted so upset at one point that he had to be given a tranquilizer by his sister, Dolores Cunningham.

Felicia's wake was crowded with mourners. Friends from the Newark area who hadn't seen Felicia in many years were there. There were her

Linda Ellis

friends from work, from the town hall, from the neighborhood, from the stores in town. Webster policemen were there to stand with their fellow officer. Members of the Gullwing Cove Lions Club, of which Larry was a member, formed an honor guard by the coffin. The Cove's senior citizens were transported in two large vans. Larry murmured to a fellow Lion that he hadn't known Felicia had so many friends.

The uneasy truce between Gerry Bucci and Larry failed to last through the wake. Gerry, still hurt by what had happened Sunday, spent a lot of time staring intently at Larry.

Once when she approached the coffin, he reacted sharply.

"Keep your fucking hands off her body," he snapped at her.

Years later, Larry said that he regretted that incident more than any of the hundreds of hostile exchanges he had had with the Girardis over the decades of his marriage to Felicia.

On Thursday morning before the funeral Mass, the family went to DeAngelis'. Before they left for church, they filed past the coffin one last time. Gerry didn't want to leave her sister at the funeral home. It all seemed like a bad dream. She looked at Felicia in the coffin and remembered how her sister used to wink at her. She remembered how her sister taught her the right way to brush her teeth. She remembered the hair-coloring disaster, the hilarious quest for green hair.

Gerry wanted to pull Felicia out of the coffin and say, "Wake up. Wake up."

The church was three miles from the funeral home. So many cars were in the cortege that police were needed to direct traffic. From the Webster police alone, there were 22 cars. The pews at the church filled quickly when the cortege arrived.

Felicia's coffin was carried up the front steps of the church, put on a casket carriage and wheeled down the aisle to a spot just in front of the altar. Pallbearers covered the coffin with a white pall. Fr. James Doyle, the parish priest at St. Genevieve's, said the funeral Mass and gave the eulogy. After the Mass ended, Fr. Doyle walked down to Felicia's coffin with an altar boy carrying a cross. The priest blessed the coffin with holy water one last time in the church, and everyone was ready to leave. The cemetery was only a mile from the church. The plot was one that Larry and Felicia had chosen when they moved to The Cove.

When the coffin was placed over the open grave, Fr. Doyle said final prayers before the burial.

"May her soul and all the souls of all the faithful departed rest in peace," the priest said.

"Amen," the mourners answered.

The service was over. People left the graveside and returned to their cars to leave for a reception at the Gullwing Cove First Aid Squad.

The Cove squad wanted to do something for Felicia. She had not been a member of the squad, but the volunteers considered her an honorary member. Felicia had raised money for the squad to pay the mortgage on a new building.

Since Monday, the squad had been getting donations of food for the lunch. Felicia's brother Carmen, Jr., who owned a restaurant in Newark, brought equipment and utensils.

Tables held huge platters of baked ziti and ravioli, pans of lasagna, a baked ham, a roast turkey, cold cuts, mounds of cole slaw, Tupperware bowls filled with tossed salad, potato and macaroni salads, baked beans, rolls, bread, and for dessert, chocolate sheet cake, lemon pound cake, fruit salad and chocolate chip cookies.

Larry told his friends and co-workers that they would see people drinking and having a good time at the rescue team headquarters. They shouldn't think it out of place. It was just an Italian thing, a way to let off steam, he said. Maloney, Larry's partner, was annoyed at the Italian reference. Don't Polish mourners eat food after funerals? Maloney wanted to ask Larry. Larry hated references to his being of Polish descent, Maloney knew. Probably this time of grieving was not the right time to tease Larry.

Larry, however, didn't strike his partner as particularly grief-stricken.

"Hey, Larry, the only place there's not enough food is at some kind of country club party, any party for rich people," Maloney teased Cusack.

The Girardis barely touched the food. They stood apart, accepting condolences and just waiting until they could politely leave.

Larry had a few drinks and walked up to Joey Girardi.

"I'll never forget her, Joey. She had so many friends. She did so much for people. I loved her so much."

Larry then did something he had never done before. He grabbed Joey by the shoulders and kissed him on the mouth. This was like something out of *The Godfather*, Joey thought.

Joey looked long and hard at his brother-in-law.

"I'm going to find the son-of-a-bitch who killed her, Larry. And when I do, I'm going to kill the bastard myself."

Part II

The Mystery

Chapter 3

The Victim

Felicia Girardi Cusack was an exemplary daughter, a devoted wife, a prized employee and an outstanding mother.

That's standard obituary material shared by millions of others at a cemetery near you. Here's the difference: were the critical elements of Felicia's life to be sifted through a filter, the gold nuggets remaining would be her children. Their mutual love slipped the bounds of earth.

"It was like that movie that came out later, 'Ghost', where the dead husband guards the wife? Demi Moore," Denyce Buckley said. "Felicia was there for them, to protect them."

John had written notes to his mother several times a week from the time he first learned to print. I love you mommy He hid them where he knew she would find them the next day. He would draw stick figures of himself John, his sister Grace, his Mom and Dad and Dime, the Chihuahua.

When his Aunt Gerry took him to a child psychologist three weeks after his mother's death, the psychologist had John draw the stick figures. In that picture, John and his mother did not exist. Larry was lying on the street in front of their home and Grace and Dime were their usual sizes.

Mommy We love you and we find you...where are you?

Linda Ellis

No amount of diligence or devotion had lent her protective garb against a murderer or cushioned those savage slashes. Duty and diligence were, in fact, all too large a chunk of Felicia's foreshortened life. There had been far too little opportunity for frivolity during her 44 years on earth.

Felicia Girardi was born into an Italian-American, working class family in Newark NJ June 3, 1937. If Norman Rockwell had wanted to portray such a family for the cover of the old Saturday Evening Post, he could well have chosen the Girardis.

Felicia was the seventh girl and ninth child of Carmen and Dorothea Girardi. As with most of her siblings she was born at one of the city's Catholic hospitals. There would be 11 daughters and four sons before Dorothea went to her well-earned rest. Three were born at home.

By the time of Felicia's death in 1982, two of the other sisters were dead and one of the brothers. An accident, a fatal asthma attack and cancer were the causes.

Felicia was reared in a home where old-fashioned virtues of honesty, hard work, respect for others, belief in God and Democratic politicians were taught. Family love and loyalty were assumed.

The neighborhood was in Our Lady of the Angels parish and parish activities dominated the social life of everyone who lived there. Along with the Catholic Church, labor union activities were the cornerstones of their public lives.

In the Girardi house, homework was strictly enforced and chores were assigned. For an hour before bedtime, if the chores were done, the children could read or listen to the radio.

People who have one or two siblings tend to romanticize the lives of their friends who come from large families. The Girardis were a super-sized household even by the standards of the 1930s and 40s.

"The good news is that you're never alone," Josie Girardi Cooper said. "The bad news is that you're never alone."

The sisters passed favorite books back and forth. One much-thumbed copy of *Anne of Green Gables* inspired a daring act of personal vanity in the Girardi household In the book, the heroine attempts hair-coloring experiment that results in a sickly shade of green. The Girardi girls decided to replicate the experiment in the book and get green hair of their own.

"Then the whole neighborhood would say 'Look at the those Girardi girls, aren't they something'!

"What a mess," Felicia's sister Vicki recalled. "We mixed up different colors but our hair didn't turn green or any color, really, it was sort of dead, you know?

"The hair is colored reddish brown with gray roots. The hair is blood stained. The eyes are colored brown and examination of the conjunctiva and the sclera is unremarkable. Major damage is to frontal scalp."

Felicia's father, Carmen Sr., worked twelve hours a day, six days a week to support his wife and children. Each child was given a job in the home.

Felicia's daily task was cleaning the bathroom, one bathroom for a family that grew to 17. In addition, in the evenings, she would get the toddler-aged siblings to bed, police the required minutes for the toothbrushing task and read three of the littlest Girardis their bedtime stories.

...Babar..my Friend Flicka..Pat the Bunny

The household duties taught her priorities and set the pattern for what would become her life's pain and pleasure: her roles as wife and mother.

Throughout her life, she was known for her sparkling clean home. In the several houses of her adulthood, she would rarely go to bed until she had scrubbed the kitchen floor and washed everything that had accumulated during the day in the laundry hampers.

Four years before her death, Larry finally agreed that she could have a no-wax kitchen floor installed. It did not give her the result she wanted: she couldn't bring out the kind of shine she was used to with the older floors. She saw no option except to apply, three times a week, wax-like products that she could buff to a glow.

Felicia's hands were in water so much of the time that she didn't join her girlfriends in their weekly manicures. It was an indulgence that she could not afford in terms of time, money or arguments with her husband. So she joked with Denyce and Jenny that her hands were so waterlogged they'd have to be drained before they could be painted.

Located on the palm of the right hand is a defense-type wound which is intermittent in its course and measures 8 cm in length (3.15 inches)...This involves the joints of the 4th and 5th fingers as well as the palmar aspect of the hand at the base of the 1st and 2nd fingers.

Each time she visited her father, she would insist on cleaning his kitchen floor as well.

"All her life she would walk right in and begin scrubbing. Even once at 2 in the morning, after a wedding, I had to move the refrigerator to make room for her bucket and the suds," Carmen Sr. said.

It is possible that Felicia had an obsessive-compulsive disorder, said a psychiatrist who looked at the case notes two decades later. In the early 80s, this disorder was not widely diagnosed, the expert said. Spending hours each day cleaning and doing laundry was not considered unusual. For a woman to clean her house all day was not considered strange in those days.

She was that way about personal hygiene as well,

"She brushed her teeth at least five times a day," Mandy Girardi Slayton said. "Her hair was always neat because it was very thick hair and she sprayed it; we all sprayed our hair back then. Her clothing was ironed and she fought so hard to get her weight under control as well. The smoking and the weight were two things she could not control and she was so unhappy about this conflict," Andorra said.

It was all so backward, her sisters said after her death. They needed her to give them approval, not the other way around.

Even though all the Girardi children knew that they were loved when they were growing up, Felicia seemed a frightened child. She had little self-confidence, and she cried often. It puzzled the rest of the family that Felicia didn't feel OK about herself. She never felt she was doing enough.

At age 23, this sense of inadequacy would lead her into a marriage with a man who would milk that neurosis for all it was worth.

An aunt on her mother's side told her she was born with a "veil": afterbirth material clinging to her scalp and shadowing her face. This is an omen; the relative told Felicia that you will die at a young age.

"The afternoon Felicia was born, now, we thought it was a boy," Carmen, her father, said. "But when the nurse said it's another girl (there would be 11 girls, four boys} I said that's OK, I love my girls. I said to the nurse 'Is she pretty?' and the nurse said yeah, so I said that's OK then."

Is there a reason for this run of girlbabies? Carmen said to the inside of his head. We're doin' it the same way as always.

Carmen said no one told him or his wife Dorothea that Felicia was born with a veil. "If she was, though, I do believe that is an omen."

"We had nine, I think we had nine kids at the time or ten at the time when we moved away from Newark to Hilltown," Felicia's father said, "and I was supposed to go in (to serve in the Army during WW2). So I got the family moved, and I was to leave the next day, a Tuesday, and then the Germans just gave up. I got a telegram saying 'Don't bother. Don't come. The Krauts gave up' Something like that."

"All Dad's friends from Webster Street were yelling: 'Hey, come on, time to go to the station, you're gonna miss your train and be AWOL'. Dad showed them the telegram," Christine, the fourth child, third sister, remembered with a grin.

Carmen worked as a butcher until 1943 on 7th Avenue in Newark. He was making $27 a week. He worked six days a week from 7 a.m. to 7 p.m. On Sundays he worked a half-day so that people coming out from the early Mass could buy their Sunday roast. During the war, people saved up their coupons to buy meat once a week.

In December 1943, a friend told Carmen there might be an opening with the National Biscuit Company. Would he want to drive a delivery truck for $42 a week?

"Would I ever," Carmen recalled in an emotional interview a year after his daughter's murder. "National Biscuit said they would be pleased to hire me. The hitch was getting in the union. They (the Teamsters' local) called me down to union hall and ask me why I should get this job in front of all the other people ahead of me wanting the job.

"I said I want this for my family and so I don't got to get up at 4 in the morning to get to Mass before I got to be at the butcher. So the union guy says 'How many kids you got?' I says 10 and one on the way. So he says 'You start working next Monday at 9 in the morning. And you can go to any Mass you want on Sunday'."

Carmen was to be with National Biscuit for 31 years. He held two part-time jobs at other companies for many of those years as well.

"I got my first week's pay, $42, I bring it home, give it to my wife and she says I must be working too hard to be paid that much. Then I get the biggest route they have and bring home $110 a week on the big route and she asks me what is she going to do with all this money!"

The Girardis always had the biggest Christmas tree on the block, Deborah Ferraro, the second-born of the Girardi daughters recalled.

"We always got new clothes at Christmas and the neighbors would wait to see the line of 11 Girardi girls go back to school with our new clothes. Felicia

69

always got blue; she looked good in blue. Larry never bought her any clothes in blue.

"We had so much fun at Christmas as a family," Deborah recalled. "We would rewrap our presents and take them back to go under the tree. Then we'd have lunch and then we'd open the presents again."

Felicia's childhood was spent in a loving, nurturing place where children and pets spilled from every room and Dad brought home steady paychecks and Mom was at home.

There were rules to be ignored at a child's peril. Many limits were set and punishments imposed if a child stepped over any line. There were strict curfews for both the girls and the boys. The elder Girardis had to know where the children would be, with whom and the phone numbers. The Girardi children had after-school jobs, at-home jobs and homework.

Given her upbringing, Felicia's decision to marry a surly, sexy Marlon Brando wannabe who was aggressively antisocial would seem an unlikely choice.

Marrying against type, though, is usually the right thing to do. Psychological research indicates that people tend to marry someone with whom they feel no need to compete. Generally, marriage between partners with different strengths and weaknesses is more likely than not to succeed, experts say.

However, hundreds of thousands of men and women are married to spouses who exploit the weaknesses and deny the strengths. Felicia Girardi would join that legion of walking wounded.

Felicia wanted to be a wife and mother. She didn't consider college but instead went to a vocational high school to become a secretary. She was well liked by her classmates, her siblings said, and was elected treasurer of the student body.

When she graduated, she got a job at Gerard & Gerard, a maker of commercial hardware equipment in Melrose.

She did not think that she was pretty enough to be a receptionist. She was glad to have the job as a clerical worker; there was a path for advancement to secretarial duties. Appearance was very important then for someone who aspired to be a secretary.

There is blood staining located over the face diffusely from the frontal scalp wound and particularly prominent over the nose. Examination of the nose and ears revealed blood located predominantly in the left nostril as well as both ear lobes."

Had Felicia survived she would not have liked her face, Gerry thought at the wake.

Lawrence Andrew Cusack, Jr., came from a Polish-American working class family in Newark. By the time Larry was a teenager, he had experimented with sex on several levels. He and two of his sister's friends, two years older than he, formed a triangle that put Larry light years ahead of his classmates. He never talked about it or about much of anything – a personality trait that served him well until 1983 – but people found out and his friends were jealous and their parents horrified. One of his mother's friends was also terrified that her liaisons with Larry would be discovered. His friends were forbidden to hang out with him. This was the late 1940s, when what Larry was doing and learning was abnormal for a teenage boy, at least in Our Lady of the Angels parish.

Half-a-century later, psychiatrists would speculate that the problems Larry had as an adult had their roots in that precocious promiscuity.

Mr. Cusack had a good union job at a brewery but he drank and gambled much of it away. Larry's ambition was to get a good-paying, steady job in the brewery and keep the paycheck, not piss it away as his dad did, literally, each week. His brother Jake's goal was to be a cop. While Larry waited to get into the union to get the brewery job, Larry went to work at Gerard & Gerard. Larry and Felicia met there.

"Mom, I've met this really nice girl. She's really pretty but she's kind of chubby. But pretty," Larry's mother related this introduction as she spoke with Felicia's father at their wedding. Gladys, Larry's mother, thought that it was a harmless remark but Carmen Sr. saw it differently. At Felicia's funeral, the memory still enraged her father.

"The body consists of a well developed, well nourished white female measuring 62 inches in height and weighing 150 lbs...."

"Our sister was married in 1960 in Our Lady of the Angels parish," Gerry said. "She was the third of us girls to get married. He (Larry) picked out the hall for the reception, the Polish-American Hall, and he reserved the party room that only held 50 people and there were over 200 at the church."

"She was too good for him. I wanted to throw the bastard out of the house when we found that out. If her mother had been alive, she would have broken it off," Felicia's father Carmen said. "We felt bad for our

Felicia, we were embarrassed but we didn't do anything about it. I mean, it wouldn't have done any good to argue with him."

"Felicia should have realized right there that Larry would be mean because he was so mean about the wedding reception money," Gerry said. "She told us later that he was concerned he'd have to pay for some of the liquor at the reception so he wouldn't allow more than 50 people to be invited to the reception. He liked that they got so many presents but he would only let 50 be invited to the reception."

"He did give our sister a very nice-sized diamond engagement ring," Joey Girardi, the second oldest brother, said.

Felicia gave him her virginity. The groom was surprised, even amused, but that was likely the normal state of young American brides until the mid-1960s.

Felicia and Larry moved out of the city three years after they married. They wanted a better life for themselves and the children they would have. When they married, they had about $1,000 between them. At the time of her death, they owned two houses, the home in Gullwing Cove and the rental in Boothbay. Just two weeks before Felicia was murdered, when they did their taxes, they had estimated their net worth at $90,000.

Her family thought Felicia and Larry would start a family right away. It would be the fulfillment of her dream. Instead it took seven years for the Cusacks to conceive Grace.

Larry at one point told her that if a doctor found that she could not have babies, the marriage was over. He could have had an annulment from the church on that basis. He said it must be her fault

73

and she did not argue the point. Nothing was more important to her vision of success than Larry and the status of being married to Larry. She would never endanger that status.

"Felicia loved kids," her sister Vicki said. "She was wonderful with them. She was the first choice as a babysitter when we were growing up."

When Grace was born in 1967, Larry was stunned. He immediately blamed Felicia. He had been so confident that the baby was a boy. He was driving a truck at the time, delivering beer, and had told his fellow drivers that he was having a son.

"When he learned the baby was a girl, he would not go to the hospital to see Felicia or the baby for three whole days. When he finally walked into Felicia's room, he threw six roses on the bed and said 'If it'd been a boy you would've got a dozen'," Vicki, one of Felicia's sisters, recalled.

"Even after the pain of that scene Felicia kept Larry on a pedestal," her sister Christine Potter said. "It was Larry, Larry, Larry did this, he did that, he is such a great guy. He let me have a new kitchen floor. He is such a good father. I'm so lucky. Blah, blah, blah. That's why she never told us all that was wrong. When he stayed out all night, she would tell us he was working a double shift."

Christine's best friend was married to a cop and she knew that nobody got that much overtime in a suburban precinct. Everybody knew he was lying, he was meeting other women, but no one in the Girardi family would ever confront him because they knew if they did, Felicia would never speak to her family again.

"We refused to take a chance that we would lose her," Christine said, tears flowing down her face.

So in 1967, when Grace was born, her father was not a happy man either at home or on the job. He had grown bored with Felicia, he hated being a beer distributor and he didn't have the son he had expected. He wished that he had more schooling.

The only bright spot in his life, he would say later, was sex with relative strangers, women who did not want a commitment. Interviews with those women indicate that he was a bright spot in their lives as well.

When the Cusacks moved to the Jersey Shore they bought property in Boothbay, a two-family house, and made extensive improvements. They lived in one unit and rented out the other. They would move up and out, Larry said, and they'd have the income from both units of the two-family house.

Felicia decorated both sides of the duplex with yard sale acquisitions. She longed to have a house in which everything was coordinated, and she would grab a few minutes now and then to look through home decorating magazines at the Boothbay public library.

"Felicia was so excited about the move to the Shore. She totally believed that Larry would make enough money so they would be financially secure. He sold her a bill of goods," Mario Girardi, the youngest brother, said.

Felicia never cared much about money, according to her closest friends. She hoped for enough to put Grace and John through college and enough to be able to entertain her family and friends and to give Grace a nice wedding. Beyond that, she didn't see money as important.

Larry appeared to care *only* about money and the choices that money brings. His mother said that he had been that way since childhood. His father gambled and drank away much of his paycheck. Larry and his siblings never knew from one day to the next whether they'd lose their home, a modest one even by Newark standards.

Before she dated Larry, Felicia had had other opportunities to begin a serious relationship. Something was always missing. After one date with Larry, she saw only him and loved only him. Apparently Felicia had a taste for danger that no one knew existed.

Early in the marriage it became clear to Larry, however, that he and Felicia had made a bad decision. If he could have chosen a bride from a punch list of attributes, he would have ordered up a nymphomaniac with a trust fund.

And whom would Felicia have called Prince Charming? Her friend Julia Miller thought for a few minutes. "A teacher, a man with regular hours and the summer off who would have time to be kind and gentle to her and a good father to at least four children," Julia decided.

Felicia seemed to enjoy sex, Larry said, but there was no fire. She shared neither his appetite for sexual experimentation nor his lust for money. In bed, she tried hard to please but after a while that got on his nerves, Larry said.

Once the Cusacks moved to the Shore, Larry changed jobs several times. He renovated another rental property, this one for a friend, and drove a truck for a succession of wholesale distributors. During this time, Felicia was a secretary for a wholesale bakery.

In 1972, Larry got lucky. A tip from a friend steered him to the right people and after doing well on the police exam, Larry became a cop in the northern suburb of Webster. The benefits and pension plan were substantially better than those of any other job he had pursued. Being a police officer also brought him the respectability, stability and vastly improved access to women that he had sought all along.

Now all he needed was more money. He often commuted by train. He didn't need his personal car on the job, of course, and commuter traffic on the Garden State Parkway could be brutal. Taking the train saved money.

Enough was never enough for Larry. Oct. 17, 1980 he set fire to the Cusacks' rental property, the two-family house in Boothbay. He started the fire in the northeast corner of the living room, on the first floor of the two-story frame building. The building was without tenants at the time, a fact that Larry seized and used to his advantage. He put a lit cigarerette under a sofa cushion.

Although the fire was at first labeled suspicious by the Boothbay fire officials who responded to the alarm, the final ruling came down as a fire that was accidental in origin. The property could be rebuilt, the insurance company ruled, and the check to the Cusacks was for $22,554.50. That was a setback for Larry; he wanted at least $37,800.

Records at the insurance company and at the fire department indicate ongoing suspicion on the part of both agencies but not enough evidence to deny the claim.

The Cusack family moved to Gullwing Cove now that Larry's prospects were bright, and the insurance on the rental property was there for the down payment.

Linda Ellis

The first room that Felicia decorated was Grace's bedroom. She bought a canopied bed, encircled it in pink ruffles and arranged dozens of Grace's stuffed animals and dolls on the bed. She bought a stenciling kit and turned a used chest of drawers into a gleaming white bureau with small roses and little green frogs sprinkled around. Her budget didn't run to carpet in the upstairs bedrooms but she was creative with rug remnants.

Two years after Grace's birth, Felicia gave Larry the son he demanded. **I'm here dad...**

Grace often took her father's side in family discussions but she and her mother got along well – better, in fact, than do most mothers and daughters. To Larry's dismay, John was his mother's child in appearance and personality. The bond between them was extraordinary. Their closeness infuriated Larry but he didn't know how to control it, how to make them include him. Even he couldn't change the fact that John looked and behaved like Felicia.

Both the children had friends, were invited to birthday parties and were active in sports most of the year. That, to Larry, made up for what he considered their failings. He took any frustrations out on the usual suspect, his compliant and loving wife. He had a repertoire of childish ways to hurt her. He would refuse to eat more than a couple of bites of a lovingly prepared dinner. He would tell her that she wasn't putting enough starch in his uniform shirt and then the next week tell her it was too much. The worst hurt was sleeping with other women and barely attempting to hide the affairs.

Felicia did what she had to do: she refused to acknowledge these horrors unless Larry forced her to hear about them.

The most serious of these involvements lasted more than a year. The woman was in many ways a size six version of Felicia. She was a woman who loved her home and children, a widow in her late 30s with inherited money. She craved sex with Larry, even asked him to move in but, in the end, she declined to marry him. Her pre-teen children didn't like him. He went through a series of short-term affairs and then returned to Felicia, who always took him back, who always loved him and who always forgave him. He promised Felicia he would be faithful from that point on.

In 1981, Larry became involved with Amy Lee Halford, a pretty, vivacious secretary barely out of her teens. He moved in with Amy. After a month of being Larry's roommate, Amy called Felicia to ask her to divorce him.

"Not in your lifetime, you whore, and if you ever show up in this neighborhood I'll mop up the streets with you." Felicia, normally calm and collected, came unglued. She was enraged at the nerve of this woman and afraid that this might be the one for whom Larry would leave.

Larry and Amy stayed together for two months before he moved back home "to be with his children" at Christmas. He told Felicia the affair with Amy was over, but, true to form, he lied

Felicia had to tell someone about this situation. The pressure and pain were overwhelming and she feared she would lose her grip on normalcy if she kept it all inside. She chose Julia Miller, the mother of Grace's best friend. Julia was a good listener. She had the added advantage of not having known Felicia and Larry very long. Her reactions were based on what was happening now, not influenced by any

Linda Ellis

baggage from the family's past. Only with Julia would Felicia talk about the dark side of her marriage.

"She (Felicia) spoke highly of Larry, everywhere, all the time," Julia would say later. "She held him on a pedestal. Larry was not easy to know. My husband was in Lions Club with him and he would comment on how Larry carried himself as if he were above the other men. He carried himself too high on a plateau and it was hard to get into a conversation with him or really get close to him.

"Felicia wanted to live with illusions as far as Larry was concerned. And she wanted *us* to think only good things about him the same as her. We couldn't do that. He treated her bad."

Dad's bad. Dad's bad he's going to be sorry...

"While the decedent's husband was gone, the decedent was allegedly attacked and received multiple stab wounds to the chest and neck. She was rushed to Harbor Medical ...Admitted to the ER. Pupils fixed and dilated. There was no palpable pulse. Clothing removed revealing multiple stab wounds of the anterior chest...neck...inner cavities Intubated. CVP lines inserted. Chest opened & cardiac massage by Dr. Bhashkar...All measures were unsuccessful.

Cause of death: massive hemorrhage as a consequence of multiple stab wounds to the chest. Time of death: 8:30 p.m.

The pathologist began the internal examination that includes a thorough look at the brain and removal of vital organs for study. The knife wounds had gone deep in three sites. Felicia's body cavities had been savaged. Her anatomical spaces were filled with blood and bodily fluids, the result of knife wounds penetrating vital organs.

In the left pleural (lung) cavity Morrill measured 75cc (approximately 1/3 cup) of hemorrhagic (mainly blood) fluid and in the right, 300cc (approximately 1 ¼ cups).

Dr. Morrill worked through the cranial cavity and saw nothing unusual until he examined the blood vessels at the base of her brain. There was mild arteriosclerosis (a condition in which the walls of the arteries become hard and thick, sometimes interfering with blood circulation). That condition would have had to be addressed to keep Felicia healthy over an average lifetime. There would be no problems and no lifetime now, average or otherwise.

The larynx and trachea revealed some mucus but no other abnormality.

She had wanted very much to stop smoking, Jenny Russo, one of Felicia's friends, said.

"Thoracic cavity: dissection of the pulmonary arterial tree reveals the wounds of the main pulmonary artery...The lungs are sectioned to reveal focal (localized to the tissue around the wound) hemorrhage around the stab wounds. In addition, there is a granuloma measuring 1.8 cm in greatest length located in the superior lobe of the right lung (a granuloma is a benign inflammatory tumor filled with granular matter)...."

"But she was more frightened of about weight gain," Jenny said, "and that kept her smoking. She was in a very difficult position, torn between two goals."

81

Linda Ellis

Morrill posted the Cusack autopsy and closed up his office in the bowels of the county medical complex.

The pathology suite was not the place to be on a beautiful spring evening, but Morrill was a good doctor, a conscientious scientist and in addition to that, he had met Felicia Cusack and had liked her very much.

"My daughter's softball team played against the Cove team, and Mrs. Cusack was their coach. She was an extremely effective coach, very calm and controlled, and she stressed that her girls be good sports. I'm very sad that she is gone, and gone in such a violent way," the pathologist said later.

Carmen Girardi, Jr., Felicia's oldest brother, believed there was an intent to kill his sister and that it was a not a robbery gone horribly wrong.

"Consider the way my sister was attacked – stabbed in the back, with a broken jaw, black and blue marks all over her body and with no fingernails left, that's not anything to do with a robbery. That's a vicious murder done on purpose. Now what in the world could an angel like Felicia have done that someone would hate her that much?

"Located in the left anterior chest...is a group of 5 stab wounds...two puncture defects in the left cup of the bra as well as one located in the midline of the back. The bra has been cut open and is hemorrhagically stained and white panties, blood stained..

"Why would any girl, in this case my sister, be picked out in a parking lot and stabbed that many times and left to die in, practically in, the middle of a

82

garbage dump?" Carmen, Jr., asked rhetorically. "Why so many wounds? Her jaw was broken. Why?" he continued. "We're a large family. We'll take care of our own. We'll find out the answers to all those questions."

It was Felicia's practice to go home at lunch hour, make supper for the family, put a load of wash in the machine and come back to work eating an apple, which was her lunch.

Looking for ways to please her husband, she mastered Polish cooking. He told her he wanted normal American food, they were Americans, not Poles, couldn't she get that through her Italian head?

Felicia spent hours with the children, teaching them to bake and to make holiday decorations. She made their Halloween costumes each year.

Mommy, no clowns we're afraid of clowns.

Occasionally she would bring Grace and John to work when her babysitter was unavailable. The kids would sit at a desk in the back of the office and draw pictures. They were very well behaved, the town administrator, Ed Cicotte, recalled.

"For no extra pay Felicia would stay overtime to finish work, typing accounts, financial work. I gave her more responsibility than perhaps I should have, but she would eagerly take the work on. She worked as a clerk, stenographer, secretary and then her last title, housing coordinator. Her salary at the time of her death, at 20 hours a week with benefits, was $13,000 a year.

"She was very professional in the way she carried herself, the way she spoke and worked with the public. She was very efficient and was friendly to everybody. Well, she was not unfriendly to Republicans but she did not go out of her way. She had this inbred dislike of Republicans and I'll tell you she lived in the wrong town to feel that way. She had a good sense of humor and liked to listen to jokes, but she wasn't one to tell jokes herself," Cicotte said.

There were problems about Felicia's employment in Gullwing Cove. She was in the opposition political party and, in small towns, politics matter.

"Soon after I hired her, really soon, I started hearing complaints from town council about hiring a Democrat even just part-time clerical and boy, that issue just never went away," Cicotte said. "It was solidified in the year that Larry ran for council. Felicia was insulted by a question that Ed Cady, (the Republican candidate for council) asked Larry, and she stood up and really let the Republicans have it. It was so unlike her to be loud and angry but I tell you about it to show you how she was about her husband. Nobody, not her friends, not her family, nobody could insult her husband and get away with it. And this wasn't even an insult," Cicotte said. "She just couldn't stand it if anyone was critical, what she interpreted as critical of her husband."

Thus, the only people who had motive to dislike her were Gullwing Cove's Republicans. Even the county prosecutor, a Democrat, admitted the Republicans weren't killing off the opposition, at least not one at a time.

Felicia once helped give CPR to a child at a community pool near where her father and brother lived in northern New Jersey. The child was from

Calcutta. When Larry learned of the incident and his wife's role in it, he expressed great pride.

"He talked about it for weeks at work," Maloney, Larry's partner on the Webster police force said. "He said it was good publicity for him in case he decided to run for office again and besides that, as a cop, he believed in saving every life, no matter what color the kid was. All he could talk about was this thing that happened and how it could help him in his run for politics," his partner said. "When they had her picture in the paper with the kid he was so pissed off that he couldn't have gotten into that picture somehow."

"Some people said that the reason Felicia was so nice to the seniors is that their votes would help Larry when he ran for town council the next time. I personally don't believe that of her," the mayor of the Cove, Cal Winters said. "But I would never put it past him."

In the Cove, Felicia was good cop to Larry's bad cop, literally and figuratively. "He was disliked here," Mayor Winters said. "He was liked by some of the women because, well, whatever reason. You can guess. But he had few men friends of his own, not anyone that was not already part of a couple that Felicia had made friends with the wife."

He rarely hit it off with people in the right way, unlike the way Felicia was seen, Winters said. Larry drank only occasionally but when he did, he drank too much. He insulted people and never apologized when he sobered up.

"Come to think of it, he never apologized to anyone for anything as far as I know. I've actually asked people since her murder, asked if he ever apologized for the mean things he did or said, or the way he hurt Felicia's feelings in public," the mayor continued. "No one remembers one time."

Being Larry Cusack apparently meant never having to say you were sorry. Winters characterized Larry as "a nasty drunk," who used gutter language. When he drank, he was outgoing and aggressive. Sober, Larry was quiet, inside himself and he was sober most of the time. Felicia was quiet as well, Winters said, but she seemed to welcome you to go up and talk to her. When she liked you, you knew you had a friend for life.

Felicia told Julia Miller that she, Felicia, was lucky because Larry didn't hit her when he was angry or drinking too much. Julia said later that she did not know whether or not to believe Felicia. In any case, what he did with her head would have been enough without actually hitting her, her friends said. It would have hurt her less if he did physically attack her.

Denyce Buckley, Felicia's first friend in the Cove and one of the people closest to her, could not shake the images of her friend's violent death.

"The night after the murder, they began, my dreams about Felicia. She appeared to me in this dream. The streetlights went out and I thought I was awake. Felicia said 'Look, Denyce, look how I was killed. Look at these knife wounds.' And she showed me the stab wounds one by one. First on her back, more than a dozen of them. And then her chest wounds when the killer got her on the ground. And then on her hands when she tried to protect herself. She said 'Denyce, I can't rest, not yet. Something will happen about my death'."

Later, Denyce said, Felicia tried to convince her to join her, to take her hand. Denyce's spiritualist told her never to take Felicia's hand, that to do that would mean Denyce would die as well.

Denyce loved Felicia but not enough to die for her.

In 1973 Denyce's sister met Felicia at a beauty shop in town. She told Denyce that she met a girl from Newark, such a pretty thing, my sister said.

"I said 'What's her name?' My sister said 'Felicia Cusack'. I said I didn't know her but my sister said that couldn't be right because Felicia knows me. She said one of these days she's going to ring your doorbell.

"And sure enough, one day my doorbell rings and here's this beautiful woman standing by my door with these two beautiful little kids and she introduced herself and the kids. John was four years old then, so Grace would've been about six."

From that day on Felicia and Denyce were close friends.

It was at Denyce's insistence that her friend sought a diagnosis for the sharp stomach pains Felicia was having in October, five months before the murder. After three weeks in the hospital, the pain and bloating were put down to pancreatitis, an inflammation of the pancreas exacerbated by nerves. Her friends wondered what was really going on behind the careful facade the Cusacks had constructed around their private life.

Felicia was prized as a friend. In a later era, she would have had as many men friends as women. She knew how to keep a secret. She was generous with her time. She didn't interrupt. Her priorities were Larry and the children and cleaning her house but once those priorities were satisfied, she was great company.

"At the wake, she did not look like herself at all. Besides being bloated, Felicia without her voice, her warmth, her personality was not Felicia," her sister Deborah said.

Felicia had once confided to Denyce that she was dreaming of her late mother and that when she had those dreams, people in her family died. When she dreamt of her mother, she said, her brother Sammy had a heart attack and died. Again she dreamt and this time it was her sister Josephine. Again, and a nephew died at age 13 of cancer.

"My mother keeps coming to me and saying she wants Nancy and I tell her, 'Mommy, you can't have Nancy, she has three girls to take care of, her girls need her, Mommy, take me instead'.

If she had only known how much John and Grace would miss her, if she could know the pain they will have to live with, she would not have wished for that, Denyce said.

John continued his habit of making a drawing of his family. He would leave it on the kitchen table at night for Felicia to find in the morning.

"Off to bed, you two, and don't forget to brush your teeth," Felicia would say nightly, remembering that she was responsible for making sure her younger siblings brushed their teeth and it pleased her that she could remind her own children.

"Examination of the mouth reveals natural dentition in good oral hygiene...Both the fingernails

and the toenails are painted with reddish purple fingernail polish".

Felicia had kept each of John's notes and drawings in a box.

Denyce Buckley said that John continued to make the drawings and write the notes after his mother's death. He felt that if he did this every day, his mother would come back to him. If she didn't come back to him – and Fr. Doyle told him she would not – then she would at least see his notes and drawings. Fr. Doyle promised that.

Gerry Bucci, the sister whose birthday party Felicia had missed because Larry wanted to see a movie, was also visited by her murdered sister in nightly dreams. She was driving me crazy, Gerry said. She came to me every night telling me the house smelled bad, her house, and I was to go over and clean it every day. Then she'd remind me that Grace wanted designer jeans.

"Then the dreams stopped. She stopped visiting me in the night, and I wish she would come back again," Gerry said. "I wish she would bother me every night. I miss her so much."

Designer jeans, makeup, boyfriends, they were all issues between mother and daughter. Grace, at 13, was in some ways an alien being to her mother in the months before Felicia's death.

Felicia and her sisters had not been allowed to date or wear lipstick until they were 16. They wore dresses to school and were not too proud to wear hand-me-downs. Grace's friends wore makeup and tight jeans to school and talked on the phone for hours with boys. Felicia had no help from Larry. To a large extent, he refused to participate in the raising of the children, especially in their discipline.

"At the funeral, Larry was still damning Felicia with faint praise," Winters, the Cove's mayor, said. "A lot of things he did seemed false. He cried and cried. He sobbed. He had tears running down his cheeks for an hour at least. He said to me the day before, at the wake, he was sobbing heavily, and I put my arm around his back, and he said to me, 'We lost a good worker'.

"I couldn't help myself," the mayor said. "I shouted at him, right there at the wake, in front of God and everybody, 'A good worker? A good worker? This is your wife, man. What the hell's the matter with you?"

Felicia's children could not let go of her. Felicia's brothers and sisters, father and nieces and nephews could not say goodbye. Felicia's husband wept.

Forensic science, however, turned out the lights. Her body would yield no more clues:

<u>Medical examiner's checklist re: Felicia Girardi Cusack</u>

- Fingerprints logged
- Decedent's blood type is B+
- Multiple autopsy pictures posted
- Specimens sent for toxicological examination
- Fingernail clippings logged out and transferred to the prosecutor's office

where's mommy? what happened?

Chapter 4

Suspects

The Cusack murder had all the earmarks of a textbook case.

In a homicide, the finger of suspicion always locks in on the surviving spouse.

In the early hours that followed the bloody slaughter of Felicia Cusack, detectives learned a great deal about her husband's habits. He was doing everything wrong if he wanted to escape a murder charge. First, Larry Cusack was in the midst of a serious affair with a 21-year-old secretary. She was far from his first extracurricular dalliance. Second, he lied to police about her. Third, he had tried, unsuccessfully, to take out a $200,000 insurance policy on Felicia's life.

He was innocent, stupid or extremely clever.

Statistically, Larry was the leading candidate for stardom in the murder and detectives would do their best to cast him in the role. He was one of the two remaining legs of a love triangle. While there could be more women involved than police yet knew of, the likelihood was that the third leg was named Amy.

When police first talked to Larry about Amy, he lied and said the affair with her had ended. Amy, on the other hand, was candid about the affair from the start. She seemed, in fact, proud and excited about being involved in a murder investigation. Not only was the affair ongoing, she said, but she had met Larry for lunch the day his wife was murdered.

None of these circumstances mattered, however. This would not be a lay-up for police. Larry and Amy, separately, had solid alibis. Based on the evidence immediately following the murder, neither could have wielded the knife that tore Larry's wife to shreds. The widower and the girlfriend had independent verification of their alibis by sources who knew none of the principals and had no investment in any specific outcome.

A disinterested witness saw Larry 60 feet away from his wife when she was attacked. Larry had no blood on his clothes and his wife was covered with blood. Those who touched her during or after the attack could not have avoided being stained by her blood.

Amy said that she was in Atlantic City, 55 miles away, on the night of the murder. Detectives went there and found the people with whom Amy said she spent the night. They verified her story. Police checked the car she rented that Saturday for bloodstains or other evidence and found none.

Larry cooperated fully in the investigation. He agreed to be hypnotized to see if he could remember any details about the killer that he might be suppressing. Under hypnosis he again told police he thought a black man had committed the murder and that the man was "humping" Felicia as he was killing her. That never made sense, detectives knew, because Felicia's clothing, including her underwear, was in place and the autopsy showed no signs of sexual assault.

Investigators were bothered by the fact that Larry never helped Felicia.

"It should be noted that at no time following the assault on Felicia Cusack did her husband come into physical contact with her body nor did he express a desire to view her body following the conclusion of the code (a last attempt in the ER to get a heartbeat)," Boothbay Det. Luke Weathers noted in his report. "Deceased's husband did not ask at any point to see her."

I found that disgusting, Weathers said later. I still do. They were married, what, 22 years? They had raised two children together, the officer said. What a prick.

You don't know the half of it, officer. Mommy I miss you so

Larry agreed immediately to a lie detector test. He took a polygraph and three days later so did Amy. Both were asked if they had committed the murder, knew who did or hired someone to do it. They each said no to all the questions. The polygraph operator said that each was telling the truth.

While that pair received the most intense scrutiny, the investigation had begun on multiple fronts as soon as the ambulance sirens began their wail, bearing Felicia to Harbor Medical and to her final breath.

On Thursday Mar. 18, two nights *before* the murder, Rhonda Malone made a connection that would, in retrospect, be helpful to police. She and a boyfriend were on their way to a movie about Ugandan dictator Idi Amin, the feature playing next to the Richard Pryor movie that the Cusacks intended to see.

Malone reported to Boothbay police that a black male who said that he was a quarter short of the funds for a move ticket approached her and her companion. Would they give him the 25 cents? The man did not appear aggressive, Malone stated, but seemed stern. She started to reach into her pocketbook for her wallet to look for change when

93

she was rushed into the theater by her date. Approximately two hours later as the couple was leaving the theater they saw the same man in the lobby. They assumed that meant he had seen the movie.

"My date was nervous about this man," Malone said. "We rushed away from the theater."

That was March 18.

How could she or anyone know that 86 hours later she would be asked for help in catching a killer? Malone was called Sunday by Boothbay police and asked to look at a preliminary sketch of the suspect in the Cusack murder. Malone was stunned. The man asking for money outside the theater looked very much like this sketch.

As soon as police learned from Harbor County Medical's ER that Felicia Cusack was dead, two Boothbay patrolmen were detailed to Dublin restaurant as part of the investigation into the attack, now a homicide.

Police searched for the probable weapon, a knife. They wouldn't know anything definitive about the weapon until after the autopsy was done, but looking for a knife seemed to be a good use of police time. Clearly, she was killed with a sharp instrument and not shot or poisoned.

Officers looked in the municipal parking lot and along the beach for possible suspects. After that search was complete, it was show time. The movie theater would seem a likely hiding place for a killer. Two patrolmen and four detectives went to the two-screen South Strip Cinemas to speak to the patrons, ask for their cooperation and determine if any of them appeared suspicious.

Everyone in the movie house was asked to stay seated when the lights came on. Each patron left his or her name, address and phone number in case there were more questions.

After scouring the neighborhood for clues for two days, officials asked for public involvement. The Harbor County Commissioners approved a reward of $5,000 for information leading to the arrest of the killer. That reward pool would double during the investigation with contributions by a Boothbay business owner and the police union benevolent fund on behalf of Larry Cusack, a brother officer.

From the moment they buried their sister, the Girardi family began an independent investigation. They felt that Larry knew what happened and why. His behavior at the Cove house that night – the fake grief, the frantic, deliberately cruel choice of clothes for her to wear in her casket, the fury directed at all the Girardis – sealed his guilt in their eyes. He was involved, he knew about the murder, perhaps he could have prevented it. He would pay. He would suffer for this if it took the last Girardi standing to extract justice.

The Girardis would not count on law enforcement. Forget the cops. Larry was a cop, after all. Their sister had not been a celebrity or a member of the country club set; there was no pressure from the media to find her killer. What Felicia had, however, was her family.

Joseph "Joey" Girardi, the second oldest of the three brothers, sat in the county prosecutor's office until someone listened to him, point by point:

95

- Larry rarely went out of the house for social occasions without his automatic; he was very proud of it. In Dublin restaurant, especially, he could take off his sport coat and people would see it, the gun.
- The description of a "bald-headed nigger humping Felicia" was bizarre enough that it could not be believed.
- Larry moved his girlfriend Amy into the family home, allegedly to care for the children, to clean and cook and do laundry. His wife had nine sisters and Larry had his sister and mother who lived very near to the Cove; any one of them would have taken over until Larry could get more regular help.

Joey Girardi considered himself a skeptic, but he asked a psychic who had worked with police in other murders to help. The psychic went into a trance and felt a strong pain in her left side, the place where the killer landed the first blows, and she shouted out, "My Larry, My Larry," which the psychic said were Felicia's last words.

Joey spoke to Kevin Glanville, the prosecutor's detective assigned to head up the case for that office, about this information, and Glanville told Joey that Felicia had not used the possessive *my* when calling her husband and that the busboy who had given mouth-to-mouth resuscitation had heard her whispering at the end but could not be sure what was said. The word Larry, however, was not said when Felicia was very near death.

"Well, we also saw a spiritualist and she said a woman who had had an abortion killed our sister," Joey told the detective.

Glanville hated being negative with Felicia's family because he shared their belief that Larry was somehow involved and because he, Glanville, had liked their sister so much. However, he could not let them impede the investigation. He asked Joey again to advise the family to step back and let the authorities do their work.

A week later, eight of the Girardi siblings came to the prosecutor's office and demanded that Larry be apprehended. They would have a sit-in right here and not leave till Larry was arrested. The family began a shouting match with several detectives and clerical personnel (Glanville was out of the office at the time) and had to be forcibly removed.

Time for vigilante justice, declared father Carmen, Sr., brothers Joey and Mario and Carmen, Jr.

Andorra, Vicki, Sherry, Deborah, Maria, Geraldine, Josephine, Christine and Elizabeth, the sisters, agreed. The husbands and sons of the sisters agreed. The sons of their brothers agreed.

They invited Larry over for a Fourth of July celebration at Joey's house up in North Jersey. Joey was pretty successful and he had a big house. On the large property was a small furnished cottage built as a playhouse for Joey's children. It was big enough to hold four adults and even had a kitchen wing. The plan was to get Larry drunk – not difficult especially with single malt Scotch on hand – and have the brothers entice him into the playhouse and not let him out until he told the truth about Felicia's death.

Linda Ellis

Sounded like a plan. It might have worked. One of the brothers-in-law, however, had the bad manners to have a coronary and that required a call to 9-1-1. The plan evaporated the minute the call was made.

The crusade was far from over. The Girardis' rage and grief would keep them on a search for the truth about Felicia for as long as that quest took.

*   *   *

Six days after the murder, authorities were working overtime on what appeared to be a major break in the Cusack case. In Seaside, a town that borders Boothbay, a police informant called the detective division to report a lead in what the snitch termed the movie murder. A man had been overheard in the Wayside Bar saying that he knew who committed the movie murder and named the man as John Tallant. The detectives for the county and for Boothbay were alerted. They spoke with the informant and he described the conversation in the bar, in which a suspect was identified as Tallant.

Police ran a check on Tallant; his address was given as 712 Seafoam Lane, Apt. #5, in Seaside. That was oceanfront property and as soon as police learned the address, they knew that they had to proceed most cautiously on this tip.

The property on Seafoam was an exclusive and expensive cooperative building. In 1982, units started at $250,000 and monthly maintenance was $400.

"Not to say that rich people don't commit murder, of course they do," Lt. Peter Agnostelli, Boothbay chief of detectives said. "But Mrs. Cusack would seem to be a very odd choice as a victim in that

98

circumstance; it wouldn't be money he'd be looking for and Mrs. Cusack would not be mistaken by anyone as a drug source. She was not sexually attacked. There would not seem to be a motive."

Within hours, the man who tagged Tallant told police he was just getting back at the other man for a perceived insult. The instigator was charged with filing a false report and wasting police time. A $500 fine was levied.

One week after the murder, a Hoboken [NJ] police detective, Carl Lazerie, notified Luke Weathers of the Boothbay police of a call he had received from Amy Lee Halford, who lived in a Hoboken apartment building. Halford, Lazerie said, twice called the detective bureau to report threatening phone calls from an "unknown male" on Mar. 24 and the day after. In both cases, Amy told detectives, the man said "You're gonna be next" after which the subject reportedly hung up.

When Glanville saw that report, he suspected Amy was lying, that she did not receive those calls but said she did because she needed to have a part in this drama.

I think she was feeling left out and she couldn't stand that, the detective said. From the beginning, Amy saw herself as deserving a leading role in this drama, as the lover of the grieving widower. She must have thought the police are pretty stupid that we wouldn't be able to expose her reports of threatening phone calls as false, Glanville said.

Mar. 29, while on routine patrol, a Boothbay officer found a knife lying on the ground in the exact spot in which Felicia had been murdered. The knife was logged as evidence, but it was not the murder weapon. It was a single edged dinner knife, serrated but not sharp enough to have penetrated her body.

According to Agnostelli, investigators speculated that robbery could have been the motive and a search was ongoing for Mrs. Cusack's missing handbag, perhaps emptied and discarded. Police also speculated that the victim could have surprised someone in the process of breaking into a parked car. The felon could have panicked and stabbed her. Agnostelli said break-ins of parked cars in the South Strip area, especially in spring and summer, were not uncommon.

Police were uncertain as to the gender of the slayer, Agnostelli told reporters. The man or woman had been described as about 5 feet 7 inches tall, slim and wearing dark clothes.

The county prosecutor's office impounded a car that was in the parking lot for forensic tests, but Prosecutor Glenn Beatty said that was not a productive lead.

Beatty again appealed for help from the public. Two large dinner parties were catered the night of the murder at Dublin restaurant. *Someone* must have seen or heard something unusual, he said. This is a notoriously low-crime area, and there must be somebody somewhere who knows what happened, the county prosecutor concluded.

A week later, law enforcement efforts were still going unrewarded. The police were, literally, clueless.

By April 15, the rewards offered had grown to $10,000.

The description of the suspect had become much more specific: a man, medium build, average height, wearing a dark-colored coat and a dark blue or black ski mask with eye holes.

The source of this description was Edward Neville, a motorist who saw a pedestrian run in front of his car around the time and in the area of the murder. The pedestrian had what Neville recalled as a woman's pocketbook. He did not remember any details as to physical description but he wanted to cooperate. He agreed to be hypnotized.

"People are always amazed what they can remember under hypnosis," Greg Brocail, the first assistant county prosecutor, said. "Some people do better than others."

Neville changed the description of the pocketbook to "more like a briefcase" during his session with the hypnotist. He also said the person who ran in front of his car ran "like a girl" and could have been wearing running clothes.

Gullwing Cove cops passed along some names to their colleagues in Boothbay. Several women should be questioned in the murder of Felicia Cusack, the hometown officers said. Larry had broken off sexual relations with two or three women over the past three years; it was possible that one of those women wanted revenge. It was also possible that he had other women even now in addition to Amy.

Records from the investigation carry the transcripts of interviews with several of these women, including a real estate saleswoman, a Webster elementary school teacher and a female police officer. The saleswoman and the teacher reluctantly agreed to talk to police. The female police officer wasn't talking at all. Her union local provided her with an attorney immediately, and the

Linda Ellis

investigation of her – at least the visible investigation – closed.

The saleswoman had keys for empty houses and the opportunity to use these houses as meeting places. She and Cusack had indeed had a lengthy affair and she would resume that relationship at a moment's notice, she told police.

"He had great equipment; it was like being screwed by an 18-year-old because he's rough," she said. "Better, though. Much better, because he's experienced and imaginative and he knows all the right buttons and he has great control. He's so big. I think the most exciting thing about him is that he never speaks. It makes it seem like he's a total stranger, which makes it even more exciting. I'm screamin' while he has his hand over my mouth and he's doing this silent stare into my eyes... and pounds away..."

'He's really hairy," the teacher said. "His hands are hairy. So when he holds you or roughs you up or holds his hand over your mouth, somehow all that hair, it...Is he doing OK?"

The real estate agent and the teacher each had, in addition to rape fantasies, solid alibis for the time of Felicia Cusack's death, backed up by friends. They each refused to tell their husbands why they needed alibis for that particular time. The woman cop never said a word to anyone, but there had been witnesses.

"It was time to get back to basics," Kevin Glanville, the detective out of the county prosecutor's office, would say later. "But I will never understand in a million years why so many women, normal women with lives...Yeah, well, moving right along..."

102

In the course of a murder investigation, lives that are loosely lived are held up to a light that is generally unflattering. Most lives have a soft underbelly, even if it's little more than a few bounced checks or sheets too long unwashed or the random misdemeanor or two. Whatever the secret shame, in a murder investigation many people are going to know all about it.

For example, during the Cusack investigation, a Boothbay man who was unemployed and living with his parents was arrested for failure to pay child support in another state. His parents, unaware he even had a child, kicked him out.

Then, at a May graduation party in neighboring Seaside, a high school senior was bragging that he could protect his girlfriend and held up a knife to "prove" it. He was arrested. His admission to a prestigious university for the fall semester was rescinded.

Police arrested the owner of one of the cars parked near the spot of Felicia's murder when a routine search turned up marijuana in plastic bags under the passenger seat.

Because the killer was described as slight with quick moves, police concentrated on young people. That was bad luck for many weekend partygoers in the beachside towns. The club crowd felt an obligation to be on the cutting edge of bad behavior and some had to explain themselves to police.

Of the approximately 30 young people questioned the night of the Cusack murder, 18 were detained for a range of offenses and released into parental custody.

Roseanne Garcia, a professed psychic who was well known to area police, called Boothbay detective

Fred Tenney two weeks after the Cusack murder. She said she had a strong impression of the killer, and she, Garcia, was shaking like a leaf because it was as though he were in the room with her. The psychic described the killer as a black male, six feet tall with curly black hair, long, neatly trimmed mustache (possibly a Fu Manchu style) and good looking. She said that he has a pronounced forehead, bushy eyebrows and recessed eyes. The eyes are very dark with dark pupils, she continued. He has high cheekbones and full lips, the psychic described. His upper teeth are normal and very white; the lower teeth are jagged, irregular in appearance. He has long sideburns, neatly and evenly trimmed, and was wearing a white T-shirt at the time of the murder. He is meticulous about his appearance.

She stated that the subject was "maniacal and homicidal" and that the victim's husband should not feel bad. The reason he went back to the car is so their children would have a surviving parent. The husband would not have been able to save her, that "the subject would have killed them both". She also stated that the dead woman is "OK" and she only felt the first knife blow to the chest, that her screams were instinctive and that she did not feel the other blows.

Ms. Garcia also instructed police to ask the husband what the words *apricots*, *peaches* and *nectar* mean to him. Larry would later say that no one asked him about those words and he didn't know any special meaning for them anyway.

Boothbay detectives also interviewed tenants at 176 Janet Ave., the rental property owned by the Cusacks and the site of the fire in 1979. The tenants of the four apartments said that they rarely saw

Larry and had never met Felicia Cusack. All business and maintenance matters were handled by the Pulaski real estate agency in the Cove.

The Girardi family remained involved, sometimes unwillingly. In late April, Gerry Bucci, Felicia's youngest sister, began receiving phone calls from a woman identifying herself as Felicia's closest friend. The caller said she had seen the murder and the killer was the busboy from Dublin restaurant, Juan Gonzalez. The caller continued, telling Gerry that Larry Cusack planned the murder, paid the busboy to do it and watched as it was done. Michael Morland of the Barrington police department staked out the Bucci living room on the day the harasser usually called. When the phone rang, Morland answered. The caller wouldn't give any information but when she hung up Morland agreed with Gerry Bucci that it sounded like a young white female, probably in her early to mid- 20s.

Nathan Cromwell, 31, had come in at the request of the Boothbay police; his license plate had been recorded near Dublin at the relevant date and time. A long distance trucker employed by an Orlando company, he lived in Florida but came to New Jersey as often as he could to visit his children. He was divorced. Their mother had custody.

He was parked in a lot adjacent to the one used by the Cusacks. He stated that his truck had broken down. He said that he had heard a scream at about the time Felicia was being stabbed. He told police that he also saw a "bluish-tone, new-looking two-door coupe" moving onto First Avenue from Cable Court a few moments after the screams ended. Inside

105

the above-cited automobile were a white male and a white female. They "burned rubber," he said, as they pulled away. Kevin Glanville, the detective assigned to the Cusack murder by the county prosecutor's office, asked Cromwell to describe the occupants of the car.

"From the lighting I could tell it was a white couple, he was driving, she was in the passenger seat. He had short hair, cropped close. From her profile, the woman looked big. Not necessarily fat but a big built woman...She had a large, uh, beefy face, that's what I'm going by. She either had teased hair or an Afro but she was white, a lot of hair is what I mean."

Can you describe the scream that you heard? Glanville asked. Take your time. We want you to have thought it through.

"It was loud, deep. It sounded like an older woman, not a young girl. It wasn't shrill like a young girl's. One of the screams lasted, oh, four seconds. Then the second one I heard was longer," Cromwell concluded.

Police talked with many people back in Gullwing Cove to get a clearer picture of Larry and Felicia Cusack – their marriage, their friends, their role in the community. The investigators began with Jeff and Jenny Russo. It was the Russos who went to the Cusack home to pick up Grace and John when Larry called from the hospital, before Larry knew that Felicia was dead. The Russos took the Cusack children to their home, but when Larry wanted them to tell the children of their mother's death and to have them there for the night, Jeff was horrified. He told Larry to be a man and take responsibility for those matters.

The Russos said that Felicia had told them and other friends that Larry worked a great deal of overtime. If it was late, he would stay with his mother so as not to disturb his own family. Their dog Dime would bark and wake the neighbors even, he told Felicia. For this reason there would be many nights that he would be late or not come home at all

"We did a lot of things socially with them and with the kids," Jenny Russo said. "Felicia didn't want us to jump to the wrong conclusion."

The Russos told Glanville and Peters that Felicia never told them about Larry living with another woman; the Russos were not aware of any marital problems, they told police. Jeff and Larry went to a Cub Scout dinner at Dublin in mid-February. Because the Cusacks wanted to go to the Lions' Club dinner at Dublin Friday night, the Russos invited 11-year-old John Cusack to the Russo home. Felicia would not allow him to stay home alone and Grace was at a sleepover.

On the eve of the murder, then, the Cusacks dined at Dublin and arrived at the Russos to pick up their son at 10:30. They would not need a babysitter Saturday night; Grace would be home with John.

*   *   *

Law enforcement officials and representatives of the county prosecutor's office were encouraged on Jan 11, 1983. Ten months after the Cusack murder, Reggie Cleveland sat in a police interrogation room in Boothbay and he had talked. He had a lot to say that could forward the machinery of the investigation into the Cusack murder.

The Cusack murder had long ago reached the teeth-grinding stage for several of the detectives and for several of the uniformed cops in The Cove. Police had made virtually no progress. Felicia Cusack's large, loud and furious family gave detectives no peace. All this frustration welled up as police began to question Cleveland. He had been picked up on a petty theft charge and he was prepared to talk as long as authorities wanted so he could get a break on the misdemeanor charge.

"What kept you from coming to us with this information sooner? What's the matter with you, Reggie? You know how vital this is," Weathers demanded. "Were you saving it for a time like this when you needed a favor? Well it better be damned good and you're getting no special treatment at all – except if you don't tell us everything you'll get some treatment you don't like."

So Cleveland told police what he remembered of that night 10 months earlier:

"I was with Eddie Collins. We walked out of the back of the movies. What we seen, the movie, I can't remember. A comedy, I think. I seen a male and a female Caucasian which I thought was arguing. It then seemed to turn into, like he was trying to take something from her, like her handbag.

"He just wrestled her to the ground," Cleveland continued, "with what I thought was punching her and he held her down and just kept punching her. Then he got up and ran with something I think was hers and she just lied still and another guy ran after him. He couldn't catch up to him. We was walking while he was running after the guy.

"We stood there while we thought they was arguing. While he was beating her up so bad, she started to fall to the ground and he, like, a ballet dancer where the guy lowers the girl in the middle of the dance? Like I saw in that old movie *West Side Story*. Like that, and he put her on the ground real careful. But then he went down on top of her and still kept punching for a long time. Well not for a long time, but as long as we was walking. He just kept beating her, cause she was already knocked out cause when she hit the ground she didn't budge. Can I have a soda, a Coke and somethin' to eat?"

The tape was turned off while a patrolman went out for Cokes and snacks.

"I don't know what else he was trying to do," Cleveland continued. "It looked like he was trying to kill her, cause he was like wild. Then he got up and ran. He had something of hers. It looked like a briefcase. Maybe it was full of money, you know? He ran towards the beach, towards the front of the theater. Then we was behind some trees and we lost sight of the two of them."

"What made the incident notable to you?" Det. Luke Weathers asked.

"The way she was screaming."

"Did you think of trying to help her?" Weathers asked.

"Oh yes, sir, I did think about it and I almost did it but at the last minute I couldn't. This is a white neighborhood. What would happen, do you think, if folks here saw a black guy chasing a white guy? Or if you was in my neighborhood chasing a black guy? It wouldn't work out," Cleveland concluded.

*   *   *

109

Police and prosecutors were looking for threads that would lead them to a theoretical garment that was unraveling. Often those threads trailed from another crime. What connection, if any, did the Cusack murder have with the Hamilton death?

On March 6, two weeks before the Cusack murder, 22-year-old Debra Hamilton was killed and her body abandoned near Woods End Trail in Barrington. She had been stabbed once and had bled to death.

Police had few paths to follow in that investigation. When Felicia Cusack was stabbed 22 times and left to bleed to death March 20, authorities considered the possibility that the homicides were connected in some way.

The paths of the Cusack and Hamilton investigators crossed continually. The most likely suspect in the Hamilton murder was a young man who had been seen at two bars near the Boothbay movie theater, Dublin's parking lot and the scene of the Cusack slaying. Investigators zeroed in on a 20-year-old Marine Corps deserter, Rob Steinem, for the Hamilton slaying. Steinem, described in a psychiatric report as a sexual sadist with a hatred for women, had what turned out to be an unbreakable alibi in Felicia's murder. For the murder of Debra Hamilton, however, the AWOL marine was found guilty and sentenced to life in prison with a 20-year minimum parole eligibility term.

Three friends of Steinem were in the vicinity of the Dublin restaurant when Felicia Cusack was killed and one of the three bore a strong physical resemblance to the descriptions gleaned from witnesses. These witnesses, including Grace Brown, Larry Cusack and Reggie Cleveland had undergone hypnosis and those sessions helped them focus on characteristics of the assailant. After the hypnosis, a consensus had emerged and the consensus looked much like Perry Clayton.

Clayton, 22, left school after the 11th grade. He lived at home. During the day he waited tables and maintained the salad bar at a nearby Pizza Hut. At night he committed various unimaginative misdemeanors and moved with a gang that was an arrest waiting to happen.

Clayton told Glanville and Peters that on March 20th he was at Jelly's bar in Seaside with Carney Maxson. Then they met up with Dan Legere and Sean McKay at about 3 in the afternoon and they stayed at Jelly's till about suppertime. Then Clayton went home and was picked up later in the evening, about 9:30, by Carney Maxson. At 7:30, the time of the Cusack murder, he was taking a nap at home. His mother verified his timetable. After Maxson picked him up, he said, they rode around in Carney's vehicle all night drinking wine. Maxson confirmed that.

Boothbay detective Jim Whitney and Omar Rodriguez, a detective with the county prosecutor's office spoke with 28-year-old Tony Castillo, who had been seen acting suspicious near 554 First Avenue around the time of the stabbing. Castillo had been less than a block from the Dumpster. He said he had heard of the incident but had not seen anyone involved. He then went to Club Spanky where he met a woman named Mandy and they went together to her apartment at 13 Lincoln Terrace. Castillo stayed the rest of the night with her and left at 7 Sunday morning. Mandy Ellison verified Castillo's account.

He expressed concern that his wife would learn of his activity.

Mar. 23, three days after the murder, Det. Weathers had a call from Boothbay resident Anthony Uliger. Uliger said that on the day of the Cusack murder, visiting relatives had a dispute and his brother left the house in a "highly troubled" state about 7:40 p.m. The Uligers went to look for him. They were driving aimlessly and they saw a person walking west on Dune Ave., approximately 100 yards west of First Ave. Uliger described the subject as "shunning away" from the Uliger car as it passed. Uliger said that he observed the subject "ducking into" Erma's Deli.

Now the Uligers were curious and they made an effort to keep an eye on the subject, Weathers wrote later that day in his report. They passed the subject "again walking fast" three-quarters of the way toward Third St. (northbound). Uliger stated that when they passed the subject this time he broke into a run and disappeared. The Uligers described the subject as a white male 5'4" – 5'6" approximately 135 lbs having short dark hair cut in a crew cut style. He appeared about 25 years old with clean-shaven face, dark complexion but definitely Caucasian. He appeared Italian or possibly someone who came up from the south and spent a great deal of time in the sun. The Uligers believed the above-described behavior to be very suspicious.

Police followed up the information, vague and perhaps pointless information, because they had to do something about the Cusack case.

The next day Detective Weathers investigated the Cusacks' joint bank accounts and talked to the companies that had issued three credit cards. All those accounts had been frozen as her checkbook and credit cards had been in the handbag taken by the killer.

Three people tried to breath life into Felicia's lungs as the blood was leaving her body March 20th: Juan Gonzalez, the Dublin busboy, Dublin patron Phil DeVito and Ann Padgett, whose family owned the restaurant. Det. Fred Tenney of the Boothbay police questioned all three. The interrogator asked a series of routine questions – name, address, date of birth, educational background, marital status, employment and ability to read and understand English.

Then the meat of the questioning began.

"Please tell me in your own words, whatever knowledge you possess concerning the incident that occurred outside Dublin's on the 20th of March 1982 at approximately 1926 hours," Tenney said in the liturgy of police questioning.

Gonzalez, DeVito and Padgett told police what they remembered.

The routine police work continued.

Boothbay's police artist made five composite sketches of people described as suspicious by those interviewed since the slaying of Felicia Cusack. Lt. Agnostelli, the Boothbay chief of detectives, said the sketches were being shown to residents of the South Strip section and to those interviewed who were in the area at the time.

"These people were seen in the area the night of the murder or the day after, and people we interviewed thought they looked suspicious. They may have been looking around in a suspicious manner or just behaving in some way that seemed unusual," the Boothbay officer declared.

Linda Ellis

He said that none of the men described as suspicious were seen with blood on their clothing nor were any seen carrying a brown leather pocketbook. "But it was dark outside and the clothing was dark so people might not have noticed," Agnostelli said. Mrs. Cusack reportedly was carrying a brown leather purse when she was stabbed to death next to a Dumpster off Cable Court.

Investigators had been giving out an incorrect description of the purse Felicia carried the night of her murder. Grace Cusack, now 14, corrected the information. Police asked the newspapers to print a corrected sketch of a wine-colored leather purse shaped like a briefcase, sized approximately 10" by 12".

Nine days after Felicia Cusack died a loud, public and pain-wracked death, detectives Glanville and Peters interviewed the other woman (of the moment) in Larry Cusack's life. The detectives wanted to know about the day of the murder. Amy Lee Halford was with her lover, Larry Cusack, between noon and 1, his lunch hour, she said. When they parted, she went straight to Atlantic City. She said she arrived in Atlantic City between 3 and 4 in the afternoon.

"I just like to go there," she said. "I roamed around for a while and about 8 o'clock I met some people at the Paramour Club. Then I went to the Strand around 10 that night and found that they had not held my reservation because I hadn't confirmed it by 6:30. What jerks! I'd had a double reserved because I expected to be with my boyfriend now, an investment banker."

"She was looking for sympathy," Peters said, shaking his head. "Can you believe it? The wife of her lover was in the morgue by that time and this girl wants sympathy for an overbooked hotel. That's when I realized how selfish, how lacking in human feelings this person is."

She left there and arranged to share a suite at the Caprice and later returned to the Paramour Club and spent time with the same people, who included three men and two women. All she remembered is that one of them was named something like Hassin, an Arabic person, and that he had rooms 1035, 1037 and 1039.

The next morning, May 28, Larry Cusack called Det. Glanville to report harassing calls to the Cusack phone. There were 11 calls in an 18-hour period; two said "Ha ha" and hung up and the other nine were hang-ups. The prosecutor's office would investigate.

Through the state police casino gaming bureau, Glanville and Peters learned that a man named Hakim Hassan Abdul from Charlottesville VA had been given complementary rooms and meals for the weekend in question and they were rooms 1035, 1037 and 1039. Mr. Abdul was a guest of Paramour Casino host Mike Ferraro.

April 2nd, the two detectives interviewed Ferraro, who said that he was off duty Saturday but had seen Abdul Thursday and Friday with two Paramour women, Nancy Hackman and Constance Ramy. Hackman identified a photo of Amy Lee Halford and said that she first saw Amy at the Paramour Club Saturday night (the night of the murder) between midnight and 1 a.m. Ramy remembered seeing Amy with Abdul about 2:30 a.m. Sunday.

Linda Ellis

Amy gave Glanville and Peters more information about her night in Atlantic City. The people with whom she shared a two-bedroom suite at the Caprice were Andrew Kepler and his mother Barbara. She had met them at the roulette wheel and told them she had no place to stay because her original hotel had overbooked. The mother, Amy said, invited her to share their suite. It had two bedrooms and she could share the expense of $110 a night. Amy considered the possibility of some three-way sex but Kepler was not receptive. Amy could have one bedroom, Kepler said, and he and his mother would stay in the other.

*   *   *

Amy carried 125 pounds on an athletic looking 5-foot-5 frame. She liked everything about herself but felt she had small breasts, a feature that bothered her inordinately and one that she would remedy in a month. She wore her brown hair in a short simple cut, brushing bangs back on her forehead.

Her eyes were her best feature, almond shaped, slightly slanted and large. She had a high-pitched little girl voice.

"I have been going with Larry for about a year," Amy told Glanville and Peters. Glanville represented the prosecutor's office investigation staff. Peters was the liaison officer from the Boothbay police

"Last September my mom found out about the relationship. She phoned Larry and told him to break it off or she would kill him (giggle)...Hah! Protecting her little girl. Hah! So what I did was move out on my mother and get this apartment. That was last November. Three weeks after that, Larry moved in

116

with me and he was here until February, so almost three months. Then he moved back home, because of his kids."

Ms. Halford then gave us a timetable, Glanville said later, and it indicated that she last saw Cusack for lunch on Mar. 20, the day of the murder. They had lunch at a diner at the intersection of Routes 1 and 9. She didn't recall the name of the diner. That was the last time she saw him until after his wife's funeral.

She said she drove straight from the diner to Atlantic City. She had a reservation at a hotel but her other boyfriend, Moore Goodwin, couldn't make it at the last moment. She got there between 3 and 4 in the afternoon and stayed overnight.

"I learned of Felicia's death from the paper on Sunday," Amy said as the detectives left the apartment. She had this annoying habit, Glanville realized, of answering questions that weren't asked. He hated when that happened.

Sunday, the day after the murder, dawned with grey skies, light rain and brisk winds. The priest at St. Genevieve's, the Cusack's parish church, arose at 3 a.m. to prepare for what he knew would be an emotional day. Fr. James Doyle had been called, as a courtesy, to be told of the murder of a parishioner by the young priest at St. Mary's, Fr. Ed Nitkowski. Fr. Nitkowski, who had administered last rites to Felicia at Harbor County Medical seven hours ago, told Fr. Doyle that Mr. Cusack had lost control of his emotions at the hospital.

So Fr. Doyle knelt to pray for the soul of Felicia Cusack and for strength for her husband and family in the coming days.

Chapter 5

The Reaction

In every corner of Gullwing Cove there was only one topic of conversation – the Cusack murder. Most of those who knew her learned of Felicia's death Sunday via the largest area daily newspaper, *The Coastal Call*. The other area daily, *The Gazette*, didn't have the story. The bare bones of it had been played high on page one of the *Call*, barely making the paper's midnight deadline.

There was not a lot of competition for news space.

March 1982 was a relatively placid time in New Jersey and in the nation as a whole. The top grossing movies the week that Felicia died were *On Golden Pond*; *Death Wish II*; *Missing*, *Evil Under the Sun* and *Chariots of Fire*.

Best-selling books included *Spring Moon* by Bette Bao, *A Few Minutes with Andy Rooney* and *Jane Fonda's Workout Book*.

The television networks ruled in home entertainment, unconcerned about or unaware of the coming juggernaut of cable TV. High ratings went to *60 Minutes*, *Dallas*, *The Jeffersons*, *Three's Company* and *Alligator*.

In sports, The University of North Carolina defeated Georgetown 63-62 in the NCAA final. Coach Dean Smith relied on 6-foot 9-inch forward James Worthy but Worthy would get help in the second half from center Sam Perkins and a freshman guard named Michael Jordan. The Hoyas featured 7-foot freshman Patrick Ewing at center.

119

Linda Ellis

On the larger stage, rebel military officers staged a coup and seized political power in both Guatemala and Bangladesh; President Reagan agreed to a "truce" with the media, oil imports hit a seven-year low and the UAW granted key concessions to GM, averting a nationwide autoworkers' strike.

So on Mar. 21, a Sunday that started very early for the Cusacks, the world outside their grieving was stable.

Those closest to Felicia and Larry made the pilgrimage to the Cusack home. They felt a need to be with one another for comfort and information and to do what they could for the families. Plans had to be made; perhaps they could help, some of the friends thought. Everyone bought food, the universal pacifier.

At various churches in the Cove and surrounding towns, the sermons touched on random evil. At the Shell gas station in the small Cove downtown area, people who came by discussed what little was known with attendant George Barton.

School friends of Grace and John, the Cusack children, heard their parents discussing the murder. A few who were especially close to one or the other of the children telephoned the home. Grace's closest friends, Dottie Miller, Cindy Glenn and Cassie Tenison, went to be with her.

The few who had learned of the murder before midnight – the Russos, the families of Felicia and Larry, Larry's partner in the Webster cop shop and reporters covering the story – got either no sleep or very little. For others close to Felicia, the news was a rude awakening that Sunday. Denyce Buckley

120

arrived home from the engagement party at 3 a.m. Sunday, still unaware that one of her dearest friends had been murdered. Four hours later her sister Tracy phoned, waking Denyce and her husband Mark. "Have you heard?" Tracy asked Denyce, who was still fuzzy from inadequate sleep. "Felicia was murdered last night in the South Strip."

Denyce was still in denial when she went to 8 o'clock Mass.

"I won't believe it until Grace and John tell me," Denyce said. "Who saw her die anyway? If it was Larry, I don't believe it."

After the service she and Mark stopped at Gino's Bakery in Boothbay, bought buns and pastries and went to the Cusack house.

Before locking up at 1, his customary Sunday closing time, pharmacist Richard Marshall was bombarded with questions and involved in speculation at the Gullwing Cove Pharmacy, the anchor store in the village shopping plaza. His assistant, Phyllis Emmerman, a woman given to a strong belief in the occult, said she already knew of the tragedy. She and Felicia had a special bond, she said, one that went on after death. The plaza, called the shopping center by residents, is a rather incongruous collection of 14 stores, offices and restaurants that together form the hub of the shopping life in town. The pharmacy serves the functions of the fabled rural general store when Scotty's Luncheonette is closed at 2 each day, closed Sundays.

That Sunday there were many questions being asked, and few answers could be given. People recalled the last time that they had seen Felicia. Several people said they were surprised to see that

121

she had bought several packs of Carlton cigarettes at QuikChek, the center's convenience store. They thought Felicia was switching from Carltons.

Small town life has its charms, a Philadelphia reporter said during his coverage of the murder, but when people know which brand you're supposed to smoke and which you shouldn't, that's over the edge into too close and too personal.

This choice of brand would also puzzle police because her husband said that he had stopped at a 7-11 on the way to the movie, gone in and bought her a pack of Barclays. What did this mean? Did Larry Cusack lie about the 7-11 stop and if so, why?

When [if] they recovered the victim's pocketbook, they would know the answer. In the meantime, they asked Larry and he confirmed that Felicia has asked him to stop and buy that brand on the way to the movie.

Others had missed Felicia in church, went home to open their newspapers and then discovered why· one of St. Genevieve's most devout parishioners would never share Communion with them again.

Their parish priest, Fr. Doyle, was worried about Larry. "Larry was a good husband and the couple was very close and very loving. He doesn't say too much," the priest told a reporter "but he really feels bad. I don't think he realizes she's gone. He's still in shock."

Julian Buckley, brother-in-law of Denyce Buckley, was near the priest and overheard parts of the interview.

"What a load of crap that is," Julian said later to his wife, relating what he had heard after Mass. "Cusack sure pulled his (the priest's) chain on that. Everything is just the opposite: Larry was a lousy husband and he never cared about Felicia at all. He acts upset but it's not real. What planet is Fr. Doyle living on? The only thing he got right is that Larry doesn't say much."

At the end of March, authorities had no weapon, no motive and no suspects without clear alibis in the Cusack homicide. That was troubling because statistically the odds of solving a crime drop precipitously with each day that passes without an arrest. After just one week the trail is cold, witnesses forget and the press has often made a hash of the details.

Authorities did know that the Cusack murder method inflicted a density of pain that was overwhelming. The choice of weapon was particularly vicious and the number of wounds inexplicable unless this was either a crime of passion or the work of a psychopath.

Even slim leads were pursued. Could there be a connection between the murder of Felicia Cusack and the fact that her brother-in-law, a Newark cop, had been involved in the shooting of a Guardian Angel in neighboring Manhattan the prior December? Jack Galloway, Boothbay's director of public safety, said police were checking the possibility, albeit remote, of a connection between Felicia's killing and the shooting of Jeb Shula, the Guardian Angel.

Jake Cusack was accused by the Guardian Angels of firing the shot that had killed Shula, a member of the civilian anti-crime group. However, Cusack had been acquitted by a grand jury in February. Bobby Higginson, a spokesman for the New York Guardian Angels, vehemently denied any link. "The attitude here is that it's such an absurd statement that it requires no comment." Higginson said. "We're not going to get involved with any conversation with any police department. Our heartfelt sympathies to the family of Mrs. Cusack."

Jake Cusack, Larry's brother, said the link was something he had not thought about himself and doubted it would prove helpful.

Local police continued to say that robbery could be the motive because the pocketbook Felicia carried on the night she was slain had disappeared. Or, they surmised she could have surprised someone breaking into a parked car, and the thief panicked and killed her.

One of the cars behind which the killer had hidden was impounded for forensic testing and released during the week. Glenn Beatty, the county prosecutor, would not say whether fingerprints were obtained from the vehicle.

Police scoured the South Strip section of Boothbay again and again, looking for clues.

Gullwing Cove's mayor, Cal Winters, had been at a party two hours away from the Cove at the time of the murder. Cove police rang his home when they learned of the Cusack tragedy, but the duty officer stopped calling at midnight. Mayor Winters learned the news in the way of many of his constituents – from the front page of the local paper.

"I had to read down a paragraph or two to learn who was killed," Winters would later remember. "The article didn't give her name until further down." A horrified Winters got details from police when they called him shortly after he read the newspaper. Winters learned details that were not made public. "It was a particularly vicious attack, they said. They thought her jaw might be broken, for instance." Officials said later that it was not broken, but there had been intense pressure applied to her jaw.

The mayor spoke to a psychiatrist at a cocktail party the following weekend and pumped him for theories. "This doctor said that it was obviously a crime of passion. For a purse snatching, a routine mugging, a random robbery or even a regular murder, the assailant would not have stabbed her 22 times," Winters related. "He said that was unnecessary, bizarre, unless you look at it differently, as a crime of passion. The person that killed Felicia had a reason that goes beyond robbery. They need to look at someone who knew her."

The hunt continued for Felicia's purse, but it was nowhere to be found. There was no sign of the murder weapon. In the earliest days of the investigation, the police and the prosecutor's investigation squad considered the possibility that the motive was robbery, but the viciousness of the attack bothered them from the beginning. Law enforcement officials could not reconcile the brutality with simple robbery.

Winters, who was also a county councilman, had a phone call two days after the murder from Glenn Beatty, the Harbor County prosecutor. Beatty asked Winters to put before the county council the idea of offering a $5,000 reward for information leading to the arrest and conviction of Felicia's murderer. Beatty was up against a brick wall, he told Winters. The prosecutor said he was at a dead end, that he had a vague description of the killer from people near the scene, but no light at the end of the tunnel. The prosecutor was leaving no metaphor unturned, however.

The decision to offer a reward was fraught with public relations problems for county officials. The relatives of other murder victims – especially victims of color - would raise a hue and cry, and it would be impossible to defend the reward decision with logic. The only approach that county officials could take would be to admit that rewards were not offered for others but that this was a special case.

The location became the public relations escape hatch. Beatty told Winters that because the murder scene was so close to shops and restaurants and because there had been a swarm of people very near the site at the time of the murder, that a $5,000 reward might just be the spur needed to get someone to come forward. In addition, area businesses were clamoring for an arrest as the image of the South Strip was suffering.

The mayor telephoned the other county officials and the reward was approved and offered by March 26.

Ted Cruise, a Gullwing Cove councilman at the time of the murder, said that he had never known an event to grip the town's residents the way the Cusack murder did. "Nothing before this has ever affected us as a town family, if you will. The hideous death of one of our dearest friends has made all of us realize how we should treasure each other and how we should treasure each day," Cruise said. "The whole community is shaken up, very disturbed, not just because there was a homicide but because of what Felicia meant to us. She was active in so many areas of the town. She was an essential part of the daily life here," Cruise, who was to be the next mayor, continued. "I feel that many of us did not even know how important she was in our lives as a community. She coached girls' softball, she was the secretary of the Democratic Club for years, she was involved with the senior citizens. I think the word is visible. I don't think there are any people here," Cruise concluded, "who did not know her and most have had their lives enriched by her being in the community."

"She will be missed more than anyone can imagine," said Julia Miller told the persistent reporters. "Grace is doing as well as can be expected." The Cusack's daughter wanted to stay with her best friend, Julia's daughter Dottie, but for the time being both children were with family members.

"Dottie _is_ part of my family," Grace told a reporter staking out Grace's school.

Julia was the friend in whom Felicia confided her darkest fears. Asked about that, Julia thought the intimacy arose from the fact that she and Felicia had not been childhood friends and had not brought any old baggage to the friendship. Grace and Dottie would graduate that June from the eighth grade at the Lincoln School, the town's middle school for grades six through eight. The two girls had been close since kindergarten at Rushwood School, the elementary school.

Julia Miller knew Felicia's demons. As her friend, she urged Felicia to believe the truth about herself: that she was strong and special. No matter what Larry said or did, Julia insisted, Felicia had to believe she was a great person whom many people not only liked but also trusted and loved.

Her greatest sadness at Felicia's death, Julia said, was of course that her friend had died in such

Linda Ellis

terror and pain. Second, though, was that she knew that her friend had never believed in herself, that she had gone to her grave never understanding how much she would be missed.

Julia had known that her efforts to bolster her friend's self-confidence stood a slim chance of success. She knew nothing would have changed for Felicia as long as she had lived for and through a man who cared only for himself.

Julia also knew what few others did – that the Cusack marriage was on very shaky ground. Julia shared her insights into Felicia's private life with no one. People who knew the couple intimately, who worked with them, who belonged to the same clubs and lounged around the community pool in summertime with them, did not have a clue that, for the second time in the marriage, Larry was on the verge of demanding a divorce. He wanted to be free to live with Amy or anyone else who took his fancy.

Dad we can help you be free... Really free

"Felicia had so much to give," Julia said two days after the murder. "She maintained a happy home and she tried always to keep everyone happy. Grace, her daughter, felt very close to her. And I worry most about John, her son. He will not do well with this." Strangers reading that statement in the *Coastal Call* wondered why Julia Miller did not mention the reaction of Felicia's widower. Friends didn't wonder at all.

Julia was determined that the image of the normal, happy household, the image most important to her friend, would be fixed in everyone's mind now that her friend was gone.

The home that was happy on the surface would remain essentially the same. It did not occur to Larry to change anything. The four-bedroom colonial the Cusacks bought in 1977 had been built in 1974. At the time of Felicia's death in 1982 it was assessed at $88,600: $24,000 for the land, $64,600 for the house and landscaping. The lot is 131' x 100'. Property taxes were $2,170 a year in 1982.

The location was a problem, one of the worst homesites in the Cove. The town prided itself on safe play environments for its children and attractive views from the picture windows. The home at the corner of Bay and Sycamore provided neither, which was the reason that Larry was able to buy it for $63,000 five years before. The house stood at the intersection of two busy roads, one of them a route from inland towns to the beach clubs on the Atlantic Ocean. The location made a safe crossing extremely difficult. During the summer, station wagons bound for beach clubs in the town of Atlantic Beach clogged the roads. Sand umbrellas extended window to window and back seats were piled with beach towels, sand buckets, beach chairs, picnic hampers and peeling children.

The exterior of the Cusack's wood frame house, sided with cedar shakes, was looking grungy. Felicia had asked Larry for permission to have the house exterior washed, and the couple was still arguing about it at the time of her death.

Felicia, an obsessively private person, dealt with the public nature of her home by having vertical shades installed in the living room, the dining room and the den. Heavy curtains were drawn at twilight and backed the shades.

The redwood deck off the dining room, reached through sliding glass doors, was rarely used until the sun went down. It was so close to the major

129

intersection that the family and their guests were on display. The house sat on a corner lot with only two small evergreens serving as buffer between it and the intersection of the two heavily traveled streets.

The kitchen was not the geographic center of this house but was certainly its heart. In the "country" kitchen – a real estate word meaning a table fits in there – Felicia had the best times of her adulthood. She was happiest when she was cooking, surrounded by her children, extended family and friends.

To Larry, who never picked up a dirty dish or a sponge, the kitchen was the domain of women and he, as the breadwinner, the man of the house, expected to be waited on when he was not at work - and so he was, hand and foot.

The living and dining rooms were carpeted in forest green and the den in tweed. There was a fireplace in the den with a brick surround.

Reminders were everywhere that the late 70s and early 80s left a legacy of bad haircuts and shaggy carpet cuts in tweed-patterned earth tones. The green-toned wall-to-wall carpet continued up the stairs and throughout the second floor hallway. Off the hallway were four bedrooms and a full tiled bath for the children. The second upstairs bath was off the master bedroom. That bedroom was outfitted with heavy blond furniture, massive pieces of it. Felicia had wanted an Italian look, but Larry vetoed anything Italian, saying it was ugly.

The house lacked a basement. The attic was difficult to access and provided footing only intermittently via two-by-fours. Felicia was creative with limited storage space. Larry had no interest in home improvement projects so she was on her own at the hardware store. She was expert at fitting things into other things and the house was always neat as well as clean. The challenge of storage extended to the one-car garage. Her brothers installed extensive shelving there for her as well as in the laundry room. In the one-car garage, Mario put giant hooks on which the family's bicycles were hung. The family's second car was slanted into a cement apron off the driveway.

Grace's bedroom, the walls painted a turquoise blue, overlooked the front yard. John's bedroom, the walls a light beige, looked out over the back yard and, seemingly, directly into the windows of the town hall across the street. At holiday time, a giant Santa Claus balloon tethered to the town hall flagpole appeared to be looming directly over the Cusack house. John remembers how frightened he was of that Santa Claus. One of the best holidays of his life was the Christmas that his mother told him there was no Santa Claus.

The fourth bedroom was a hobby room that housed an electric train set, a pinball machine and a dollhouse. Felicia's hobby was needlework. A half-finished pillow cover was draped over a basket holding the tools of crewel embroidery, a cover that now would never be finished. Grace had it framed and has it hanging in her home. It was a small pillow, intended for Dime, the family dog, and on which a pattern of a Chihuahua was imprinted.

The Monday after the murder, customers drinking coffee at Scotty's Luncheonette in the Gullwing Cove Plaza talked of nothing else. Scotty's, between the barbershop and the sporting goods store, was the favored spot for coffee breaks and gossip. There was plenty of the latter that day. Scotty's was closed on Sundays or the gathering

131

would have begun 24 hours earlier. Stu Vosberg, a real estate developer in town and the property manager for the shopping center, reminded everyone in the restaurant about the statistics on murder.

"Nine times out of 10 it's someone close, someone in the family who does it," Vosberg said. "Who says Larry didn't do it? They say that because he had no blood on him he couldn't have done it. Well, he could have changed clothes, couldn't he?" The others, a dental assistant, two of the lawyers from the office in the plaza, three retired men who were there each morning and two construction workers from an area building firm, agreed that anything was possible.

One of the construction workers said he wouldn't put anything past Larry, that he was a shifty looking guy who had an eye for women. Across town, that sentiment was being echoed in many homes and workplaces. The idea that Larry was somehow involved began to gain widespread currency as the days after the murder went by.

At the luncheonette, Scotty had trouble keeping his mind on the orders for two eggs and toast (the $1.29 special, coffee and refills included) as he listened to Vosberg and the others.

"She was such a nice lady," Scotty said. "She used to come in here a lot, usually with the kids. She was always happy, she laughed a lot, you know, a really friendly person. You felt like you'd known her a long time. If she knew that Larry would be working a late shift, and it would be just her and the kids having dinner, she'd splurge on a couple of No.1's, the subs with ham, cappacola (a spiced ham) and provolone after she was finished with her work at the senior housing. That's right across the street there," Scotty pointed. "I was just sick that such a thing could happen to her. It's all anyone talks about in town."

The organizers of the girls' softball league in Gullwing Cove, a collection of five teams made up of girls in grades six through eight, realized they had a personnel problem. They had lost not only a good friend; they had lost a willing and dedicated volunteer.

Jenny Russo had been the assistant coach for Felicia, but she didn't see how she could add the job of coach to her already packed schedule. The 11 girls on the Red Rovers were in tears every time they thought about their coach. Mrs. Cusack had been special, Megan Tolliver, an outfielder, said. Felicia had coached their team for four years and they had learned more from her than softball strategy.

"She was terrific," Megan said. "We took her death very badly. It was on our minds a lot. Even when we made mistakes, she was super. She never yelled at us. If we muffed up, she just let us know she was behind us no matter what we did, as long as we tried and as long as we were good sports. She was very strong about that, about being good sports when we won and when we lost. We had good seasons under her. We came in second most years. We dedicated the 1982 season to her memory."

They finished, as they did historically, in second place.

Felicia and Jenny had had a good time with the girls. The Russos' involvement spread beyond time. The family business agreed to officially sponsor the Red Rovers, supplying them with red shirts with white trim. After the final game of each season, Felicia and Jenny treated the girls to pizza at Mario's in Boothbay. The team, for their part, took up a collection each year and bought small gifts, usually jewelry, for their coaches.

Andrea and Brian Downing, both high school teachers with children close in age to the Cusack children, were in disagreement from the beginning about Larry's involvement, if any, in Felicia's murder. Brian said from the get-go that Larry did it; his wife, who knew Felicia and Larry's current girlfriend, Amy, from softball coaching scoffed at that conclusion. He could never do a thing like that, she said.

A friend of Amy Halford said that she was tired of hearing her friend's reputation being trashed when she was sure that Amy had nothing to do with this murder. "Amy was looking for emotional security, for someone she could devote her life to," said Angela Fillmore, three years younger than Amy and a young woman whom Amy had coached in the Catholic Youth Organization basketball league. "She was desperate about it. From the time she met Larry Cusack, she had no time for anyone or anything else. And that hurt me, but I understood it. She had been like my older sister," Angela said. "But I lost her to Larry. It was the whole emotional security bit. She wanted someone there all the time. She pushed everybody off after she got involved with him. She was one of the only people I trusted in the whole world and I don't know where to turn now."

Amy apparently had asked friends to understand that she could no longer give time and attention to anyone but the married man with whom she had fallen in love. Until she met Cusack, Amy had been a model friend: supportive, sensitive and caring, Angela said.

In any competition for friends, however, Felicia would have won hands down. Her sisters threw a surprise 40th birthday party for her and hired a hall that held 150. The place was packed, and by the end of the night it was standing room only. "Felicia was one of the good ones," said Martha Fullerton, the municipal assessor's assistant said. Some years ago, Fullerton had worked with Felicia and they had been good friends. "She did her job well. We had many a laugh together."

Felicia had been principal secretary to Ed Cicotte, the director of the town's public works department. She was laid off that job eight months before her death because the federal funding for her project was not renewed. She was a top-notch secretary with an excellent resume and she got another job quickly in Barrington, a private-sector job this time with no political overtones. She was only three minutes from her sister and often they shared lunch breaks. The new job was part-time by her choice because she wanted to continue to work with the seniors in the Cove.

When the news of her death reached the senior citizens' apartment complex across Cove Avenue from the shopping plaza, the building became a hotbed of rumor and speculation. Several residents remembered the fights that Felicia used to have with Tony Giglio, a former building superintendent there. Giglio had been gone more than a year by that time, but the recollections of their battles were fresh in many minds. There was much routine and boredom in the lives of many of the seniors, and shouting matches were replayed and remembered.

Felicia was their friend, champion and guide through the maze of bureaucracy. She had worked

Linda Ellis

there as the liaison between the seniors and the town, a paid position. Unofficially, she was considered the personal angel to the seniors. She knew which residents had had surgery, who was sick or feeling depressed about a specific issue, whose children had visited over the Christmas holidays and who was not speaking to whom in the laundry room.

For some, she was literally a lifeline to the sometimes hostile outside world. The reaction at the building was severe. Steve Gagne, who had taken over from the unpopular Tony as superintendent at Gullwing Cove Gardens, said the residents were horrified at the news. They were also frightened for themselves, convinced that if Felicia could be stabbed to death in nearby Boothbay, they were not safe in the Cove location. Activists among the seniors demanded that the Long Island [NY]-based management company, the building owners, provide them with more security and install more lighting in their parking lot.

Non-residents who frequented the building on a volunteer basis become hesitant about going there after dark. Gloria Loomis, a staff member with the county library who conducted special programs and routinely substituted for absent librarians, was one of those. Loomis stopped going to the seniors' building in the evenings to conduct outreach sessions and deliver books to the bedridden. "It was something of a mass paranoia," Loomis recalled. "We each of us took it personally, what happened to Felicia. We became frightened all out of proportion to the odds."

"They (the seniors) didn't expect anything to happen to Felicia. They saw her as so young," Gagne said. "They didn't think about young people dying.

136

They all wondered, 'Why Felicia?' They felt cheated, because she had been there for them, and now she was gone."

There was great concern amongst the residents who had friends and relatives who were waiting [or hoping]to enter in the complex. Rents were heavily subsidized. Competition for residency was fierce; qualifiers had to fit under stringent low-income ceilings and be able to care for themselves. Beyond that the seniors sensed a pecking order that they did not understand and could not influence. As a consequence they put their trust in Felicia Cusack.

"There is a committee that makes the admission decisions and Felicia was on it," another committee member said two weeks after her death. They selected on location and need, he explained.

Ohmigod now what're wegoingtodo the committeemembersaidto the insideofhishead. Now who's goingto explainit allto them on abad day?

If the senior was already a Cove resident he or she got first crack. They also had to show financial need, show their income as low enough to qualify. Their net worth - often substantial - was not counted, so many seniors qualified and there was intense competition. Felicia had kept the notes and all the files. She kept everything organized. The seniors figured she was the key figure in all this. The liaison committee knew she was. When she was killed, they all felt injured. Who was going to keep everything straight now?

"The whole town can't think about anything else," Dania Sher, a fellow Democratic Club stalwart, told a reporter. "She was truly special. When I joined the club in 1975, I was really attracted to her as a friend. She was one of the warmest people I've ever known."

She's not warm anymore now she's cold forever. I miss you Mom

Testimonials to her kindness were legion. She often seemed to have a bottomless pit of energy and she always had a novel idea for fundraising. Those who were boosters for worthy causes knew a telephone call to Felicia would result in help in some form. Where others were generous with money donations, Felicia gave time and creativity. She would have given money as well if she had had more of it. Felicia never seemed to have much disposable income, her friends recall. If she had $20 in her wallet at any given time, she felt flush.

For example, Denyce related, there was the liquor situation. Felicia needed some for a holiday party that Felicia and Larry hosted on New Year's Day 1982. Denyce and her husband Mark insisted that Felicia take several bottles from their large selection in return for all the favors she had done for them over the years. Felicia was visibly embarrassed but took them up on the offer. Denyce thinks she didn't have the money to buy a comparable supply and that she would not have accepted the gift otherwise.

"She just never had much cash on her," Denyce remembered. "Larry made the spending decisions and he's money crazy. Everything in their life was measured by the cost. He couldn't stand it when someone in the family spent what he considered 'his' money."

*   *   *

Twelve days after the murder some of the people who were near Felicia when she was attacked were being asked by Boothbay police to relive that experience.

Juan Gonzalez was asked about the night Felicia died.

"I was working that night," the busboy related. "I was carrying a tray from the dining room to the kitchen, as I was going, Mr. Larry, he came to the door and said 'someone has stabbed my wife!' and for someone to call an ambulance. I put down the tray and went to the hat check girl and I asked her what was happening and she said someone had stabbed someone outside. I ran outside and Mr. Larry was leaning against one of the cars," Gonzalez said.

"So he was saying 'oh my God' so I asked him if he was all right and he said it was not him but it was his wife. I went to see her. I checked her pulse, her breathing and heartbeat...she was breathing but her pulse was low. The boss' wife, (Ann Padgett) came over. She had some rags and she cleaned the lady's face because it was full of blood... So then the young girl (a nurse who had been in the restaurant) came from across the street and as she was coming the lady stopped breathing.

"So I tried to give her mouth-to-mouth but the blood just kept coming from the mouth and the nose. But she started to breathe again! I was thanking the Lord, saying prayers while I worked and then the nurse took my place...My boss came out and asked me why I had blood all over my face so I told him what happened. So I went inside and saw Mr. Larry and I told him his wife was going to be okay.

"Then when I learned that the lady died, I was not surprised, she had lost so much blood, but I felt so bad that I told Mr. Larry that his wife would be OK," Gonzalez said.

It appeared to many in The Cove that "Mr. Larry" was not OK himself.

He would walk the shaded streets of the town by himself, sometimes just as dawn was beginning to crowd out moonlight. He left the spillage of family and friends in his wake, crowds of grievers coming and going at his house. He would later say that if he had not been able to walk out for quiet time he would have had to check himself into a hospital or just disappear.

Never much for family gatherings at the best of times, Cusack had zero tolerance for outward emotion and shared grief. He said he also needed solitude to remember the good times shared with Felicia and to figure out how best the children could be cared for after school. His compassionate leave ran out April 3; he had to go back to his job as a Webster cop. He would say later that he looked forward to going back.

"I felt so guilty that I had not gone to her, to help her, to stop the bleeding, something! I needed to get away from people who cared about her," Larry said.

Guilt has become fashionable again, according to Dr. Jason Long, a New York psychotherapist. "As well it should," Long said. "Guilt, the sense of anguish that we have fallen short of our own standards, is the guardian of our goodness...The failure to feel guilt is the basic flaw of the psychopath, who is capable of committing crimes of the vilest nature."

The people offering to help Larry with arrangements were doing so not for his sake but out of affection for his late wife and concern for Grace and John. John's religion teacher at St. Genevieve's, the Cusack's church, organized a memorial program for Felicia two weeks after the murder. The half-hour program, a family Rosary crusade, was broadcast over a local radio station. Carrie O'Donnell, the teacher, said the 13 fifth-grade boys in the religion class helped collect money to pay for the program, which cost $90.

During the program, prayers were said in memory of Felicia. The choir sang *Amazing Grace,* Felicia's favorite hymn.. The program was taped and the tape given to the Cusack family, Mrs. O'Donnell said. The program gave those who were unable to attend the funeral an opportunity to tune in and say the Rosary prayers. Besides the boys in the class, the proprietors of Gullwing Cove Wine & Liquor and several private citizens contributed money and helped with the program.

Larry didn't seem to be worried about support for himself and the kids, about who was going to cook for him, do the laundry. Felicia had made so many friends that he would have help no matter how people felt about him.

Larry's primary concern was, as per usual, getting laid. He knew he was under such close scrutiny by so many people that even he didn't dare visit any of his regulars.

While many knew he had an obvious alibi for the moments surrounding his wife's death, no one could understand his inability to act. The biggest problem residents of the Cove had with Cusack was that he did nothing to help Felicia as she was being stabbed and nothing to comfort her as she lay bleeding into the muck and gravel.

The town could not accept that he had none of her blood on him. The town could not accept that he did not intervene as she was being stabbed. The

141

Linda Ellis

town could not accept that he, a policeman, had not begun extensive cardiopulmonary resuscitation. "How the hell can you be 50 feet away or what the hell ever, how can you let that happen," Winters, the mayor, said, pounding his fist into a wall. "Maybe he panicked and was afraid for himself? Not an acceptable response for any man, but at least a way to explain his being such a wimp. People could understand that maybe the shock of seeing her that way froze him in place, but the witness, Mrs. Brown, she saw him start forward and then retreat and then do that again, so he wasn't frozen. Besides that, it takes time to stab someone 22 times and he could have shaken off the fright and had plenty of time to help her."

Cusack was not passive by nature; anything but. He was quiet, but that's very different from passive. It was completely outside his normal behavior to stand by or be indecisive in a crisis. He was a cop, after all, and even his detractors said he was a good cop. *WellOK a little roughbut cops hadto be careful thesedays maloney said to the insideof hiscop head*

Some thought of him as hostile. No one ever saw him as indecisive. In those few moments of horror at the crime scene, however, he wavered and waited passively for somebody else to do something

Moreover, if the town could not accept the scenario, Felicia's family was beyond skepticism and into full-blown conspiracy.

Many decided that Cusack was a coward; many thought he was somehow involved in his wife's death but no one could pin the actual murder on him. Grace Brown, the impeccable witness, stood in the way of that theory.

"People here were also very interested in Amy Halford and any role she might be playing in this besides comforting her boyfriend," said a Cove patrolman. "Most of the people who knew the Cusacks knew about her, about Amy. Everyone tried to keep it from Felicia while Felicia was trying to keep it from everyone else. Talk about a vicious circle. Lots of guys knew that Larry was sleeping with her. She loved cops, that Amy. A little nutty, a little slutty, you see that type around here, around cops. She loved to hang around police stations. It's like ballparks and ballplayers. She was known in Boothbay and Seaside and Atlantic Beach besides here. We finally had to tell her not to come back to the station anymore," recalled the Cove police officer.

"I obviously had no problem with Amy having been around the block a few times," Larry would say later. "So she screwed other guys, yeah. So I didn't take chances, I always wore a condom. It wasn't because of disease necessarily, although gonorrhea is pretty nasty. And there are other diseases women can give you. It was mainly because I never wanted to hear about a pregnancy that I'd be paying out on for years." Amy's reaction to Felicia's death was to wonder what to pack for her move into Larry's house and into his bed. Now that Felicia had been murdered, the way was clear for Amy to become part of his household. She would give up the Hoboken apartment and they could commute together on the train just like married couples did. Larry's response to her idea was that she had to wait for at least a month and if she did move in with him, she would have to say that she was there to care for the children and clean the house.

Linda Ellis

"Amy had better just be the maid and be there for the kids," Felicia's sister Vicki said. "If we'd found out they were doin' the nasty and the kids bein' in the next rooms, being subjected to that with their mother hardly in her grave, we would've got a court order to remove John and Grace from that home in a heartbeat."

Part III

The Break

Chapter 6

The Confession

It was nearly 3 in the morning on Saturday, the first day of the Memorial Day weekend 1983. Amy Lee Halford picked up the telephone in her apartment in Manhattan and dialed the number for the Harbor County Prosecutor's Office in New Jersey. She was alone. Her roommates, Alice Chilton and Mimi Goldberg, were out. The time was right. It had to be now.

Amy was frantic. For too long now she would be asleep in the apartment with the thermostat at 80 degrees and still wake up feeling cold. She couldn't stop shivering. Alice and Mimi and their boyfriends complained about the heat, found it unbearable and moved in with their men. Now Amy was left to sleep alone in the three-bedroom apartment.

Nothing helped keep the nightmares away, the terrifying dreams in which Larry Cusack was trying to kill her.

Somehow everything that had happened to her in the last year seemed like a game, but the game wasn't fun anymore. She certainly hadn't won the prize. Cusack, the man she loved, had another woman now.

Amy had lived with Larry. She had had the best sex of her life in his arms and at his feet, at his head, just about everywhere actually. They had talked about a shared future. All that was over now.

Did he think she would just take this rejection lying down (hah, hah)? He finds a blonde, that slut Julianna, to take to bed, and she, Amy, is supposed

147

to wish him luck and get on with her life? Think again, Larry, Amy said aloud to the walls of the [*rivvu,24hrDrman,3br,2ba,wbfp,eik*] apartment.

No one was in the prosecutor's office when Amy called. At 3 in the morning, a police dispatcher in the Harbor County radio room took their calls. Amy, who didn't identify herself, said she had to speak to Kevin Glanville, a homicide detective in the prosecutor's office. The dispatcher knew that Glanville and his team had three active cases. If this girl knew something that could help with any of them, he'd be toast if he didn't alert the detective.

On the other hand, it can be dangerous to call a guy's home at this hour because what if he wasn't where he was supposed to be? Just do it, the dispatcher told himself. That's the drill. Besides, the way Glanville talked about his wife and kids, not a problem.

The dispatcher rang Glanville's number at the Gullwing Cove house. Glanville answered after two rings.

"We've got some girl on the other end of the phone. She's asking for you personally," the dispatcher told Glanville. "She says she's got to talk to you. Should I patch her through?" What the hell does some girl want at 3 in the morning, Glanville thought. He hadn't fallen asleep till 1:30 and was sound asleep when the phone rang. Being awakened from a sound sleep wasn't a new experience for him. Homicide detectives were on call throughout their working lives. This call went with the territory.

"Sure," Glanville told the dispatcher. "Put the call through."

"Who is this?" Glanville said with irritation in his voice.

"It's Amy."

Glanville recognized her voice immediately. She was Larry Cusack's lover, or had been and maybe still was. After Felicia Cusack's murder, he and John Peters, a Long Branch detective, had interviewed her at her apartment in Hoboken. That day she had gushed out personal information about herself and her affair with Larry.

As the investigation into the Cusack murder took on a life of its own, Glanville realized that Amy had taken a liking to him, that she saw him as a potential conquest. There were many sacrifices Glanville would make for the job, but adultery was not one of them. Nothing would have been worth that.

With Amy, Glanville was extremely cautious. In their every interaction, he was aware that she was hanging on his every word and watching his body language. His first rule was never to be alone with her. On the other hand, he made sure she felt that she could trust him, that he would see she came to no harm. If she chose to read more into that, it wasn't anything he could help.

Although there were times he knew she was telling stupid lies, although there were times he had wanted to tell her to go to hell, it never showed. He made it a practice in general to hide his feelings, negative or positive. In his work, he never knew when someone would have information he could use. He did not want to alienate anyone until he knew they were of no value to an investigation.

Now, as the holiday weekend began, he hoped that she had something of value for him. Knowing Amy as he did, knowing how needy she was, he figured that she might just want to talk. However, before he could ask her why she was calling, she started to cry. "I got to talk to you," Amy said. "I got to tell you what happened. I can't live with it anymore. I can't live with it anymore. I'm having nightmares."

"Calm down, Amy. Just be calm. Slow down."

"I did it, Kevin. I fucking killed her. Larry got me to do it, Kevin. He made me do it. I was afraid he would kill me if I didn't do the killing. It wasn't my idea. He got me to kill his wife."

Ooooh, When Mommy wakes up you're going to be sorry Amy...

Now Glanville was wide awake and already making a mental action plan. He sat up straight in bed and flipped the switch of the lamp on the bedside stand. Glanville realized he needed a pen and paper to take notes, but he didn't want to interrupt Amy. His wife had heard his part of the conversation and was awake now. He motioned to her to get the pad he had on the dresser. When she brought him the pad, he blew her a kiss and motioned to her to make some coffee. He knew it would be a long time before he had a chance to sleep again.

Amy told Glanville how she and Larry had bought the hat and coat she had worn on the night she killed Felicia. A few days before the murder they had bought the apparel in a store in New York. Amy was speaking in short bursts, beginning a story somewhere in the middle. Glanville just let her rip.

"I threw her purse in the river on my way to Atlantic City and the knife, I threw that in too. Larry bought it, the knife I killed her with at a Strand sporting goods store. I think the one in Harbor Mall. He used his Visa." Months after the murder she

150

bought a knife just like the one she had used that night, Amy said. She did it so they would have it in case anyone ever asked what had happened to the knife Larry bought before the murder.

"Why did you stab her so many times?" Glanville asked.

"Larry told me to make sure she was dead. He told me that over and over. If Felicia didn't die, she'd be able to identify me. I mustn't say anything to her, because if she lived she'd know me from my voice. *Allof HarborCounty knows your freakin'voice Glanville said totheinside of his head.*

"My part of this was to make sure she was dead before I ran away," Amy said.

"I don't want to live anymore," she said more than once. She sounded heartbroken to Glanville. "Hang on, Amy. Don't do anything foolish." *Idon't want tolose this collar this is a career-maker glanvillesaid..i want to be the player to named later...he whisperedto theinside of hishead..where'sthat coffee?*

Several times he spoke to Amy gently, kindly, trying to get her to calm down. He didn't want her to lose control. He wanted her to go on.

"Kevin, come and get me. I want you to come here and bring me in. Right now." This was the Amy Lee Halford that Glanville had come to know in the investigation in the past year. She had just confessed to a murder and now she was giving him orders. He decided that he had better take command of the situation. "You're not around the corner. It'll take some time to make the arrangements to pick you up. I'll call you up before I leave," he said. After he hung up, Glanville phoned Heath Murray, a captain in the prosecutor's office, and told him what he'd just heard. "Do you think she's telling the truth?" Murray

151

asked. "It seems so to me," Glanville said. "But that's neither here nor there at this point. Whether she is or she isn't, we gotta find out."

Then Glanville called Peters, the Long Branch detective who had worked the Cusack case with him, and told him what Amy had just said. It was now about 3:40 a.m. "Get your ass out of bed, we're goin' to Second Ave and 90th. It's showtime," Glanville said, quickly outlining the events.

"Good to go," Peters answered. "Finally."

As soon as she hung up with Glanville, Amy called Jack Leonardo, a lawyer for whom she had once worked, in the upright as well as in the prone and kneeling positions. She realized that she would need help, at the very least legal advice, on what to do now and in the future. At about 3:30 she called his home in New Rochelle. He wouldn't mind, she thought. Leonardo hadn't been in Amy's bed in about a year but she was right about him. He didn't mind the call. It was obvious to the lawyer that Amy needed help. Not that this would be *pro bono*; he'd get paid back in several ways. He called a New York reporter while he shrugged into a turtleneck and jeans, a friend who was looking for a good case to turn into a book.

Amy called one of her roommates, Mimi Goldberg, who was at a friend's apartment. When Mimi returned to their apartment, she found Amy crying and confused. "I don't know what to wear," Amy kept saying. "What do you wear to confess to a murder?"

Mimi looked for signs of what Amy was truly feeling at that moment. She hoped her roommate would be feeling some guilt. She didn't sense that, however. Amy didn't seem very empathetic as Mimi cast her mind back to situations that could have shown guilt one way or the other. She couldn't think of any. Mimi was afraid Amy was tipping over the edge into hysteria. "I want the police to get here, Mimi. I wish they were here now. Shouldn't they be here soon? I killed this woman. I stabbed her five times and killed her."

Mimi was stunned. Her roommate was talking about *herself*. Felicia Cusack was obviously not important in this narration, only Amy. Me, me, me. Same old, same old. What a bitch. Good riddance. Wait till I tell Alice. *Now we can can turn the freakin'heat backtonormal mimisaidto theinsideofher sweaty head*

Amy had in fact stabbed Felicia 22 times. Later, she would brag about the number of thrusts but at this early stage in her short but dramatic criminal career she was still trying out various story lines to assess their impact.

Mimi had known Amy only a few months. Mimi later told the police that Amy had confided only a few facts about her affair with Larry Cusack and nothing about its aftermath. I've been seeing a married guy with two kids, Amy had told Mimi shortly after they moved into the apartment.

Glanville called Amy back at 4:05. "How are you doing?"

"I've calmed down some. Mimi's here. I called my lawyer, Jack Leonardo."

"What did he say, Amy?"

"He told me not to say anything."

"Well, do you still want me to come get you and bring you back here to the county if your lawyer told you not to say anything?"

153

Linda Ellis

"I want you to come just as fast as you can get here, Kevin. Please come soon. I can't live with this anymore. I want to cooperate with you. Jack asked me to call him back when you get to my apartment. I'll expect you in an hour and a half."

Glanville picked up Peters at his home. As they drove to New York, Glanville told his partner about the call from Amy. Detectives who handle murders learn a great deal about many different people and Glanville and Peters had learned a lot about Amy. Within hours after Felicia Cusack had been killed, they knew that Amy was one of Larry Cusack's current girlfriends. They learned that this was not a one-off or even an occasional nooner but a fairly serious affair. At least in Amy's mind it was serious; who knew what Larry felt when he was zipping up, getting ready to leave another warm body?

When they had interviewed Amy shortly after the Cusack murder, she had tried to control the flow and content even then. Instead of having to coax her to talk, police had to ask her repeatedly to slow down. The tape recorder couldn't keep up with the flood of her words. Amy answered questions before they were asked. The first week after the Cusack murder, 14 months ago, Glanville and Peters had been amazed at how freely Amy spilled private events and thoughts. She gave them information about herself that Glanville thought most people would never talk about with strangers. She volunteered far more than necessary or even appropriate. She gave them details of her love affair with Cusack.

She gave them the abortion scorecard. She claimed to have had four. When medical records were accessible to investigators in 1983, and the four abortions verified, Amy still refused to name the man or men responsible for two of them. A lawyer close to the case figured that at least one of the pregnancies was the result of sex with commuting strangers during the routinely hour-long train ride from central coastal New Jersey to Penn Station in Manhattan.

Psychologist/best-selling novelist Erica (*Fear of Flying. 1973*) Jong had hit the feminist wave with that book and created a sensation by describing the ideal sex act for strong, independent women. Jong called it the zipless fuck. Why should men be the only ones with the right to anonymous and commitment-free coupling, anywhere, anytime, with anyone? Jong asked. Damn straight, women's liberationists answered. Restrooms on planes and trains, back seats of taxis and corporate cars and nosebleed seats at Knicks games became hot-sheet motel substitutes. There were three rules: minimum conversation, maximum protection, no networking. This kind of coupling was not for the fastidious or the faint of heart. Fans of random sex among the cognitive elite said wearing men's ties to work was not enough; women had to behave like men in all the ways possible.

Amy's fourth pregnancy remained a mystery.

*   *   *

Early in the investigation when detectives considered Amy a suspect, they came up against a blank wall. There was no evidence to link her to the murder. On top of that, she had passed a lie detector test. A trained polygraph operator said that she was telling the truth when she said she knew nothing about the murder. They had to give her the benefit of the doubt. Glanville and Peters, though, had always been bothered by Amy's lack of a rock solid alibi. She had told them she was in Atlantic City on the night of the murder. The detectives could prove that Amy was in Atlantic City, but the earliest they could put her there with independent verification was at 10 that night, two hours and 20 minutes after Grace Brown saw a figure flee the spot where Felicia lay dying.

Ask Dad. He knows where Amy was.

If police had found proof that Amy was in Atlantic City at 8 or 8:30 that would have satisfied them that she couldn't have been the murderer. Just two weeks before Amy's call, Glanville and Peters had talked about going back to Atlantic City to see if they could do anything more to test her alibi.

During the trip to New York, Glanville and Peters talked about how best to manage Amy when they reached the apartment. They'd have to handle her very carefully. If Amy decided she didn't want to return to New Jersey voluntarily, there was nothing they could do to get her back immediately.

Since they were going to be in New York and had no legal jurisdiction, they didn't have the right to arrest her. They didn't have time to get an arrest warrant and even if they did get a warrant, Amy could still fight extradition. If Amy decided not to go back with them to New Jersey, it would still be possible to make her return with them, but it would take some time - maybe hours, maybe days. Time was important to the detectives. If Amy had time to think about what she had said to Glanville, she could change her story. If Larry learned that Amy had confessed, it could become difficult, if not impossible, to get enough evidence to make a case against him. Her life could be endangered on two

156

fronts: Larry and the Girardis; the latter were perhaps the more dangerous.

Glanville and Peters decided not to question Amy until they returned to the prosecutor's office where there wouldn't be any distractions. "I told her I'd like to be able to start at the beginning and go through to the end - seamless. I didn't want, for instance, to debrief her in her apartment or on the ride back. There would be interruptions. I wanted to keep conversation in the car to a minimum," Glanville recalled.

Now that it seemed there was a break in the case, Glanville had to deal with contradictory emotions. There was excitement. There was relief. There was enormous satisfaction in finally being able to say that he had an answer in the Cusack case - and he had a sense that this was the answer, that Amy had told him the truth. If so, Amy could help his career.

Yet, because he really was a nice guy [even nice guys wanted something from Amy] he was concerned that the truth would bring enormous pain. He thought of the children, Grace and John, who were facing adolescence without their mother. "Really deep down inside I had hoped Larry was not involved, for just one reason - those poor kids. I did not let my emotions affect my approach to the case in any way, but I hoped from the beginning it wasn't him. You've got those two kids. They've lost their mother.

We've lost that lovin' feeling...oohoh that lovinfeelin

"So, I thought, wouldn't it be horrible if it is their father? These kids - if Amy is telling the truth - will have to live with this now, that their father is involved in their mother's death. It's bad enough you have a beautiful mother and you lose her by a brutal

157

murder. Then to put the icing on the cake, you lose your father. You find out he's the one who did this to your mother. If you're a compassionate person, you know you have - I have - a lot of problems at times with things like that," Glanville said.

At 6:05 a.m. Glanville and Peters arrived at Amy's apartment. The building was a modern high-rise at East 90th St. and Second Avenue; not bad at all for three young women just starting out. This was a city neighborhood that was improving, not declining. It was a neighborhood for young career people like Amy and her roommates. It was a place for people who wanted the excitement of living in New York, who were ambitious and whose lives seemed to be filled with promise. Glanville and Peters left the elevator at the 29th floor and walked down the narrow corridor toward apartment 29-B. When the door to the apartment opened, the life of Amy Lee Halford, a life filled with ambition, promise and psychotic behavior was going to be changed forever.

Mimi Goldberg let them in. Amy was packing some things to bring along, Mimi told the investigators. Mimi seemed very concerned about her friend. "Take care of her," she said. *Get herthehell out of here Mimisaid totheinsideof her head*

Since Amy wasn't under arrest, Glanville and Peters made it a point to let her do whatever she wanted. She could go anywhere and talk freely to Mimi. They didn't want a defense lawyer to be able to say later on they had coerced Amy in any way. Soon, however, Glanville felt that Amy was trying - it was in her nature, her insecurity - to take command of the situation. He was very good at reining her in but it wore him out in the best of times. The scenario the detectives had sketched out was one requiring a combination of sensitivity and discipline. Here we go again, Glanville said to himself. Calm down Kevin. Get it right and you never have to do it again because her little ass will be in women's prison.

"What would you do if I said I wasn't coming back with you?" Amy asked the man whom, three hours earlier, she had ordered to pick her up. Her dramatic entrance and her challenge did not surprise the detectives. Nothing was going to be simple with this case now that Amy was ready to talk. Amy called Jack Leonardo, the lawyer she had called earlier, and gave Peters the phone. He told the lawyer about Amy's call to Glanville, that she admitted killing Felicia Cusack and that she had asked to be picked up. She said she wanted to give a statement, Peters declared. Amy talked to Leonardo again and then gave Glanville the phone.

"What are you planning to do?" Leonardo asked.

"I want to take her back to Harbor County and interview her," Glanville said. "We're talking about a murder, a woman who was murdered on March 20 of last year. When your client called me this morning she told me she had killed the woman. She also told me the victim's husband, Larry Cusack, set up the whole thing."

As long as Amy was willing to go and wanted to cooperate, then you are free to take her back with you, Leonardo told Glanville. A friend of Mimi, Rafael Mentor, came to the apartment and spoke to Amy in her bedroom. Peters stood at the bedroom door. You can't take your eyes off this woman for a minute, he muttered to Glanville. Mimi had been with Mentor earlier that night. Glanville and Peters let Amy talk to Mentor because, just as with Mimi, they didn't want

159

Linda Ellis

anyone to say later they had stopped Amy from doing anything or coerced her into going with them.

Mentor irritated Glanville. "He's lucky we weren't in Jersey. He was a wise guy, showing off in front of the women, trying to put his two cents in," Glanville said later. "He was trying to intimidate us by taking notes about what we were doing." If they had been in New Jersey instead of New York, Glanville might have charged Mentor with obstructing a police officer. An hour after Glanville and Peters reached the apartment, they left with Amy. As soon as they entered the car, Glanville gave Amy her Miranda warnings. She and Peters sat in the back. Glanville drove. She told them she understood her rights and was willing to tell them everything they needed to know. Glanville asked Amy not to talk about the case while they were in the car, but she said that she felt the need to talk. What a surprise, Glanville and Peters muttered under their breath. She told them how she had thrown the knife she used to kill Felicia and the purse she had taken from her into a bay near Atlantic City.

They stopped for breakfast on the Garden State Parkway and she kept on talking. *OmiGod does this woman ever just shut her damn mouth? Peters asked theinside his head I don't care how good she is in bed the price is way too high and no wonder Cusack dumpedher but now he is going to pay again, big time thistime the idiot I think you'd pull yourcock out of her and your cock wouldstart a conversation.*

They got to the prosecutor's office at 10:14 a.m. Amy called Mimi for reassurance and 15 minutes

160

later, the marathon session of questions and answers began.

Amy took them back two years and five months to the day she met Larry on a commuter train. She spotted Larry, thought he was handsome and asked him if he was a policeman.

Larry wondered much later when he had a lot of time to think what would have happened could he have savedhimself if he'd said: Me? A policeman? Not me babe. I'm acircus clownunder the big top.Would she have still gone to bed and fucked aclown? clowns wear a sort of a uniform he said to the inside of his head and he heaved adeep sigh. John my littleboy used to be so afraid of clowns.

They rode to work on the same train and Amy ran into Larry repeatedly. One morning she asked him how he felt about sharing the bathroom on the train. It was unisex, wasn't it? He said he didn't follow and Amy laughed. So lead, then, she said to him. If he entered the car at the front of the train, she followed. If he got on the last car, she was right behind him. She would stare at his wedding ring. Larry, who was between women at the time, was flattered by the attention from a pretty girl young enough to be his daughter. What the hell, go for it. He asked her for a date, a movie in Jersey City.

When they met for their first date, Amy told him there wasn't enough time for a movie and sex, so shouldn't they go to a motel right away? *man, this is my lucky day.Larry said to the inside of his head Wonder if she'll pay half.*

"We very quickly established a love affair," she said into the tape recorder on the first day of that holiday weekend. To call this a love affair was dressing up mutton as lamb but Amy was

161

determined that this be a cut above a weekday matinee, the norm for the people with whom she worked at the brokerage house.

Few would call their first date an expression of love. Nevertheless, whatever Larry and Amy felt for one another after one sweaty afternoon under dubious sheets would grow and endure and do great harm to a great many people.

During their first time in bed, Larry told Amy about his wife and his guilt about cheating on her. Amy didn't care. That was the standard *blah blah blah* that she had heard from other married men. She wondered if they thought anyone ever believed them. His professed feelings of guilt, however, didn't interfere with marathon sex in fairly nasty places. At some point, he recalled, he complained about being bitten by bugs. Amy immediately said she would get her own apartment and she did. Amy generally did what she said she was going to do and she did it fast.

Amy ducked out on a lease in Jersey City she shared with two other women and got an apartment of her own in Hoboken.

We saw each other three or four times a week and I was head over heels in love with him, she said, and he says he was with me. Amy found Larry loving and understanding *and hard don't forget HARD.* They talked *there right THERE* often. She told him about her childhood. Whatever she said, no matter how stupid she might sound to someone else, he never put her down *down already down on her knees.*

It was the sex that signed Felicia Cusack's death warrant. Once Amy and Larry discovered their potential, learned what they had going for themselves in bed, there was no stopping them and no going back. The classic Woody Allen line could have been

162

written with them in mind: Is sex dirty? Only if you do it right.

Amy, now 22, had lost her virginity at 13 with a 14-year-old boy. Amy soon tired of 14-year-old boys who could care less about her satisfaction. She moved up to men in their 20s when she was in her teens. When she was 20 she was ready for men in their 40s. Shazaam! Here came Larry. For her, for reasons hard to fathom, nobody did it better.

Even during pre-trial hearings and private conversations, with all the fury and hurt showing on her face, she still went out of her way to focus on sex with Larry. It was as though all her behavior could be excused because he had that power over her. Read my diary, please, she asked Glanville. There's a lot in there about how I came under his power. He has amazing endurance, she had written in her diary after her first afternoon with Larry. He's so unselfish. He always made sure I was just about there, just at the edge of coming before he allowed himself to catch up.

Dear diary, "We practiced till we could come together. That was great. We didn't even need to talk about where we were, how close we were. He doesn't like to talk during sex. He won't talk. He just looks at me."

More tomorrow, diary,
Love, Amy

Consideration from a sex partner was a new experience for Amy. No one had ever done that for her before, timed himself, trained himself, to make it this good for her as well as himself. Most men

Linda Ellis

rushed through foreplay and would climax when
they wanted to and if she wasn't ready, too bad.

Dear diary,

*Men just want me down on my knees sometimes
and to hell with my pleasure. I like to be with the
traders from my firm, to have drinks after the market
closes, get stock tips. I've learned a lot about the
market. If they don't have time for me, to bring me
home [not that kind of home, diary] that's OK I guess.
I'm building up a trophy tie collection; I ask for a tie
before they unzip. They have their rules [no kissing,
no penetration) so That's MY rule. Tie first. Some of
the ties cost $100.*

Love, Amy

Dear diary,

*This is it. I can stop worrying about who I can
marry. No more guys in a hurry who just unzip and
stand there, or bend me over or give me a signal on
the train as though I'm just a body part. I've fallen for
a married guy but he will get a divorce, He loves all
my body parts!*

Love, Amy

Are we in the right line of work? Glanville and
Peters wondered after reading the parts of her diary
that Amy had bookmarked for them. She just wants
to get you hot, Kevin, Peters joked. She wrote it all
last night. I don't think so, Glanville replied.

When she moved to Hoboken in November 1981, Amy was near Larry's precinct. They saw each other almost every day. Two months later, he moved out of his house in Gullwing Cove and into her apartment. They talked about staying together forever, but he said there was a problem.

Yes, he wanted to marry her, and yes, he wanted to divorce his wife. But he couldn't, he said, because Felicia would never give him a divorce. Felicia was so set against divorce that she was prepared to blackmail him to stop him from breaking up their marriage, Larry told his lover. Felicia had evidence that he had burned down a house they owned in Long Branch in order to collect the insurance, Larry said. He had put a cigarette under the cushion of a chair to start the fire. Felicia also suspected him of "borrowing" funds from the local Democratic Party that had not yet been repaid. If he tried to get a divorce, Felicia was ready to tell the police about these crimes. Since he was a policeman, he would be ruined if any of that became public, Larry told Amy. He said the only way he could have me was to have her dead, Amy told the detectives.

This was the motive for murder the police had considered more than a year ago, but could never prove. Now they had the motive. Next they had to find out from Amy how she and Larry planned the murder. In a pretty sloppy fashion, actually, but Amy was confident that Larry had thought it through well.

"First he discussed guns as a method to kill his wife, the whole time implying that I was to do it. But he changed his mind quickly because if he had to ask around for a throwaway gun, people would remember. Then soon after his wife was dead

165

everyone would know he did it even though he wanted me to do it."

Larry brought a huge pellet gun from home to her apartment, she told the detectives, and tried out a murder method with her playing the part of Felicia. He put two phone books together and wrapped a towel around them. He had her stand about 15 feet away holding the wrapped phone books. He shot the books but the pellets didn't make a dent.

Time to think about a car accident.

"He wanted to have a car accident for her, but he said if he fiddled with the brakes he'd be implicated and he didn't want that," Amy said. "He decided that having her slip in the shower probably wouldn't work either and he couldn't figure out a way to get any sort of drugs that would cause her death without it being detected that he gave it to her. Anyway, he wanted me to do it, the killing."

Larry's final decision was death at knifepoint.

"So he decided that a knife was the right thing to use because he said it would be less emotional for me. He said he would plan everything and let me know when and where."

Larry bought a fishing knife with a long, thin blade at a sporting goods store and paid for it with a credit card. Two days before the murder, Larry had a Lions Club meeting at Dublin. He got to the parking lot early and scouted the area in a way that he hoped would not arouse suspicion.

"He planned on taking her to the movies at the South Strip theater, parking the car in a lot about a block and a half from the theater, near Dublin, because he told her that after the movie they would go to Dublin for a drink," Amy continued in her recitation of events to Brocail, Glanville, Peters and the tape recorder in one of the interview rooms at the prosecutor's office in Garrison, the county seat.

Larry added some refinements to his plan, she said. "He moved home in February of 1982. He was going to be the perfect husband for everyone's eyes because he wanted everybody to see he was trying to make the marriage work. So when she did die, it would look like a robbery and not a murder. Subsequently, he took her out frequently to establish a reason for going to the movies that night."

"He never did that," Denyce Buckley said, "took her out specially. If he had taken her out she would have known something was very wrong because in 22 years of marriage I think he took her to a tablecloth restaurant maybe 10 times."

A few days before the murder Larry picked Amy up at her office in New York, she said. They bought the clothes that she wore on the night of the murder - a blue ski mask with cut-outs for the eyes, nose and mouth, a blue bomber jacket. Larry made her pay for them, she said. This bizarre preoccupation with who paid for what in their relationship was to crop up repeatedly, the investigators would note.

"The whole time he was planning the murder he kept telling me that he loved me and he could only be with me if she was dead and that we wouldn't get caught and that everything would be OK. The morning of the murder he came to my apartment before he went to work. He arrived at about 7 a.m. He handed me the knife, took it back, wiped off the fingerprints and taped the handle with black electrical tape. He made me practice holding the knife. He told me the reason he was taping the knife was so it wouldn't slip. I went to see him at lunchtime at a derailment. He had given me the plans either in the morning or at lunch. I don't remember which. The plans were the layout of the murder. He had explained to me where I would be sitting, where he would be going and the general area where she was to be killed. He told me that he would tell her that he had dropped his keys and had to go find them."

After Larry left work, they met at a diner in Elizabeth. Larry told Amy to be at Dublin by 7:25. They headed south on the Garden State Parkway and stopped at a gas station on the Parkway to say a last goodbye. They knew they couldn't see one another for a few days without arousing suspicions. Larry went home to have dinner with Felicia. Amy had some time before leaving for the restaurant. She waited in a parking lot near the Parkway and then drove to Boothbay. She parked her car at a meter on First Avenue near Dublin restaurant.

I waited and I waited, she said, petulance returning to her voice. A man in his late 50s - pudgy belly, silver hair - pulled up his car beside mine. I believe he might have seen me, but he didn't get a very good look at me. He walked in the direction of Dublin. To my knowledge nobody else saw me although I saw what looked to me to be an old black bum, but I don't think I saw him after 7:15.

I was about ready to leave, because it was about 7:30 and they hadn't shown up yet. But then I saw his car, Larry's car. So I stayed. They parked and they were walking towards me and I was crouched between the Dumpster and the big four-door black or blue car. I was close to the hood of the car. They got about 10 to 15 feet away from me, and Larry and I saw eye to eye. He quickly whirled Felicia around - she was walking on his right side - and proceeded to tell her that he had dropped his keys and he was going to find them. She told him to make sure that the car doors were locked. Felicia's back was to me.

I then got up and trotted over and proceeded to try to stab her in the back with an upward thrust. I am not sure if the knife penetrated her back. I think I recall it going up near her left shoulder blade, but I'm not sure. She screamed Larry's name. I tried to put my hand around her mouth to stifle her yell and she started to fall. I believe while she was falling - and I was helping her fall - I may have tried to stab her in the back once again.

I don't believe I am hearing this glanville saidto the insideofhishead. She talks as though she's playing soccer here.

"So Felicia was lying on the ground on her back and I proceeded to stab away while I was straddling her. I didn't realize how many times I stabbed her. Larry had said to me, 'She must be dead. In case she doesn't die, don't say anything to her.' He could only marry me if she was dead."

Make sure she's dead. Make sure she's dead, was all Amy thought as she stabbed Felicia.

I had no feeling while I was stabbing her

We can help you feel things later, Amy! Lots of things! and my mind was a complete blank. But I do know she did gurgle. Gargle? Gurgle.[Let the record show the tape was stopped at 12:45 p.m. so first assistant prosecutor Greg Brocail could leave the room. He said he was indisposed].

I didn't know how long I had been stabbing her but after I heard her gurgle, I proceeded to stab her a few more times because when I heard that gurgle, I

169

figured she had to be close to death. Then I got up, ran to the car. When I was halfway there, I pulled off my ski mask and I also had her pocketbook. Larry told me to take her pocketbook because it would look like a robbery.

Amy said she then got in her car and drove toward the Garden State Parkway, the road to Atlantic City. On the way, a police car passed her with its siren and lights on.

"I thought he was going to pull me over," she continued after a break for lunch. "I was scared to death. I nearly shit my pants. I didn't realize what I had done until after it was over and the idea of being put in jail bothered me more than her death. The reason her death did not upset me was because the two people that ever loved me were already dead, so there was nothing left to lose."

The only people Amy ever thought had loved her were her paternal grandmother and her mother's Godmother, both deceased.

On the way to Atlantic City, Amy stopped and changed her clothes. She had cut her left thumb and had wiped some of her own blood on her pants. Before she reached to Atlantic City, Amy searched through Felicia's purse. She found $60, a cigarette lighter and a gold cross that was in the change purse in the wallet. She kept those contents, but she knew she had to get rid of the bloody clothes, the purse and the knife. She stopped on the causeway into Atlantic City and threw the purse and the knife into the water. When she arrived in Atlantic City, she drove to the bus station, went into the ladies' room and stuffed the clothes into a trashcan. The bathroom was so filthy and smelled so bad, she said, that no one would notice a smell of blood.

Zero mistakes so far, Beatty thought later, listening over and over to this tape of the first interrogation. Cold as zero, too, this bitch, he said to Brocail. Brocail had recovered his composure but had feared for a moment in the interview room that he was going to launch over the table and break Amy's neck just to hear her *gurgle gargle gurgle.*

Before Amy had called Glanville on the morning of her confession, she had little reason to fear that she would ever be arrested for the murder of Felicia Cusack. Now she had voluntarily confessed to the killing. Before the day was over, she had signed a written confession. In the face of all this reality, Amy refused to understand the consequences of what she had done. She acted as if everything would be fine now that the detectives knew what had happened. Several times during the day, she talked to Glanville about going back to her parents' home in Gullwing Cove. Glanville didn't argue with her, although her expectations were so patently ridiculous.

"Did she really think she was going to go home?" Glanville would say later. "I don't know whether that was an act on her part or whether it was sincere that she thought she could tell her story and then get to go home."

Others had heard the story before and didn't believe it. Amy said she had told six men about the murder - two priests and four businessmen. One of the businessmen denied ever hearing the story. Another said he had, but he was waiting for her to give him more information before telling police. The other two men told police they just didn't believe her. The priests weren't talking to anybody.

"Amy said to me that she had killed somebody," one of the businessmen later told Glanville. "I said,

'Yeah, sure Amy. ' Amy said, 'Yes, I did.' I just didn't believe she did it."

Another businessman to whom she told the tale said that she should get psychological help.

"Did you ever consider reporting this information to the authorities?" Glanville later asked him. "Or maybe your lawyer?"

"No."

"Why?"

"I wasn't sure I believed her." *And I'm married See? Wedding ring idiot.*

The question that remained for the detectives to answer was whether *they* could believe Amy. She had certainly fooled the polygraph people from New York, as had Larry. Gaylord Serry, the owner of the company that trained the operators was called on the carpet by the prosecutor's office and asked to explain himself.

"This happens about once a year; a mistake was made with her but I can explain the husband," Serry, nervously slicking back his hair, began.

"This oughtta be good," Glanville muttered to Bryan Carlyle, another of the prosecutor's office detectives.

'It was immediately obvious to me that the husband was lying in that he was attempting to control his breathing," Serry said with a straight face. "I know of no truthful person ever having done this. However, in discussing this with the operator, Pete Lily, he said he was treating the husband's examination as he would that of a victim and/or witness. Since the husband claimed that he saw his wife stabbed to death, if he is truthful then indeed he is both a victim and witness."

"Huh?" Peters muttered to Glanville.

172

"And, in future, please conduct the polygraph examination before the burial of the suspect's spouse as that also had an effect," Serry said as he went out the door.

"What a load of bullshit that was," Carlyle said. "I don't think he has to worry about 'in future' around here. We'll find another company. Cusack and Halford are just really good liars, they were too much for him."

So when the prosecutor's people began their questioning, Glanville saw a red flag behind every statement Amy made. They had to consider the possibility Amy was inventing everything. They had to consider the possibility that Amy had killed Felicia but had acted alone and was trying to frame Larry. After all, he had a new lover. For a high-strung young woman who was willing to kill for sex and security, couldn't revenge be a strong motive to make her lie about him now? Would Amy sacrifice her own freedom to make sure that Larry couldn't be with someone else?

"After the entire interview was finished, my feeling was that she was telling the truth," Glanville said. "There were a number of things she told us that walked right, looked right, quacked right so probably we were looking at a duck." Glenn Beatty, the county prosecutor, Greg Brocail, Beatty's first assistant, and Steve Balterri, the prosecutor's chief trial lawyer queried Glanville about events so far and asked his impressions. They listened to the tape of the interrogation, re-running several parts, stopping the tape, conferring, starting the tape again.

Is she telling the truth? Beatty asked.

Glanville voted yes. Beatty said to run with it. In the weeks to come, Glanville would work through

173

Linda Ellis

layers of Amy's mind and he would emerge somewhat
shaken by what he learned. Now that the detectives
and prosecutors believed Amy about Larry's
involvement in the murder, they needed proof. They
needed evidence that would convince a jury. Larry
may not have been a faithful husband before his wife
was killed. He may not have acted the way a
policeman should have acted when he found his wife
brutally attacked. He may not have shown the
interest in solving the crime that people almost
always show when a close relative is killed. He may
have taken up with another woman a short time after
his wife was killed - a time when most husbands
would still be grieving. This was all circumstantial
evidence, however. Taken alone, it didn't prove that
Larry plotted to kill his wife.

Even Amy's confession wasn't enough evidence to
convict Larry. In a murder conspiracy, just the word
of one conspirator isn't enough to make a case
against another conspirator. Larry needed to admit
his involvement - something he hadn't done for 14
months and something authorities doubted that he
would ever do of his own accord.

The plan the prosecutor's office now devised was
to use Amy to discover whether Larry truly was
involved. If he were, Amy would trap Larry with his
own words.

"You've been used and abused," Beatty had told
her that afternoon as she was confessing. It was
something she would never forget. She wouldn't
forget what else Beatty told her.

"We have to get that son-of-a-bitch."

Chapter 7

The Trap

Amy Lee Halford had always wanted to be a cop.

"1 would be a good cop," she said. "I'm honest. I'm always willing to work. I always wanted to work in New York City. I have a young face. I could do stuff like they do on *Mission Impossible* and stuff like that. I'd be terrific."

Now that Saturday afternoon, 14 hours after confessing to the murder of Felicia Cusack, Amy was going to get her time in the spotlight.

Kevin Glanville, the prosecutor's investigator that Amy had chosen as her confessor, asked if she would help them arrest Larry.

Does a bear shit in the woods? she shot back. She would, he told her, have to make Larry admit that he had helped plan the murder. She would talk to Larry and investigators would tape the conversations. When she met him in person, she would wear a transmitter. Detectives would be standing by for protection if Larry should try anything.

"She was all she was for it, 100 percent for it," Glanville said. "Amy wanted us, the investigators, to believe that she was telling the truth. I think there was a combination of things - this is only my opinion. She wanted to prove to us that she was telling the truth. If she could prove to us that she was telling the truth, it was obviously not going to hurt her and probably there was some self-

Linda Ellis

satisfaction on her part to make everyone think that she was not the worst one in this whole thing."

She liked being in harm's way, one of the psychiatrists she visited said later. And to be put in harm's way by a detective with whom she wanted to have sex, to know Glanville would be listening to every word she and Larry said, could get her close, then to the top and then spilling right over. Larry would think it was him. What a jerk.

Glanville laid out the story Amy would tell Larry. Amy was to say that the detective had called her and wanted to meet her that night. So she needed to see him, Larry, immediately. She didn't know what to do and she was scared. When Amy and Larry met, Amy was to lead him into talking about the murder.

Have him talk about how the two of you planned the killing and then carried it out, Glanville told Amy.

She took a few sheets of paper and made notes for herself:

1. Checking things with <u>Visa</u>, she wrote. Amy told the detectives that Larry paid for the knife she used to kill Felicia with his credit card.
2. He (Glanville) said he was talking with Paul <u>Harper</u> and Harper told them interesting things. Harper was a private investigator from Long Island. Amy had told him about the murder in March.
3. What if he talks to Father <u>Bailey</u>? He was one of the two priests she had told about the murder.
4. Why <u>aren't you worried</u>? She scribbled. . What if he talks to friends and everyone I know?

5. I'm convinced <u>they know something</u>... I stuck to story but it's hard to do, Larry.
6. Before we hung up, Kevin said listen, Amy, you better start thinking hard and do what's right to make it <u>easier for yourself</u>. If they are that close, maybe we should talk to him, Larry, so they go easier on us.

Amy was determined to shine. Here it was - her big chance. She could hardly wait.

She thought of the situation as a game. She would be playing cop. She was going to be playing a role to catch a murderer. There was a hint of danger. There would be secret meetings, a tape running on a hidden transmitter. Although she thought of her role as a game, she wasn't playing.

"You've been used and abused," Glenn Beatty, the county prosecutor, told her that afternoon as she was confessing. She would never forget that phrase. It sounded just right.

"We have to get that son-of-a-bitch," Beatty said.

To tape record Larry's conversations with Amy, Beatty, as the county prosecutor, had to approve. At 3:22 that afternoon, he signed the consent.

The first attempt to reach Larry came at 3:26. An investigator put a bug on the telephone and Amy called three numbers. She tried his house in Gullwing, his work and his brother Jake's house in Brick Township, but she couldn't find him.

At 7:18 they got lucky at the home number.

"Hello," Larry said.

"Hi.

"Hi, there, how you doin'?" Larry said.

He didn't have to ask who it was. Amy's little-girl voice was distinctive. Today she was nervous and her voice was even higher than usual.

She settled down to business.

"Um, Larry, I've gotta see you. Glanville called me today. And I, I don't know, I don't know what he wants. Why is he calling me after all this time? I'm really upset."

She talked fast, so fast that it was difficult for him to understand her. In contrast, Larry's responses were slow, deliberate.

"I don't know," he said.

"And he, he wants to talk to me tonight, and I told him I'd get back to him, 'cause I'm down at my girlfriend's house in Cotswald. Can you meet me about 8:30 or 9 tonight, you know that one park in Boothbay...?" At breakneck speed, she spilled out her prepared speech.

"Yeah, Amy."

"That we went to before with the gravel and everything?"

Larry told her to calm down. For his part, he was completely in control.

"Larry, I'm so upset, my girlfriend's gonna give me the car so I can see you."

"What time, Amy?" he asked.

"I've gotta talk to ya. Between 8:30, 9 o'clock. At that one park..."

"In West Boothbay," he said, his voice rising for the first time, his anger evident. "Okay, all right."

"You know the one with the..."

"Yes," he shouted. "Yes!"

"Casa Cantina."

"I know'" he yelled. He rarely showed anger. "I know. Okay. Why there?"

"Because that's where I know," she answered with impatience in her voice and condescension in her tone.

Then Larry suggested they meet somewhere for a drink.

For a few moments there was silence on the other end of the telephone line. Amy didn't know what to say.

"No, because there'll be too many people around.. We can't talk and besides, I don't wanna be seen with you."

"I'll meet you at the park at 8:30," Larry told her.

"You know because, Larry, I think he wants to talk to me about the murder."

"No, he doesn't'" Larry insisted. "Now stop this fuckin' shit, will you please? You know you had nothin' to do with it, you know, so what the hell is this?"

Cusack hadn't dug a hole for himself yet. But then, Amy was just taking her warm-up pitches.

"Because I'm really upset, Larry and if, and if he talks to me I think I'm gonna crack."

They agreed again to meet at 8:30 and said their good-byes.

When Amy hung up, Cy Blandon, the prosecutor's expert on electronic surveillance, took the cassette out of the recorder. He broke the tabs on the original cassette and copied it. He put the original tape in the electronic surveillance unit's evidence locker. This was the routine that he followed with all the tapes.

Amy had been in no hurry to end the conversation. She wanted to get the most out of her first adventure playing cop. After all, it wasn't every day she could act out a fantasy - be part of a secret team, the critical link in a murder investigation.

There are different versions of the story as to why Larry agreed to meet Amy that night. He would later say that he was frightened of her; that she was acting crazy and he feared she would say things she shouldn't. When he dropped her for another woman, he knew that had hurt her. He didn't want her to hurt him in return.

Cusack' lawyer, Robert Schwarz, has a simpler, though hardly elegant explanation: "He was horny. His current girlfriend was out of town and he wanted to get laid. He knew Amy would come across so he agreed to meet her."

The call was made from the prosecutor's office in Garrison. To arrive at the meeting with Larry, they had to drive 18 miles to the park in Boothbay. They pulled in the parking lot of a roller rink in Boothbay at 8:30. Blandon put a transmitter on Amy's body and gave her a car to drive to the park, which was less than a mile away.

Their plan was to have five detectives near the park where Amy was to meet Larry. Glanville and Johns would be nearby, but would remain out of sight. If Larry recognized either of them, he would bolt.

Leland Halliday, the chief of detectives in the county prosecutor's office, Blandon and Bonnie Boudreau, a prosecutor's investigator, were to park in a car where they could keep Amy in view. The radio receiver was in their car so they could follow the conversation. Glanville and Johns were hooked up to the conversation as well. If Larry found the transmitter or tried to hurt Amy, Blandon would give the signal and they would rush the car.

Amy drove away from the roller-skating rink. It was 8:35. She reached Landover Park and pulled up to a parking spot. However, by 9, she knew that he wasn't coming.

Everyone drove back to the roller rink. Glanville wasn't worried because Larry hadn't shown up. When he had listened to the call to set up the meeting, Glanville thought Larry was confused about where he was supposed to go.

Call him up again, Amy, and find out what happened, Glanville told her.

He went inside the building with her. This time the call wasn't recorded. When she hung up, she said there had been a misunderstanding about the park. Larry told Amy he thought it was a different park and he'd been waiting there. When she didn't come, he just went home.

They all drove back to the park and took up their positions again. This time Cusack was there. Blandon activated the recorder.

Amy and Larry began with an argument about the mix-up. He had trouble making her understand in what park he had waited for her.

"There's a park on the left-hand side like near the animal hospital in Broadview," Larry explained.

"Huh?"

"Go around the circle, go around the circle, three-quarters of the way around the fuckin' circle then you make a right-hand turn in there"

"We never went there, Larry. I don't know what you're talking about," Amy said. ["Jeez, women," Blandon said in the van, "Can't follow directions."] Larry's voice started to rise."I met you once on

181

[highway] 16, I waved to you and you said 'Let's go to the park'."

Larry finally gave Amy enough details so that she remembered that particular meeting spot. All this time she was sitting in the car from the prosecutor's pool. Larry had exited his car and was standing beside the unmarked police car.

"Anybody in your car?" Larry asked.

"No, why would anyone be in my car? This is Alice's (Alice Chilton, one of Amy's roommates) mom's car," Amy demurred, her voice high and tense.

[And this guy collects a paycheck for impersonating a cop? Blandon muttered in the van.]

"Larry, I've got to call Glanville back."

When Larry asked her why, she said that Glanville had called her at her apartment in New York that morning. He said that he had to talk to her. Amy told Larry she'd put him off by telling him she had a lot to do, she was busy but Glanville kept insisting they meet today.

"He has nothing, he's got..."

"No, Larry, what if he's got your Visa, that you purchased the knife, do you still have the other knife in the garage?"

"I don't have any knife, Amy."

"The knife we bought at Strand, you still have that one?"

"I have the knife I originally bought. It's in the garage on the table." Slowly, patiently, Larry parried each of her awkward thrusts.

"No, not . . ."

"Get in this car," he demanded, not angrily, but firmly.

"I'm not getting in your car, Larry. We'll talk like this."

"Amy, they have fuckin' absolutely nothing on you, they can't have anything."

"Larry, why would they call me if they don't have anything, why would they all of a sudden call out of the blue? I haven't seen you since December, I don't wanna see you..."

"I don't know, Amy. I don't know what they want. It's, you know, any number of reasons."

"Larry, I'm scared and I have been, I've been, I'm so upset. I have been waking up, I've been having nightmares, I've been waking up in 80 degrees and I've been freezing cold. I'm freezing cold right now. Larry, I think they know we did it and I can't handle it. I know I'm gonna crack if he talks to me. You've gotta tell me what to do, what to say, you gotta tell me because I'm gonna crack."

Amy babbled. She tripped over her words. There was an overdrive of panic in her voice as if she were afraid he would leave before she could make him say something incriminating. This is exactly what she feared – that she would fail to entice him to say the words that would confirm the conspiracy.

The question will always remain about Larry – how could fail to detect a trap? How could he not become suspicious? He knew this woman very well. He should have realized something was wrong.

The generally accepted answer is the one his lawyer gave from the beginning. Larry wanted to get laid. Period. His brain had gone south.

He was willing to shut out the nagging voice of reason and suspicion because he knew what Amy could deliver when she was in the mood. He had a taste today for the kind of sex in which Amy specialized.

"First of all, Amy, you don't know what he's going to ask you at all. Second..."

"I can't hear you."

"Let's take a walk somewhere, Amy, let's walk and then maybe we can fuck."

"I don't... Larry, no, I don't wanna be seen. I don't wanna fuck right now. Larry, you've gotta tell me what to do, what to say. Larry, come on, they could have researched your Visa [card] and they could have done a lotta other stuff that we don't know about. Now, you know you've been afraid about your Visa."

"Amy, Amy, you knew nothin' about anything."

"Larry, come on, you've got me very upset. You set me up for this and you took my soul," she whined. "You know you set me up for this."

"Let me hold you, Amy."

"Don't touch me; don't hold me. Maybe when I've gotten through this meeting with Kevin. Then you can touch me," she said petulantly. "Come on, you set me up for this."

"I didn't set you up."

"You did set me up and you know what else pisses me off, is the fact that because you set me up to kill your wife, now all of a sudden she's dead and you don't wanna see me anymore, you don't wanna go out. "

There, she said it. Amy laid the most obvious trap she dared and now everything depended on Larry falling into it.

"See you? What am I doing here?" Larry said.

"You always see me when I call you and we both know that, and we know why. It's because we're both scared to death they're gonna find out we did it," she nagged Larry.

"We didn't do it, Amy."

"Bullshit, Larry. We did too do it and stop, would you finally admit the truth, Larry. I mean, my God, it's drivin' me crazy, I can't handle it. I've gotta tell the truth to somebody," Amy wailed, on the verge of tears.

"You already told a couple of people."

"Yeah, I know I have told a couple of people," she said defiantly.

"Keep your mouth shut."

"But I feel, not right, it's like, I, nightmares all the time. I can't function. Larry I can't get upset like this. I'm ready to crack. He could say anything, I still might crack. You've gotta give me somethin' to go on, to say to Kevin. Telling me to just say over and over 'I don't know what you're talking about, Kevin, I don't know what you're talking about, Kevin.' That's not helpin' me, dammit. It's bullshit."

Amy whined like a small child who needs a nap. She was doing a superb job of acting. In the surveillance van, they were impressed. She adopted a taunting tone with Larry. "That ain't gonna work," she said. "It's not gonna cut the mustard - I can't handle it. Get that through your thick head."

Larry didn't know what Amy was trying to do to him. But he didn't seem to much care. All Larry was thinking about was sex. Nothing new going on there. He wanted to get his hands on her and get her clothes off. He didn't care if he did her in her car or in the middle of the road or on a countertop in the friggin' drugstore across the street.

He asked Amy if he could sit in her car. He had, all this time, been standing outside, leaning on a car that had a decal that should have set off alarms in his head.

Amy gave him permission to get in, but he changed his mind. He would say, much later, that he thought the car might be wired and that the wire would be activated if he got in.

He asked her again to get out of the car, but she wouldn't.

"Where does Glanville want to see you at?" he asked her after an awkward pause.

Amy said she would choose the place because she had to return the car to her friend in Cotswald, a resort community 10 miles south of Boothbay.

Larry reached for her.

"I'm not wired," Amy said [Oh shit Blandon said in the van. What the hell is she doing, saying that? Don't screw this up now Amy.]

You can trust her Dad, she's not like the others

Glanville needn't have worried. Larry was so focused on getting at her that he was barely listening.

"So stop feelin' me. Get your hands off of me, Larry. I don't wanna be touched by you."

"Okay, Amy," he said with resignation. "How do you feel now?"

"I feel..."

"Physically. With the last abortion."

"With the last abortion, Larry? I'm getting over the infection, it's fine."

"I'm trying, I'm trying to calm you down, OK?"

He was trying to find out if she was physically able to have sex.

"Well, you're not calming me down by talking about my last abortion, you have got, God, I can't

186

walk in to this guy and just say, 'Oh, Kevin, I don't know anything. I was in Atlantic City,' 'cause he's gonna come at me with something and I know it. What if he went to Atlantic City and, and, and, searched and, and scuba dived and did all that other stuff to find the knife and stuff and the pocketbook and we don't know it..."

"Okay, so they found it..."

"What if it's...

"All right, so they found it, now this is where you gotta be cool," he said. Now he was the cop, logical, rational. She seemed to needed some reassurance and he gave it to her, telling her step-by-step what she had to say. If he calmed her down, then they could...[focus, Larry he whispered].

"So they found the knife or Felicia's purse. You say, 'Hey, I don't know anything about it. I went down to Atlantic City.' If you stumble on your story and he says that's not what you said the first time, then you tell Kevin, 'It was so fuckin' long ago, I mean, I forgot. Kevin, I forgot.' Amy, I'm nervous now too. I, my throat is dry."

"Mine's extremely dry," Amy offered.

"Okay, you went to Atlantic City and, and if they try to, they're gonna try to pop you with something, something they know that you shouldn't know and you're just gonna have to play it. You shouldn't know a lotta things about it, and if they say how'd you find that out, well. Say Larry talked a lot to me when we were, when Larry and I were going out after it, after she died. Larry told me a lot of things and he, you know, he told me his story.

"He said he went to start back for the keys. He turned. Felicia called. He turned. He saw this black figure over Felicia. He started to run, he thinks he ran, he's not sure he ran. He's positive he ran, he don't know. Even with the hypnotism, he's not sure. Both times, he told me, he described a black person under a ski mask. Do you understand?"

Amy understood him perfectly. They had been over this ground so many times before. "Yeah, Larry, but when you go under hypnosis, you have got to want to tell them things. So what do you think they caught you lying about?"

"Nothing. Nothing significant. They asked me if I hired this guy to kill Felicia. They mentioned a man's name and I got very adamant. I said, 'Fuck no' and when they were all done, they said 'Look, we know we've put you through a lotta hell and we're sorry. So they apologized. Beatty shook my hand and, you know it's, it was just, ah, they probably just 100 percent believed my story."

"What happened?" she asked, genuinely fascinated with his ability to focus like this, to remember these things.

"And they believed it 'cause I believe it. Do you understand, Amy? I told it as if it was true, that's what you gotta do. I would say to Glanville, Kevin, this is very unorthodox. If he was going to question you, he would have to apprise you of your rights, the right to remain silent, other stuff, have a lawyer.

Hey, dad, You have a right to blow your head off with your police pistol doesn't he Mommy? I love y

"What the fuck is he gonna do on a Saturday night talkin' to you?" Larry demanded.

"Kevin's trying to scare me," Amy said to the tape on her chest. And he's doin' a damn good job of it too, Larry, and you're not doin' anything but tellin' me how you..."

"What would you really like me to tell you, Amy? What can I say?" he said, trying to calm her down.

"You had nothing to do with it, we don't know any fuckin' thing about it."

This isn't what Amy needed to hear from Larry. She wasn't going to give up until she got him to say what she wanted.

"Larry, you know that's not true," she said angrily.

"You do too know it's true," Larry contradicted her. "You know that we had nothing to do with it."

"No, Larry, that's not..."

"Just try to keep telling yourself. If you can't keep telling yourself that you had nothing to do with it, think about this - think about ladies' prison. Think about spending the rest of your natural fuckin' life there." Larry threatened her with what he knew faced her if she ever talked. "Think about being some bull's girlfriend, never having it again from a man, never having a man touch you like.."

"DON'T TOUCH ME! godammit how many times do I have to tell you not to touch me..."

"OK, Amy. OK. Calm down. Are you tellin' me you want me to get rough here? Do you want the rape thing here?

"Not right now, thanks anyway, Larry. I'm too scared to want it. I know this is bad. I'm scared that they're gonna have somethin' on us."

"They don't have anything, honey. If they had any material evidence on us we'd have been gone a long, long time ago. They have no material evidence. The only thing they have right now is they're gonna work on you psychologically, they're gonna work on you and you just have to say, 'hey, I don't know what the fuck these people are talking about. You say, I never

189

got over this, I, um, I spoke to you freely and many times. I haven't seen Larry now since December. I do call him once in a while. Now I recall the phone bills, whatever. See, I, I call Larry to see how he's feeling. When I have a problem I think he can help me with, I call him, and we talk about it. He's been very helpful to me. Fuck it, his head's screwed up too about this whole thing.' You tell them that, Amy."

"You're so full of shit," Amy laughed at him. "You wanted her dead and you know it. You even told me that night when I left. Are you still glad she's dead?"

"Yes," Larry said. "Yes, I'm glad. I, I broke up with Julianne this weekend. I broke up with her Friday and I'm very upset, very lonely and when you called, I half thought you were just jerkin' me off to get me to come here to see you.

"I says, aw, jeez, don't let this be the reason that she's tryin' this. You don't have to do it, and, uh, you're a lifesaver in more ways than one. You don't have to scare me to see me. I will see you anytime. You just call and say 'Lar, I wanna see you, I wanna just talk.' That's all you have to do, all right? Can you understand that?"

Amy just sighed.

"Don't, don't work on me like this 'cause it, it fucks, it fucks everything up," Larry said. "It fucks my head up, it fucks everything up."

"Well, how do you think my head has been Larry? When they call, I wanna see you because I need you to tell me what we did. You're the only one besides me that knows the truth."

"You don't have to see 'em, Amy." He reached his hand out, perhaps in solidarity, perhaps just because he was so horny...

"Please don't touch me. I don't wanna be touched by you."

"Alright. I'm sorry. I'm sorry. You really hate me now."

"Yeah, Larry, I mean you said to me the only way I can marry you is if Felicia's dead. You lied."

"I never lied to you, Amy. I never would."

"You, oh, you're so full of shit... Larry, you took my soul. I can never trust anybody anymore... Get that through your head. You fucked me up good."

"You hate me."

"And you're damn right I hate you."

"I'm sorry. I'm fuckin' sorry. I fucked up."

"Well, why did you pick on me? How long were you wanting somebody to kill Felicia because you didn't have enough guts to do it?"

"We, we both did it, okay. We both did it. We both actively fucking did it, you know."

In the surveillance van it was two down in the bottom of the ninth, full count, tie game.

Now Amy had what she wanted and the investigators needed. She had worn Larry down and he acknowledged the truth. She stopped for about 10 seconds as if she understood what had happened. Then she went on, keeping up the cover of the meeting.

"So, I'm just gonna tell him I don't know anything," Amy said.

"Maybe Glanville is just trying to trap you into saying something that would prove I did it," Larry said.

"Why would they move on you?" she asked.

"Because I am the most likely fuckin' suspect. They have nobody else. The only thing they can figure is I paid somebody to do it and then he's probably gonna ask you, do you think Larry had anything at all to do with it? Do you think, did he ever say anything, did he ever suggest anything? That's where I think he's coming from. To tie you into it, it's, its, it's impossible, Amy. They haven't been able to, through the lab tests or through everything else so I can't figure it.

"They can say that the lab tests and they said this and they said that and in respect to that point, you say 'look, you're gonna make these kinda accusations, I want a lawyer. I don't wanna talk. I don't wanna say anything else more to you.'

"But the fact that he's not telling you that you can have a lawyer, he wants to meet you at this fuckin' hour of the night, on a Saturday night. What the hell is he doin' this for?"

"Maybe he wants to get laid?" Amy giggled.

"Yeah, that might be it."

"I doubt it, Larry. Um, what if they lock me up? What if they try to detain me?"

"For what? They can't. Legally, they cannot detain you. You have the right to a lawyer, and you have a right to, they start to read your Miranda to you, the Miranda warning. You have the right to remain silent. Then just say, 'OK, fine. If I have all these rights, I want 'em all.' And just, don't say anything else to 'em. They can't possibly have anything. If they had, they would have had it a long, long, long time ago."

"What if they just got it and that's why they just called?"

"How could they just get it?"

"My God, Larry! You know they, they could have checked all the wind currents. I mean, I know it would have taken a long time to get all the experts to

192

check all the wind currents and all the, the lakes and rivers from here to Atlantic City. But my God, it coulda been done and they could have traced this stuff. They could have followed it and eventually found it."

"Get it out of your head," he lectured her. "If you dumped the purse and the knife in Atlantic City, it went out to the ocean. all of those little bays, all of those harbors, all those inlets all go out to the ocean. That shit's out in the ocean, Amy. You say, 'yeah, I read in the paper there's somethin' about a pocketbook' or some shit like that. Any number of things."

"Alright. Look I gotta go call Glanville," Amy said, putting the key in the ignition.

Larry sighed deeply. "Can I touch you?"

"My God, Larry, do you ever think of anything besides doin' me or whoever's around?"

"That's pretty funny, Amy, coming from you. Get outta the car."

"No. Please go, Larry. Thank you for seeing me."

Larry asked her to call him after tonight. She agreed to do that.

"I always call you after I talk to them," she said, "and you always call me. We cahooted on everything. I wonder how they never figured out we did that?"

"We did what'?'

"Cahooted on everything."

"I don't know, Amy. I just hope you haven't been wired, and tried to set me up."

"I haven't set you up, I'm not wired. Look, Larry, I don't wanna go to jail either."

"OK. Be cool."

"I will, Larry."

Linda Ellis

At 9:48 p.m., she drove away from the park and back to the roller rink where the law enforcement team had met earlier. Blandon removed the transmitter. Amy's work was done for the night. She still wasn't under arrest, but Glanville didn't want her to run around loose. The prosecutor's office put her up for the night in a hotel in Garrison. The next morning, police and prosecutors reviewed the tape from the meeting in the park. They had Larry's admission on the tape, but they decided they wanted more from him.

The plan was to have Amy talk to him again, this time saying that she hadn't met with Glanville. The meeting with Larry in the park had lasted too long for her to meet the detective, she was to tell Larry. When Glanville had called, he had told her they would talk another time. She was to tell Larry that she had spent the night at friend's house in Cotswald, the oceanfront resort town south of Gullwing.

Beatty, the prosecutor, called people at the Manderlay Hotel in Cotswald and asked them to let him use a phone there. They wanted to make sure that if Larry got suspicious and asked Amy for a phone number to call her back, they would have a number with a Cotswald exchange.

Glanville and Peters drove her to the hotel. She made the call on a phone line that was being recorded.

At 11:19 a.m. Larry answered.

"You're not working today?" she asked Larry after they greeted each other.

"No. No, 'member I took the three-day weekend?"

"Ooh. Oh boy."

"What?" Larry asked her.

194

"Um, alright, I went back to Cotswald last night."

"Yeah?"

"And I called the radio room."

"Um hum."

"And Kevin called me back at my girlfriend's house."

"Um hum.

"He was a little upset."

"Yeah?"

"Because I called him so late, you know, 'cause I told him I'd call him like about 9 and I called him about 10:30."

Larry was not reacting. Amy decided to plow ahead and see if she could get a rise out of him.

"Oh my God Larry, I'm so upset. And, oh shit..."

"It's a game, Glanville's playing a game just like he did with me, remember? He said they wanted to see me and they never saw me. I thought about that after I left last night. Remember what they did with me? Remember that I said Kevin and Peters both called and said they wanted to see me. . See how I would react?"

"Well, my God, Larry, Kevin said on the telephone, he said that he was talkin' with a man named Harper and that he told him some interesting things and he said, you know, Amy, you know Harper."

"Yeah, he's playin' a game," Larry sounded relieved. "You don't know a guy named Harper."

"Larry, that's one of the people I told."

"You fuckin' idiot. You fuckin' idiot," Larry said, desperation in his voice.

"What if he talks with Father Bradley? He's one of the priests I confessed to." She had confided in two priests. Larry said Glanville couldn't talk to the priest

195

about anything Amy or anyone else said, because priests had to keep things secret. The priest didn't count, but this Harper sounded like bad news.

"Who the hell is Harper?" he asked her.

"Oh I don't know. He's some guy in New York, a friend of mine brought him along."

"To where?"

"When I met him for drinks one day."

"And you just blurted it out to him?"

"Yeah, I kinda had a few drinks in me."

"You fuckin' idiot. alright, just tell him... alright, here's the game. You have been in a state because you were cheating with me. Then she (Felicia, his wife) got killed and you're putting yourself through a guilt trip. You didn't go into any details with this guy, did you? Did you go into details with Harper when you met him that day?" Larry asked.

"I told him the whole story." That news was like a knife in Larry's gut. "You fuckin' idiot" Larry spoke now with near-total despair in his voice.

"You know," Amy said, rubbing his nose in it, taking some chances on contaminating the testimony but having too much fun to be careful, *this is so much fun shesaidtothe voiceinsideherhead.the voicesaidshutup AmyI'mtired of hearingyou*

"What if they start talking to, to some more friends and some people that know."

"What do they know? What friggin' people? Who now? How many?"

"About four people know."

"You dumb fuck," Larry said with a deep sigh. "You have to keep your mouth shut from now on and if anybody says anything you just, you know, he starts that shit you say look, 'I'm on a heavy fuckin' guilt trip and in my mind I already believed, you know, that I had something to do with it'."

"Um hum."

"Okay. Now carry that along. Amy, they cannot break you on this as long as you know what you want to say and just keeping saying it. After a while you'll start to believe it yourself. That's the secret.

"So you say to him, 'But in fact, Kevin, I didn't have (anything to do with it). Sure, I may have said something to these fuckin' people but I may have been drunk out of my mind when I said that.. And from what Larry has told me, I pieced it all together and I made myself as the villain because I was on such a guilt trip."

"Larry, then why would he say to me, 'Listen Amy,' he said, 'you'd better start thinking hard and do what's right to make things easier for yourself'. Listen, Larry, if he's getting close to settling it, all right, my God, I think we ought to turn ourselves in because he'll make it easier on us."

"Sure, Amy, sure. What does that do to my kids?"

"I can't worry about your kids, I gotta worry about myself. If they're gonna solve the case and come get us, that's just gonna sit us in jail."

"Amy, you are going to spend the rest of your natural life and so am I in fucking prison if we open our mouths, Amy," Larry said angrily. "If we shut up, the fucking boast in a bar doesn't mean shit. If he had that much conclusive evidence he'd be down to Cotswald to pick you up. Understand that, Amy?"

Amy told Larry she thought Glanville knew everything and authorities were just trying to give her a break, give her a chance to confess and get an easier sentence before they came to arrest them both.

"He's gonna let me sweat it out and he's gonna maybe give me until Tuesday, Larry, and then he's gonna come get me. I can't be embarrassed like that at my job and have him pick me up there. I think it'd be a lot easier if I went to him now."

"Don't do it. Amy, please, hon, I beg you. Don't do it. You'd be a fool if you did that. It'd be just fucking idiotic. They don't have anything on us. They've just been fishing. Somebody could have just went in and said, 'Look, I don't know how true this is. She was drunk and she kept, she admitted this.' You say, 'Kevin, I was drunk. I don't know what the fuck I said'. You're home free. They can't do anything."

Amy brought the conversation back to the subject of the second knife that Larry had bought as a red herring. What if they check his Visa card and the sales records at the sporting goods store, she said. The receipts will show he bought two knives, not the just one knife he still has, she said.

"Amy, Amy, don't do this," Larry pleaded, desperation in his voice. "Amy please. What more can I say but please? We have made a huge mistake and we're both paying for it now. Let's not pay anymore and make other people pay too, people we care about.

"Think about all those people, your family, my family, my kids. We've done one fucking injustice. If we just shut our mouths and just say, 'Yeah, I may have boasted, Kevin. But ya know, come on, I was drunk out of my mind. I didn't know what I was saying'."

He wasn't getting through to her. Larry was not insightful by nature but he did have a clear perception of what other people really believed or thought. Part of being a good cop. So he knew now with virtual certainty that he could stay here, leaning on this damn car door

And there's somethingabout this car, something not right. Uh-huh. It has that littleBarringtonbeach decal in the window and her girlfriend lives in Cotswald anditcould be from thepreviousowner? Larry pleaded with the inside of hishead, a head filling fast with righteous panic and stay here all night and he wouldn't change her attitude.

"I'll call you back after I have a meeting with Kevin," Amy said.

"Please, Amy, please. I am begging you with all my heart and soul. Please don't be fuckin' stupid. Keep your mouth shut, Amy. Please. Please."

"Are you gonna be home? Listen. Stay home," Amy urged.

"I'll be home all fucking day," he said. "Be strong, OK? You got me scared now too we gotta keep strong, OK? We gotta be strong now," Larry pleaded, not strong at all anymore. "This is it. This is the last fuckin' chance to be strong and to stay out of jail. And if I could just touch you I'd feel better...If we could just go to someplace for a coupla hours I think we'd both feel better."

She completely blew him off. She'd never seen this Larry, Weak Larry and she hated him for being weak and begging for it and nearly crying for it.

"Won't we get a better deal if we confess?" Amy asked.

"They're not gonna go easier, honey. You're not gonna get a deal. You're talkin' about life, life, life the rest of your fuckin' life. And you can't claim insanity or any other shit. You went with me to get the jacket, the hood."

199

Then came the words Amy and her comrades in crime fighting had been waiting for:

"We planned it, it was perfect, we did it and it's over. You can't say you didn't know what the fuck was happening. You have to be cool. You can be. You're tough. Now baby, pull it off."

[Headfakes in the surveillance van. Silent cheers in the unmarked. Strike three. Nailed him with a heavy sinker, inside corner. Ballgame.]

Iam NOT theplayertobenamedlater Glanville said to the inside of hisHappyhead. Iam NOW the franchise.tobenamedNOW.

Amy and Larry said their good-byes. *Casablanca* it wasn't. For Amy, the game was almost over. She had played the role of cop to the hilt. She had done what the prosecutors and the investigators wanted. She had succeeded in the real-life *Mission Impossible* episode. She had done something the real police couldn't do. She had done better than the prosecutors and investigators could have wanted.

All that was left to do now was to arrest Larry. Now that the police had enough evidence to arrest him, they had to decide when and where to do it and who would do it.

They didn't want to arrest him at his house. Because he was a policeman, he had guns at home. They didn't want to risk the chance that he would reach for a weapon. If the children were in the house, there was the chance that Larry could try to hold them hostage, Beatty said.

Glenn, Glanville said to Beatty, I know this guy and there's almost nothing he cares about besides getting money and getting laid but he loves his kids.

In his own way, he loves them more than anything. He would never ever endanger their lives.

The top guys still didn't like the idea of arresting him in front of his children. They wanted to cuff him away from the home.

The children would know soon enough that their father was arrested for their mother's murder. But there was no need for them to see him arrested.

Not a problem. be our guests. We can sell tickets and put on a show!

Glanville decided to have Amy call Larry again and set up a meeting outside the house. At 1:50, Amy called Larry and said she had spoken to Glanville and she wanted to meet with Larry. As soon as possible, she told him.

"Listen I gotta take the car back to Cotswald but I'm hungry. I haven't eaten anything since like 12 o'clock last night," she said.

Larry suggested a diner in Southfield Township. She agreed.

The chief of the prosecutor's detectives and his top investigators, Glanville and Carlyle as well as Lt. Agnostelli of the Boothbay Police drove to the diner.

They took a table where they had a clear view of the entrance. And waited. Within five minutes, Larry arrived. He walked in the door and looked for Amy. When he didn't see her, he turned to leave.

They walked up to him, fingers ready to grab a gun if Larry pulled one. They took him without a struggle.

Amy was arrested and transported to the women's unit of Harbor County Correctional Institution. She would be held there as a material witness in a homicide.

Larry was taken to the men's unit of HCCI.

Law enforcement authorities had made the arrests after 18 months of misleading public statements on their part, escalating anguish for Felicia's children, siblings, father and friends and mounting horror for the Halford family.

Now the private back-of-the-envelope deals would begin. Amy loved games. This would be quite a ride through the debris-strewn tunnel of Amy's mind and down the chutes and up the ladders of Larry's libido.

Chapter 8

The Couch

In *Hannibal*, (Dell, 1999) Thomas Harris' sequel to *Silence of the Lambs*, Harris describes roller pigeons. There are two kinds: deep and shallow. The offspring of two purebred deep rollers plummet to the ground and die. The behavior is hard-wired; the pigeon has no option. That there is a similar genetic flaw in some humans is likely.

For Amy Halford and Larry Cusack, the doctors were in.

Amy was an old hand at talking to psychiatrists. Larry would have had a root canal on every tooth in his head rather than be analyzed, his lawyer told a reporter for one of the Newark NJ papers covering the case.

Larry submitted to one session with a psychiatrist at his lawyer, Robert Schwarz's, insistence.

Amy, on the other hand, had her psychiatric visits planned out on her calendar in county jail and looked forward to them.

At the end of it all, Larry gave little more than his name rank and serial number. It was a "He said, she said" thing and all the talking in the world wouldn't change that, Larry sighed:

He said: "This was her plan. She planned to kill my wife, made it into a game. I played along with her because I was afraid for my kids and, frankly, for myself. Amy killed Felicia. I went along with what I thought was game-playing for protection. By the time

I realized she was serious about killing my wife, it was too late. Felicia was dead."

<u>She said</u>: "Larry played games and messed with my head. He drew the blueprint, bribed me with marriage in the future, bought the knife, showed me how to use it. He pretty much said 'Go, girlfriend. I like to watch.' Pretty much that was it," Amy said.

"You know I never wanted her to die. I just wanted him to get a divorce."

The lawyers, Larry's for his defense in a capital murder case and Amy's for her "Let's Make a Deal" situation wanted divergent outcomes from the psychiatric exams. Robert Schwarz for the defense sought a finding that Amy was unfit and incompetent to testify against Larry Cusack. The prosecution wanted to use the physicians' findings to prove that she knew full well the difference between right and wrong, making her fully qualified to testify. Amy's personal attorney, Colin Pascoe, wanted that latter outcome as well.

From: Matthew R. Donohue M.D., Department of Forensic Psychiatry
To: Robert Schwarz, Esq. (Cusack lawyer)
Re: Amy Lee Halford

Dear Mr. Schwarz:

I examined Miss Halford at the County Correctional Institution on June 9 and at that time she was administered a Minnesota Multiphasic Personality Inventory (MMPI). She had a second examination in my office on August 4 and was administered a second MMPI at that time.

She said she likes uniformed cops because they made her feel safe and they have all that heavy stuff hanging from their belts, the gun and handcuffs. The look and feel of weapons and handcuffs turn her on to the point, she said, that she ignores danger signals in these relationships.

She works at not acknowledging reality; she made a choice to play a game in which she denied any difference between her fantasy and everyone else's reality. Her complete lack of interest in her victim was particularly striking; she mentioned Felicia Cusack only once and that was to say that Larry told her to make sure Felicia was dead. She was proud that she was successful in killing Mrs. Cusack.

She said everything happened rapidly and it seemed like she (Felicia Cusack) was here one day and dead the next. The killing "didn't mean anything to me. It's like a game. I'm waiting for someone to come and tell me I can go home."

She was able to relate the murder incident, although she claims some memory loss for the time of the actual stabbing and for that of her trip to Atlantic City. She also stated that she could re-enact the crime "if the guys from the prosecutors' office" would take her back to the scene. She said this in a way that someone else might say "the guys" would take her out for ice cream.

DEVELOPMENTAL HISTORY: Began talking at six months old. Walked at nine months old. Toilet trained at two.

FAMILY HISTORY: mother, in good health, father, also well. One brother and one sister, both living and well. No familial disease.

PSYCHIATRIC EXAMINATION: Miss Halford is oriented in all three spheres: person, place and time

205

Linda Ellis

[she knows who she is, where she is and approximately what time it is]. Her memory for recent and remote events is somewhat impaired since she claims "to have to write everything down or else I forget it." Her affect is silly and childlike and inappropriate to the situation in which she finds herself. She is able to think abstractly. She is not depressed or suicidal. She evidenced some hypnogogic hallucinations on the first night in jail as well as a couple of months ago. [Hypnogogia is the condition similar to the suspended state of awareness a person has when falling asleep, the transient state that bridges waking and sleeping.] However, she did not have any true hallucinations. She says she does not trust anyone and she says everyone is out to get her. She asks for a cigarette frequently, and I supply them. She seems inexperienced at smoking. I asked if she smokes often. No, mostly just after sex, and did not elaborate.

She is not delusional. She is able to do serial sevens. [Counting backwards by 7s starting from 100 is an exercise that tests the ability to concentrate and is often used to diagnose depression and/or other mental illness.] Her cognitive functions are intact. Her judgment is obviously defective. I could not arrive at a firm psychiatric diagnosis during the first interview.

<u>She is, at the time of this session, competent to testify.</u>

There is some possibility that the clinical report is an exaggerated picture of the client's present situation and problems. She is presenting an unusual number of psychological symptoms. These extreme responses could result from poor reading ability, confusion, disorientation, stress or a need for attention for her problems.

Determining the sources of her confusion, whether conscious distortion or personality deterioration, is important since immediate attention may be required. She may be showing a high degree of distress and personality deterioration.

Hey, doc! You should see the other guy! [That would be our Mom].. deterioration everywhere there.

Individuals with this [test] profile tend to be chronically maladjusted, narcissistic and self-indulgent. This client is somewhat dependent and demands attention from others. She appears to be rather hostile and irritable and tends to resent others.

She has great trouble showing anger and may express it in passive-aggressive ways. She tends to blame her own difficulties on others and refuses to accept responsibility for her own problems, feels she should be treated as a special person and feels that she is getting a raw deal out of life. She is somewhat aloof, cold, non-giving and uncompromising.

*   *   *

There was a vast accumulation of these findings from therapists who were hired to evaluate Amy with regard to her fitness to testify against Larry. The evaluations all said she was fit to testify.

Interestingly, the evaluations also could be used to present a case that she was easily led by Larry Cusack or by anyone who promised her a rose garden and that, perhaps, she was not completely responsible for the fact that she stabbed Felicia

207

Cusack 22 times when 8 or 10 would have been enough.

The common diagnosis from three psychiatrists: borderline personality disorder.

DIAGNOSTIC CONSIDERATIONS: An individual with this profile is usually viewed as having a Personality Disorder, such as Passive-Aggressive or Paranoid Personality.

The following are characteristic of this client's current and long term functioning:

[1] Impulsivity or unpredictability in at least two areas that are potentially self-damaging, e.g., spending, sex, gambling, substance use, shoplifting, overeating, physically self-damaging acts.

[2] A pattern of unstable and intense interpersonal relationships, e.g., marked shifts of attitude, idealization, devaluation, and manipulation (consistently using others for one's own ends).

[3] Inappropriate, intense anger or lacks control of anger, e.g., frequent displays of temper, constant anger.

[4] Identity disturbance manifested by uncertainty about several issues relating to identity, such as self-image, gender identity, long-term goals or career choice, friendship patterns, values, and loyalties, e.g., Who am I?

[5] Affective instability: marked shifts from normal mood to depression, irritability or anxiety, using lasting a few hours and only rarely more than a few days with return to normal mood.

[6] Intolerance of being alone, e.g. frantic efforts to avoid being alone, depressed when alone.

I asked Miss Halford how she felt about Larry after the murder. She said she began to wonder when he would kill her. She said that he had tried once. She had asked him to come to her apartment. She told him to go home and write a suicide note and kill himself, or she would kill herself with sleeping pills. She took some sleeping pills. She told him to call the paramedics. He said he would. He didn't. She wouldn't get in the car with him for fear he would drop her in the woods. She cut her phone cords so that he would go down the stairs and call for help. He wouldn't. He was afraid she would tell. He tried to get her to take coffee, but she wouldn't take it. She didn't remember him leaving; he must have drugged her some way.

She had undergone four abortions, she said; two were Larry's babies. The first one Larry told her to abort because it wasn't the right time. At the fourth one, she had broken up with Larry. She didn't know until after they had broken up that she was pregnant. She told Larry to pay for it. He said she still owed him $1500 more for the $2500 breast augmentation so she would have to pay for this abortion herself.

The second abortion, she said, resulted from sex at work. The guy responsible, a currency trader, denied paternity. She had to go to a clinic in Midtown that charged on a sliding scale. She vowed never to have to go to a "charity" clinic again because she was "of a different social status from the other girls".

The third abortion was the result of a blind date arranged by another student at her secretarial school in New York. This guy, a football player at Fordham University, paid the full charge, she said. Even though it was full surgery with anesthesia so it was very expensive, about $4,000. The guy had wanted the baby to be up for adoption because he is a very strong Catholic. She refused to have the baby even though by the time they finished arguing she was six months gone and beginning to show.

She told him she had to stay in school and then get a good secretarial job. She couldn't achieve her goals if she had to carry the baby to full term and then give birth. She would have to miss many classes and tell the school the reason for her absence and they might expel her.

It was difficult to steer Miss Halford back to her current situation. I asked about her current legal status, she said she had pleaded guilty, and was awaiting sentencing. She perceives the prosecutor's office and anyone in authority as on her side. The prosecutor told her, "You were used and abused by him. We have to get that son-of-a-bitch."

"Everything I did was to help get Larry," she told the doctor, "to nail him because this is his fault. He did it, he forced me to kill his wife. We had to catch him and I had to make him confess. I was scared but it was fun. It was like being a cop, like an undercover cop, who trapped people by setting them up. The prosecutors didn't want anything bad to happen to me. They made a game out of it. It was all planned for my protection."

I asked her to describe her plans for the future. She said that she wants a marriage and somebody to come home to; she said that is all she wants.

That was true for Mommy. Amy, you're a lying bitch. Sincerely yours, your (worst)nightmares

I asked Miss Halford to interpret the adage "People who live in glass houses shouldn't throw stones". She said "That's like the pot calling the kettle black." I asked her to interpret another adage,

"You can lead a horse to water but you can't make him drink." She said that you cannot force someone to ...and she paused for a very, very long time. Then she finished by saying, "You cannot force someone to do something they don't want to do." Then she went on: "If you stick a burr under the horse's saddle, then the horse doesn't have much choice. Or if you keep him from water he doesn't have much choice. I asked if that applied to her. She said Larry kept her away from people, and added, "I just wanted to go to bed with him. I didn't want to fall in love with him."

I asked what was going to happen to her. She said that her sentence could be no more than thirty years She didn't know for sure because she didn't know how long she would have to serve before parole. My fate is up to the judge, she said. If I were the judge I wouldn't make me go to jail. Jail is a place for bad people. I'm not a bad, mean person. I am very impressionable. I asked what that meant. She said, I have the innocence of a child. There is no reason to punish me for something I had no control over. I didn't want this to happen anyway.

Now, she said, she has special circumstances.

" I'm in the medical wing because I am so important to this case. There are only four women in there, including me. If there is a problem, if anyone bothers me, the other person is always moved out. I asked if she had any visitors, and she said her family. I asked if she had seen any psychiatrists, and she named others. In 1979 she saw a doctor in Barrington. I asked why she went to see him. "I was just mad that day. I didn't like him. Now, from jail, I have consented to be interviewed and analyzed by psychiatrists and a psychologist and now I am given this time to come and see you and others. To help the case."

*   *   *

After high school, the psychiatrist reported, Miss Halford went to school in New York City, the Partridge Secretarial Institute, for one year.

She worked part-time for an attorney's firm for a short period of time while going to school. Then she got a job with a bank for six months. She hated the job. She transferred to a brokerage house for a month. She left by mutual agreement. She was disgusted with the manager. They gave her a choice: stay and we make you miserable or leave on your own with a glowing recommendation. She chose to leave because she said "the bosses" at the brokerage were out to get her and ruin her career. She would not elaborate. She next went to work at a Wall Street brokerage firm and she said she loved it there. For two years and six months she had a job she loved, she felt like a valued member of the team there. Then Larry ruined it all. I asked her how he did that. She said that by involving her in murder, Larry ruined her life. She said the brokerage was the best job she ever had. She would still be there if it weren't for Larry. For 18 months she worked for three partners in mergers and acquisitions and then was put in research. In May 1982 [two months after the murder] she was promoted. She was administrative assistant to the grandson of one of the founders. She ran his office and loved it.

She denies any homosexual problems and has no hang-ups of any kind about sex. They had a lot of sex, good sex before "they" killed Felicia. After that, the sex was never as good. He would come to the apartment but would not stay all night. He wouldn't leave the children overnight alone and he said he couldn't very well ask for help without explaining where he'd be. Miss Halford related this in an extremely petulant manner. She said she is a "victim". In what sense? I asked.

I am a victim just as much as his kids are and Felicia's family, she complained. I shouldn't have to go to jail. I never figured I would. I'm not a murderer. What happened was not my fault. I had no control over it. Prison is for bad people, mean people. I have the innocence of a child. Emotionally I never grew up and Larry preferred me that way. All men like me that way. I asked what she meant about not growing up. I do not know the answer, she said, but you should, you and the other psychiatrists. They make me talk, talk, talk and then never give me any answers.

Miss Halford had a breast augmentation in November 1982. I asked the reason for the breast enlargement and Miss Halford said Larry was always looking at women's tits. She figured that if hers were larger he wouldn't look anymore, plus the fact that she wanted to. She didn't feel that hers were big enough. It was done at Doctors' Hospital in New York City. She also had arthroscopic knee surgery in September 1982 at that same hospital.

I asked Miss Halford if she had ever been in difficulty with the police. She said no. That was a stupid question, she said, because she wanted to be a police officer and she still does. I asked if she thought she could still make it. She said sure and she would be a good one, too.

Linda Ellis

I'm honest, she said. I'm always willing to work. I always wanted to work in New York City. I have a young face.

She said spontaneously, "He'll never get out of jail. If he does, I know he will try to kill me. But her family, Felicia's family, will kill him before he can get to me so I have to live out this misery, my life".

*   *   *

From: Kevin C. Pearson, M.D.
Re: Amy Halford

Dear Mr. Pascoe:

I received your letters regarding information from a psychiatric interview re your client Amy Lee Halford. I am afraid I can only be of minimal assistance to you in this case, as I only saw Miss Halford on one occasion and that nearly two years ago.

At that time she had come on very short notice and I was able to do only a partial examination. It was extremely difficult soliciting information from her during the interview, and I was not able to form a clear impression of her mental status at that time. She tended to be guarded and jumped from topic to topic so that I was unable to arrive at a chief complaint or specific reason for her consulting me. The patient did tell me that she was engaged to a 42-year-old man who was currently in the process of getting a divorce. She did not identify that as a specific problem however, nor did she complain about her work.

Any other complaints focused around a difficulty she had had with high school friends and some

214

feelings that she did not fit in well with her peer group. However, the patient did not admit to suffering any serious disturbance during the interview.

I then had the patient fill out a symptom checklist which she then left in the office to be scored. On the basis of the symptom checklist, it appears that she was suffering from a much more serious disturbance than she presented in the interview. She scored fairly high in symptoms of paranoid ideation, psychoticism, as well as hostility and interpersonal insensitivity. I did not have a chance to discuss this with her as she cancelled her next appointment and all future appointments.

Sincerely yours, etc.

Amy had filled out a symptom checklist for that psychiatrist in 1981, a list that was later to be seen as a whole string of red flags.

Would Felicia have lived if someone had analyzed those symptoms and asked Amy to return for follow-up treatment?

She indicated thoughts of others dying, an urge to smash things, feeling lonely even when with people she knew, restlessness, inability to sit still, shouting or throwing things, having thoughts and images of a frightening nature and a firm belief that most people cannot be trusted.

She had no feelings of worthlessness, however, nor did she ever have panic attacks. She did not feel guilt, inferiority to others or blocked in getting things done.

She dreaded being alone.

Amy would not be alone for a long time.

215

Part IV

The Trial. 1983

Chapter 9

The Half Court Press

Now the machinery of the legal system began to grind its gears.

In early June, Larry Cusack appeared in court for arraignment. The suspended cop was somber as he pleaded not guilty to charges of soliciting Amy Lee Halford to murder his wife, to felony murder and to conspiracy to commit murder.

Larry and Amy were each charged with felony murder because the killing occurred during an armed robbery and with conspiracy to commit murder. Additionally, Amy was charged with armed robbery.

However, she was testifying against her former lover and for the state in exchange for a plea bargain. That arrangement would limit the amount of time she would serve for murder to 30 years. The minimum time to parole eligibility varied and was the decision of the trial judge. Amy could wind up with as little as six years in prison for the murder or she could get the maximum, 17 years to parole.

Larry, if convicted, faced life imprisonment without the possibility of parole for a minimum of 30 years.

Their dance cards read arraignment, grand jury proceedings, plea bargaining session (hers), jury trial (his), testimony, jury ruling and sentencing (his & hers).

Larry would not face the death penalty because the crime had been committed four months before capital punishment went on the books in New Jersey.

the death penalty works for us, Dad... Mommy, we miss you

A few minutes after Larry's exit, Amy appeared in court for arraignment. Her demeanor was calm and she was smiling a bit. Amy wore summer clothes in primary colors and appeared to be without a care in the world. She was well groomed despite her complaints that she could not prepare for her "public appearances" if she couldn't use a blow dryer for her hair. She looked trim despite her constant complaints about prison food.

Before Superior Court Judge Gillian McDonnell gaveled the court to order, Amy was carrying on a subdued conversation with her personal lawyer, Colin Pascoe. It appeared that Amy was beginning to understand the gravity of her situation and that she had her emotions in check. Pascoe was making her realize that Judge McDonnell was the single most important person in Amy's life.

Bryan Carlyle and Kevin Glanville, the two prosecutor's office investigators who had been Amy's most constant companions, were relieved at her demeanor.

She'sgonnashut up thankyouGod she's stable today because we need some credible testimony from this sillylittle.. and then I don't have to be nice to hereveragain Glanville said to the inside of his head I'd liketostrangle her sometimes just toshut herup...remembershe's myticket to ride

As the prosecutor's point men and Amy's minders, the detectives had had enough histrionics from the troubled young woman to last them the rest of their careers.

Today, apparently, the reporters and the court would see I'm-Under-Control Amy. That was good for the prosecution.

Let her stay that way pleaselordjust for a few more minutes what did the cop in the Cove call her? Slightly slutty, slightly nutty which is gross understatement but not right now pleaselord let her seem normal she's the bigenchilada for our case and if we spent all that time with this sillylittleslut for nothing I'll kill hermyselfCarlyle said to the inside of his head.

Just when the prosecution team was ready to sit back and enjoy its good fortune, Out-of-Control Amy popped up like a heart-stopping Chuckie doll. Amy/Chuckie is bored! Her body language is talking loud and clear: "Hey everybody! This is about me! It's always been about me!"

Out-of control-Amy swiveled to wink at Glanville, her personal favorite, and he shaded his eyes with his right hand and tried to disappear.

Amy threw her head back and laughed raucously in a sustained excess of all the wrong emotions. She seemed hysterical. But those amongst the spectators who knew her recognized this role, knew it was orchestrated. The outburst lasted perhaps 45 seconds, seemed forever, a huge gift to the defense. The prosecution team held its collective breath. Glanville flashed on a fantasy that Amy's head would detach from her body (*and it was a goodbody*) and roll right down the aisle and out the door and down the marble hallway. It would still be talking and

221

winking and laughing [*goodteeth*] as it bounced down the courthouse steps and was gone.

Judge O'Donnell, the detectives and prosecutors and spectators were at first shocked at Amy's behavior, then angry.

Pascoe, her lawyer, skipped shock and went immediately to anger. He had not seen his client this way before. He had seen Angry Amy, Hurt Amy, Seductive Amy and Martyr Amy. Those were bad enough. This was humiliating and bad for his image. She reverted to quiet conversation but Pascoe did not respond to her, furious at her lack of impulse control.

When the judge called for order, Amy began smiling at spectators again, appearing to pay scant attention to the business of the court. Throughout the proceedings, she laughed and waved at people in the gallery whether she knew them or not.

She pleaded not guilty to felony murder, conspiracy and armed robbery but gave no indication that she took any of this seriously. She was excused and had to be told to vacate the witness stand.

Pascoe, a highly respected trial attorney who asked for and received large fees and who had a contract with a reporter for a book on the case, was so troubled by his client's manic behavior that he had psychiatrists from outside the county look at Amy's prior psychiatric exams and her test results.

At this point he was hoping to get a diagnosis of diminished capacity, anything so that he didn't have to be associated with her anymore. Having a large role in a true crime book was a dream but it might have to be a dream deferred. He wanted someone to state that she was incompetent to stand trial.

However, the new lineup of psychiatrists agreed with the earlier ones: she was competent to stand trial.

There was no more money. That did not make the lawyer happy. He couldn't drop the case at this point because of the book contract and his good reputation. He would just have to kiss goodbye to some substantial billable hours.

The grand jury heard taped testimony from the alleged co-conspirators.

With regard to Larry, the jury members heard his original account of the murder. He maintained complete innocence. He testified that he had no idea that Amy had killed Felicia. He said again that he had seen a "bald-headed nigger humping" his wife as she died.

In the case of Amy, they heard her confession to the murder of her rival.

Several of the grand jurors had questions that were answered by Greg Brocail, the first assistant prosecutor.

Was the weapon ever found?

No, ma'am.

Have attempts been made to locate that weapon?

Yes sir, they have, and the attempts are ongoing.

Do either of these two people have any history of drugs?

Ma'am, that's not a proper question for you to ask. That really has no bearing on the evidence that you have before you. Whether or not they had a bad history of drugs that's not what you should consider. You should consider only the evidence you have and not whether or not they are good or bad people.

Linda Ellis

How long did she wait to move into his house after the wife was killed?

A week.

Mr. Brocail, why did this woman confess when she knew she would be arrested and probably jailed?

She said she couldn't sleep at night or stay warm, that she had a guilty conscience.

"Any further questions from the grand jury? Then proceed to your deliberations and thank you for your time and attention."

* * *

The 44-year-old widower and his 22-year-old former lover were indicted for murder by the grand jury in mid-June, 15 months after Felicia Cusack's death. Larry was bound over for trial – *State of New Jersey v. Cusack* - with the date set for October 3, 1983.

Later, one of the grand jurors said that it was clear to her that If Larry had not broken off with Amy and then rubbed her nose in it by moving another woman into his bed, no one would ever have been charged with the murder of Felicia Cusack.

One of the arresting detectives agreed.

A good woman lost her life for two pathetic reasons, theorized Fred Tenney, a Boothbay police department liaison to the prosecutor's office. One, Larry wanted sex with no strings and no boundaries and two, he would not risk his assets and paycheck in a divorce action. Felicia might make good on her threat to turn him in for the Boothbay rental arson. She told him a divorce would bring shame to her family and would damage the children.

224

Even if she kept quiet about the arson, and about the time he'd borrowed some funds from the Cove Democratic Club, she'd still get half his assets and he'd have to shell out child support.

It was always about sex and money and that order could probably be flipped depending on the woman, Tunney concluded.

Cusack was not stupid as much as he was greedy and horny, the detective said, and keeping the money and getting his freedom blinded him to the escape route. He should either have married Amy or killed her. Dumping her was the absolute worst move he could have made. Obviously, the detective said, rolling his eyes.

*   *   *

A week before the arraignment, Amy had written a five-page letter to Brocail. In the letter, she asked that a separate note be given to Judge O'Donnell on her behalf. In the main letter and the separate note she asked to be released from jail. These are requests that must be adhered to before I testify, she wrote.

"I've done you all a big favor and now I want to go to my parents' home," she wrote. "I do not get my proper diet here and I will get sick if I am made to eat white bread every day. I need whole wheat bread with fiber."

She enclosed a diet – mainly fruit, vegetables and whole grains and a strict sugar limit - and said it must be strictly followed. Next, she was to be driven to the state prison to meet with the warden so that he understood that she was a special case. At the state prison she wanted privileges for all the "extra" facilities like the pool. Before she has to testify, she

225

must have five hours at her parent's house to pack her clothes. She has to pick out her outfits because her mother still likes to dress her.

"I want to have what I want," she wrote. It is probable that she did not realize that was a statement defining her entire life, not just picking out a wardrobe.

Amy continued her letter to Greg Brocail, first assistant prosecutor and the man who would present the state's case against her former lover. "The guards and inmates are jealous of me here (county jail) I'm the spoiled girl who gets special treatment. Besides, Greg, I'm cute, and there are not very many cute girls in jail with me, believe it or not. I'm not the type of girl who should be in jail. I can read and write." (Smile face drawn in margin of letter.)

She said she had every intention of being there for Larry's trial. [Sad face] "Once I start a game, I always finish it!" Amy claimed to present no risk of flight. "I could have done that anytime [run away]. I helped you [the prosecution team) get Larry even though he could have easily killed me because I wanted to help you. I wouldn't miss the end after all this."

The jail won't let her just take care of herself in general, she wrote. Ask the judge to lower her bail so that her folks can afford it, she asked. Once in state prison, she demands protective custody, a guard by her side "from the time I awaken till I go to sleep." She said that as long as she is in county jail, Investigator Carlyle must still be allowed to accept collect calls from her at least once a day so that he knows she is OK. If he doesn't hear from her, he is to drive to the jail immediately because something is wrong. Also, Carlyle and Kevin Glanville will drive her to state prison after sentencing. She will not accept any other drivers.

"Please, Greg, come to see me as soon as possible or just go straight to the judge and work it out for me – please."

"And Glenn (county prosecutor), you lied to me once already – we never did have breakfast like you promised!!! (Smile face)

"Please don't disappoint me again!" (Sad face)

*   *   *

Larry and Amy were held at county jail in Garrison in lieu of one million dollars in bail each.

Amy asked prosecutors to lower her bail. She was, after all, the reason there would be a trial; without her confession they would have nothing. Not their call, the prosecutor's office, in the person of Bryan Carlyle, told Amy. That was purely at the discretion of Judge O'Donnell. Therefore, Amy wrote a letter to the judge. The judge wrote a letter to Pascoe. Tell your client, the judge wrote, that the answer is no. Further instruct her that all correspondence goes through your office.

Amy just didn't get it yet. She didn't realize there were people in charge of her life now who didn't care if she drew a happy face or a sad face on her letters. The state of her inner child was of no consequence to anyone. She was in the legal system and she had barely begun to realize that it's a steep learning curve in there.

Meanwhile, Larry told his lawyer, Robert Schwarz, to ask for reduction of bail to $150,000 and for permission for his client to put up the Gullwing Cove house as collateral. Schwarz reminded his

227

client that putting his children's home at risk would not be a good public relations move. John and Grace were now 13 and 15, living with friends and relatives and had rights to a portion of any family asset.

When Larry phoned periodically, neither of his children would talk to him. Grace believed that her father had her mother killed. John would say nothing about his father to anyone, even his Aunt Gerry, his favorite among his mother's sisters. He would talk only about his mother. A year after her death, her 12-year-old son had not come to grips with the fact that he would never see his mother again. He wanted every day to move back to the Cove house because he didn't want his mother to come home to a dark house with no one there to meet her.

He pleaded that a light be left on inside and one on the porch. A neighbor obliged **Thank you for leaving the light on for mom** even though John was living eight miles away.

The Miller family had moved to Atlantic Beach and Grace Cusack went with them, to be with her best friend Dottie. Dime, the Cusack's pet Chihuahua, became a problem. Dottie's father Cal had an allergy to dogs, so Dime had to live outside. Over the winter, even in a specially insulated doghouse, the all-but-hairless dog nearly froze to death. Julia put an ad in the paper, asking for someone to take Dime. Within a week, a neighbor back in the Cove adopted the seven-year-old dog.

Grace was drifting into a netherworld, hanging with the kinds of kids she used to scorn. The Millers were greatly worried. Grace had seemed to hold onto at least a fragile connection to her past through her pet; once Dime was gone, Grace seemed to lose heart, to give up any pretense that life would ever be OK again.

Fortunately, one of the priests at St. Genevieve's began counseling sessions with Grace at the Millers' request. Grace tried to dwell on good memories of the past, not the awful realities of the present.

John and Grace gradually became estranged and they grew up in different towns. John could not understand why Grace would not talk about their mother. In 1990, Grace married and the next year had a child. She wrote her brother that her husband wanted John to be their son's Godfather and that now she was a mother, she understood better how John had suffered. It worked. Felicia's psychic friend from the town drugstore, Phyllis Emmerman, said that Felicia told her in a dream that the reconciliation mended her broken heart.

Neither child ever lived in the Cove house again but they owned half the equity if Larry were freed, all the equity if he were found guilty. His lawyer told Larry that he could not use the Cove house as collateral even if the judge would approve a lowered bail.

You think I would run, then? Larry asked Schwarz, his lawyer.

Not my call, Schwarz said, but if I were the judge I wouldn't take a chance like that, that you might skip town. It could worry your children. It should worry you, Larry because just between you and me, when you consider the feelings of Felicia's people, the Girardi family, if you just think about that for a few minutes, you will agree that you do not want to be out there. You want to stay right here. You are safe in jail.

You catch my drift, Larry?

Linda Ellis

There are degrees of murder – first and second.

The difference between first degree and second-degree murder is based on the suspect's intent in committing the crime or the manner in which he carries it out. Punishment, which can include the death penalty, is more severe for first-degree murder.

The charges against Larry and Amy were way up there on the first-degree list.

First degree murder is willful, deliberate and premeditated. It includes killings committed in the course of certain felonies, usually arson, burglary, robbery, rape and mayhem.

Murder in the second degree includes murder in which the suspect intended to kill the victim but the killing was not premeditated (a spur-of-the-moment killing as opposed to killing in cold blood), murder in which the suspect intended to seriously harm but not to kill the victim and killings committed in the course of a felony, other than those felonies listed under first-degree murder.

Manslaughter is killing when no malice or intent to kill is present or provable.

Voluntary manslaughter is intentional killing when no malice existed before the triggering event, usually in the heat of passion. A classic example is a man finding his wife in bed with his best friend. There was no existing intention that led him to shoot his friend and/or his wife.

Involuntary manslaughter is unintentional killing caused by criminal negligence. An example from today's headlines is the death of a driver if his vehicle has faulty tires and those tire faults were known by the manufacturer.

230

In all measured categories, the percentage of female culprits has been ratcheting up since 1975, according to the U. S. Bureau of the Census and federal crime statistics. Before the mid-70s, women accounted for nine percent of homicides where there was an arrest. In 1998, the last period for which data are available, that percentage had grown to 14 percent.

In August, Judge O'Donnell refused to reduce Larry's bail and denied a change of venue for the Gullwing Cove resident's trial. Schwarz had asked that the proceedings be moved to a more neutral county.

A month before she murdered Felicia, during a time when she and Larry had to stay away from other another, Amy began a sexual relationship with a 28-year-old man in her high-rise apartment building in Hoboken.

She dated Moore Goodwin sporadically from February 1982, a month before she killed Felicia Cusack, until May 1983 when she turned herself in for the murder and then nailed Larry. Moore and Amy had separate apartments in a building filled with people working on their first million. For all intents and purposes their building was deserted from 7 a.m. until 7 p.m. weekdays and Saturday mornings. The neighborhood delis, takeout storefronts, boutique restaurants and cafes feed the 20-somethings on their own for the first time. Hoboken, a 20-minute train ride under the Hudson River to lower Manhattan, is hugely popular with people who want a doorman, safe streets and a reasonable commute at affordable rents.

Goodwin was everything Amy had ever wanted. He, on the other hand, had no intention of getting serious with her. She was a great party girl, a good dancer, didn't drink too much or require illegal substances. He liked their easy relationship; no obligation and no tension on his side of the bed.

After the arraignment but before the trial, Amy told one of the county jail guards that she was pregnant. She said she wasn't sure who the father was but she joked that one was young and rich and the other was in his 40s and in jail. "Which one do you think I should choose to be the father?" she asked the guard playfully.

In analyzing the turbulence of her life in the relevant months, the father actually could have been either Cusack or Goodwin.

Goodwin would be called as a witness for the prosecution. To avoid any surprises, Bryan Carlyle, a detective and colleague of Kevin Glanville in the prosecutor's office, interviewed Goodwin before the trial date.

Amy had said that she was with him Mar.19, the eve of the slaughter of Felicia Cusack. That was true.

"I met her in the lobby of our building at about 8 p.m. that night for dinner," Goodwin said. "She had rented a car and she had it parked on the street near our building. We drove to downtown in the city, to Soho, for dinner and then drove around Manhattan to a few clubs and bars and we ended up back downtown, in the Village," Goodwin told Carlyle. Their last stop had been a favorite Village club, They Shoot Horses.

"Did you know she was going to Atlantic City the next day?" Carlyle asked.

In fact, Amy had asked him to meet her here,
Goodwin said. He told her he had to work, which he
said he had told her numerous times. He had told
her often enough that to make that first million you
had to work at least 100 hours a week.

She had told him she had scheduled breast
augmentation surgery so that she would have some
down time as well. That's the reason she wanted to
have fun this weekend, and Atlantic City was fun.

The two got back to Hoboken from Manhattan
around 2 Saturday morning.

In 18 hours Felicia Cusack would die at the
hands of this good-time girl named Amy, a girl who
just wanted to have fun.

Amy was known to Hutch, one of the bartenders
at They Shoot Horses. He remembered her as a
"cheerleader type," who promised to show him her
new breasts after her surgery.

When Hutch read the May 30, 1983, *New York
Post* story of how Amy persuaded Larry to admit the
murder on tape (*Post* headline: <u>Cop Popsie Tricks
Dick</u>), Hutch was stunned. He thanked his lucky
stars that he passed the last time she asked him to
take her home. The Amy he knew was a poster girl
for a party girl. This murder thing was hard to
believe.

Well, as they say in the outer boroughs, go figure.

*   *   *

Amy had confessed voluntarily on Memorial Day
weekend. Although she had a legal right to a trial, it
was not in her best interests. The only sensible
course of action was to make the best bargain she

233

could with the state, the best bargain her lawyer, Colin Pascoe, could make.

Sept. 7 she came to court for the plea bargain. The plea was guilty. This time her demeanor was serious. After she testified against Larry, her sentence would be left to Judge O'Donnell, who could give her up to 30 years, with a maximum of 17 years before a chance for parole. Amy was scheduled as the star witness for the prosecution and was more than ready for her close-up.

On the infamous *"I'm not wired but don't feel me up"* tapes, Larry apparently admitted his role in the slaying of his wife and told Amy he was glad his wife was dead.

"We did it, we both did it, we both actively fucking did it," he was recorded as saying to Amy and thus to the wires on Amy's upper body, proving he was never the brightest bulb on the tree. He told the grand jury that he meant they both had the love affair together.

But again, the apparent voice of doom:

"He told me to wait behind the green Dumpster between two cars," Amy had told the grand jury. "He said he was going to pretend to be taking Felicia to the movies..."

A few minutes later, Larry said on the tape that he hoped Amy was not wired. She said she wasn't, she just wasn't in the mood to get laid.

So what thehell amIdoing here wastingmytime? Theonly reason I'mhereis toscrewyour tinybrains outstupid, Larry saidtothe insideofhishead that fateful day...

Greg Brocail, the first assistant county prosecutor, would be first chair for the state's case. The first assistant, the second in command in the prosecutor's office, normally doesn't appear at trials because his job is to supervise other prosecutors and investigators and to direct sensitive investigations. This, however, was a case Brocail asked to try; he had known Felicia as a friend and a fellow political minority in The Cove. In addition, these cases could be make or break a career and Brocail had a good feeling about this one.

Based on pre-trial motions, the state intended to present as evidence the media-dubbed Amy tapes.

Amy and her tapes were, in fact, the state's entire case. Beatty, the prosecutor, admitted that without her they had nothing. However, they did have her, she wasn't going anywhere and the state had a slam-dunk.

Beatty and Brocail, his point man, made sure Amy was treated with kid gloves at every step along the way. Carlyle had been assigned to make sure she got special treatment in the jail. Glanville was finally able to hand her off.

Ohshit, Bryan said to theinside ofhishead as the first of a flood of demands began rolling out of the women's wing of county jail. It was worse than that, Bryan Carlyle moaned. It was more like someone took the lid off popping popcorn.Poor Bryanindeed as Bryan Carlyle wondered if there would be any limits set on this lunatic's laundry list.

Amy, predictably, responded to the offer of special treatment from somewhere out in the ozone layer. She wrote a letter to Beatty and Carlyle with a copy to the judge saying that she could not testify if she wasn't happy with her appearance. She wrote to the office that she also needed tools for a pedicure.

Seewhatl mean? Carlyle said to anyone who would listen. She has no friggin' concept of where she

*is. You're infriggin jailAmy! The cop said to the inside
of his head. You want tools?Toolthis!*

Amy knew that she was in the driver's seat on
this case and with these cops and she did not want
to leave any opportunity unexplored. She wanted
unrestricted and regular visits with Glanville, Brocail
and Carlyle. Conjugal visits would be great, she said
to a guard with no sense of humor. She wanted an
hour with Leland Halliday, the chief of detectives for
the prosecutor's office. She saw him as a father
figure.

Amy never once asked how Larry was doing; the
only times she mentioned him was to the *insideof
herhead* where she could call him a
stinkingbastardwhohad ruinedherlife. However, she
wouldn't mind a couple of hours with him in his cell.
Be like on the train. A zipless fuck with an audience.
She'd never done that before.

Amy never mentioned Felicia; if asked, she
shrugged and ignored the question. In the picture
Amy was painting of her life, Felicia wasn't even a
silhouette.

Halliday, the chief of detectives, was new to the
Amy watch and was totally unprepared for her
antics. She wanted a special diet in jail. She
demanded weekend furloughs in New York City and
said there was no reason why she should not be
allowed to go home and stay with her parents. She
wanted tranquilizers. She wanted Moore Goodwin for
private time.

Because she was pregnant, Amy was allowed a
visit to her obstetrician-gynecologist in Manhattan,
Gary Prentice. Carlyle and Glanville accompanied
her, and a female detective from Harbor County was
present as Dr. Prentice examined Amy. He told the

236

detectives to phone him the following week for the results of some tests. He did not tell the police, but Dr. Prentice was not happy with the development of the fetus. He also said that Amy had a respiratory infection and a yeast infection and he wrote prescriptions for medications to treat the infections.

Amy wanted her cell locked when she wasn't in it because she was being robbed. That was actually a valid request, prison officials reported. She acted as though she had discretionary income and had thus made herself a target.

Prisoners are allowed very few personal items, and they treasure those they have. Shower shoes, for example, are crucial possessions. Deborah, a prisoner who had status in the group, took Amy's shower shoes. Amy had no protectors in county lockup and she was vulnerable. She had had several fistfights with Deborah and altercations with other inmates about programs on TV and the location of each woman's mat in front of the TV. The view each inmate had of the television set and the input on programming choices are serious matters in jails at all levels. Amy had gone out of her way to make herself different from the other prisoners and then wondered why nobody liked her.

She felt the other inmates at the county lock-up hated her so much that she might have been in danger. They certainly hated her enough to let her miscarry, to watch her blood soak the concrete on a bright sunny day in the exercise yard and not call for help. By the time a guard spotted Amy lying on the ground bleeding and shrieking, Amy had to be hospitalized.

Hospitalized is how she remained the rest of her time in county jail. Prosecutors were so anxious to keep her stable, healthy and loyal to them that they had her moved to the medical wing of the county lockup, where doors could be locked in her absence, her medications would be delivered on time and security was tight. There were only five women per TV set and everyone had a decent viewing spot.

It was October 3rd, opening day at the courthouse for *State of New Jersey vs. Cusack*. It was nineteen months since Felicia Cusack was told to wait with her back to a Dumpster and since a ski mask of indifference was likely the last thing she saw on this earth.

Cusack went on trial before a jury of his peers on charges that he had solicited Amy Halford to murder Felicia Cusack.

Mrs. Cusack died of multiple stab wounds to the chest, neck and back after she was attacked by Miss Halford as Mrs. Cusack walked to a movie theater in the South Strip section of Boothbay, the jury was told by Brocail for the state.

Brocail told the jury that Cusack plotted the murder with Miss Halford and led his wife of 22 years to the slaughter.

"Much of what you need to know about this person on trial is that when he stopped his wife and told her the lie that he had to go back to find his keys, he turned her toward him so that her back, her vulnerable back, was an easy target for the vicious killer bent on slaughter and waiting behind the Dumpster."

Defense lawyer Robert Schwarz denied that Cusack turned his wife on purpose. Schwarz said Miss Halford was an emotionally disturbed young woman who committed the murder and then tried to place some of the responsibility on Cusack as revenge for leaving her for another woman.

Spectators queued up two hours ahead of the opening gavel to gain a seat at the trial, hoping to hear some melodramatic testimony. Attendants turned away late arrivals.

Both the defense and the prosecution gave dramatic presentations of what they intended to prove to the jury. "A dark figure slithered through the night and stabbed and stabbed and stabbed and then left. After the attack...Cusack stood to the side, not a hair out of place. Not once did he go over to caress and comfort his dying wife," Brocail said.

Schwarz, Larry's lawyer, planned his assault on the flanks of the state's case and trained his guns on Amy. "She is a very troubled young lady, not at all a normal 22-year-old. She has a Dr. Jekyl-Mr. Hyde personality, efficient at work, then after work a screaming creature who can't or won't control her emotions."

He said his client would testify, not because he must but because Cusack wanted to expose the web of deceit spun by his former lover. He broke off the relationship because he met another woman. Amy went to the police with the conspiracy "fiction" not long afterward.

The opening arguments were followed by testimony from Ann Padgett, co-owner of Dublin, Grace Brown, the widow who observed the Cusacks in the parking lot across from Dublin and Dr. John Morrill, the pathologist who performed the autopsy.

Linda Ellis

The next day was Amy's close-up, her special moment, a chunk of time in which everyone would study her and hang on her every word.

"I spoke with Mrs. Cusack last year, in February, and I told her I meant her no harm," Amy testified. "All I knew was I wanted to be loved and Larry said he loved me," Amy said. "Mrs. Cusack called me a whore and a tramp." Even now, Amy seemed genuinely puzzled that Felicia would have felt animosity towards her.

The phone call originated when Larry phoned Amy to say he would not be moving back to her Hoboken apartment as planned.

"Do you want to talk to Felicia?" he asked Amy.

A grotesque suggestion, surely.

However, this being that fun couple Amy and Larry, who between them had the sensitivity of a stone wall, Amy said she would love to. Felicia did as her husband directed.

"She (Felicia) said she loved her husband and he loved her and he has cheated on her many times but he always came back to her. She told me Larry would get tired of me and that he had told her everything about us. "So I asked her 'Did you know I slept in your bed while you were in the hospital'?

"She said 'no'. She started to cry."

Amy Halford should have been very grateful she was not herself on trial. In that moment, that jury would have ordered her lashed to a tumbrel and trundled off to the guillotine.

*   *   *

In October of '81, Felicia had been hospitalized for 20 days with severe abdominal pain. It was that

240

time to which Amy had referred. A cornucopia of tests was administered with no definitive diagnosis. On admission she was thought to have pancreatitis, an inflammation of that gland. It was trouble in the liver, however, that was eluding diagnosis. For each day that she was hospitalized, her liver function test results grew markedly worse. Doctors never did discover what was wrong with her liver. The abdominal pain, the reason she had been hospitalized, gradually disappeared after she was taken off an anti-inflammatory medication prescribed for a prior condition. After nearly three weeks of hospitalization, she was released with a diagnosis of pancreatitis. The liver problem must have disappeared because five months later a physician saw it and found nothing wrong.

On the stainless steel table that Felicia occupied briefly in the county morgue, her liver and pancreas were revealed, removed, examined, weighed and catalogued as "unremarkable." If her husband had been trying to poison her, there was no evidence of it at autopsy.

"When he knew she'd be in the hospital awhile, he had the children go to his sister's house because he had to be at work and sometimes he got home late. So they weren't there the three weeks she was in the hospital, so I stayed over," Amy told the court. "It was near my birthday and he gave me a diamond 'pre-engagement' ring."

In December, Larry left his wife and children and moved into the Hoboken apartment with Amy. In late January, he left Amy and moved back to the Cove. He told Amy that Felicia was blackmailing him and that if he left again, Felicia would go to the police about the arson at the rental property and about funds he had allegedly stolen from the Cove Democratic Club funds.

"He told me he used the stolen money to pay for our motels when they first met," Amy testified. "And he said she had proof that he had burned the rental house down with a cigarette butt in a cushion."

Brocail brought Amy forward to Feb.13.

By then, Felicia had a little more than a month to live.

On the night of February 12, Amy testified, she and Larry had a prolonged discussion about murder methods. Larry decided that she should use a knife. He picked her up at work the next day, Feb.13, and they went shopping. The knife could wait; he wanted to get the clothes she would wear. She bought a blue bomber jacket and a ski mask with red stripes.

On cross-examination, Amy denied telling Larry she was buying the jacket and mask for her brother for a ski trip.

"Larry made me have abortions when I got pregnant by him," Amy said sulkily, in response to nothing, putting the procedure on a par with scrubbing greasy pans or taking out the garbage.

For the first and only time at his trial for murder, Larry rocketed out of his chair at the defense table and vented. "I wear condoms you evil stupid bitch and they weren't pregnancies by me. Just one, just one if any at all and that's because I was hammered that one time and I would give anything to just shut you up forever."

If you had none of us would have tobegoing through this youdumbfuck, Amy's lawyer said to the · *inside of his headachefilled head.*

Too late,youdamnedfool,youhad chances Larry's lawyer said to the inside of his headachefilled head.

Larry had finished his outburst before Judge O'Donnell could even get a bailiff over to drag him out of the courtroom.

"Mr. Schwarz, ·approach the bench...Control your client, Mr. Schwarz, and stress to him that if he does anything remotely resembling that again in my courtroom he will be charged with contempt and removed. "Mr. Cusack, can you control yourself here?"

Stonefaced, Larry nodded. Schwarz elbowed him in the side.

"Yes, your honor," Larry said.

Amy, determined to turn herself into Martyr Amy, acted as though there had been no interruption of her discourse on sex and its occasional consequences.

What the hell is the matter with thiswoman? JudgeGillianO'Donnell said to the inside of herhead. I want tosee those psych reports because if she isnot competent I don't want a mistrial onmyrecord.

"Miss Halford, you are allegedly a grownup. Begin to act like one or there will be penalties," Judge O'Donnell instructed.

Larry's lawyer, on the other hand, liked where this was going, so he asked Amy the questions she wanted so desperately to answer.

"Two (abortions) he paid for (Amy points to Larry) Then another by someone I know in Hoboken and the other that was about two years ago."

When that testimony appeared in the next day's New York and New Jersey papers, Moore Goodwin was nauseous with fear. He knew about DNA. He also knew Amy was an habitual liar. He had checked with the small liberal arts college of which she claimed to be a graduate; they had no record of her. The thought that he might have fathered a child with someone who didn't even have an undergraduate degree was beyond imagining.

On the second day of testimony Amy admitted stabbing Felicia Cusack "about 20" times on the evening of March 20 1982. Five days after the murder, she said, she tried to commit suicide by swallowing 13 sleeping pills. She said Cusack offered to drive her to a hospital but would not call an ambulance for her. "I was afraid to get into his car because I was afraid he'd leave me in the woods to die," Amy said.

"I was afraid he'd find out about the jewelry too."

Cusack had told Amy, very specifically, not to wear any jewelry to the killing ground. As a cop, she said, Larry knew that a dying person would grab at anything and that if the killer had jewelry, the victim could grab it and be holding it in a death grip.

Amy told the court that she wore all the jewelry she had to do the murder.

"I wanted to be caught. It would ease my guilt," she testified.

She said she should not have to go to jail.

Shortly after the killing, she testified that she moved into the Cove house with Larry and the children. However, she had trouble disciplining the children, she was treated badly by Felicia's family when they came to visit the children and Larry would not help her with any of that.

She didn't like his not letting her sleep with him in his bedroom. He said it would be bad for the children to see that arrangement. Grace and John were old enough to know what was going on, Amy thought.

"So a week before Christmas I left him. New Year's Eve he had a new girlfriend. He had her, I had guilt. I found people to tell about the killing, to just dump it all out there. Two priests and a few other people," Amy said, "businessmen I met in bars or through friends."

On the third day of her testimony, she said that after turning herself in she tried to kill herself in the county jail by swallowing cleaning fluid, but her cellmate stopped her. No one is sure about the chain of events, but she had swallowed something that made her sick. Jail records are unclear.

Steve Lemke was a securities analyst in the midst of a divorce when he met Amy at a bar near their building on Wall Street. He was the last witness called by the prosecution and one of the last men to have taken Amy to bed.

"She told me she had done it," Lemke told the court.

"Told you she had done what?" asked Brocail for the prosecution.

"That she had murdered her ex-lover's wife. Here we were skiing for the weekend in New England and she tells me that the previous March she had stabbed this woman 22 times because the woman

245

wouldn't give her husband a divorce to marry Amy," Lemke recounted.

"What did you say to that admission?" the prosecutor asked him.

"I told her I didn't believe her and that she should see a shrink. I told her to pack her stuff because we were going back to New York. She kept feeding me details of this alleged murder and I told her if she didn't shut up I'd pull over and put her out of the car." *Amenbrother a dozenmenin the courtroom saidto theinsides oftheirheads*

Amy said she told two other men, both of them in March of '83. She called Mark Ocasio, a banker with whom she had had a prolonged affair in 1980, and asked him to meet her for a drink. Ocasio had not seen her for a while but he remembered that she was very seductive and also a bit strange.

Not at all a bad combination given the purposes for which he used her.

He brought protection along in the form of Paul Harper, a friend who was a private investigator.

"It was me, and Amy and a friend named Paul," Ocasio said. "We had a few drinks and I was bouncing around at the bar and Amy was having a conversation with Paul. I got back to the table and inquired what the conversation was about.

"As I recall, Amy said to me that she had killed somebody. I said, yeah, sure you did. Amy insisted she had and I could see Paul believed her. That made me scared. She said she had killed the wife of a man she was having an affair with.

"I asked her how and she said she stabbed her," Ocasio testified. "Somewhere in the conversation she said the husband was involved in the killing. She mentioned his name but I didn't remember it until I saw it in the paper today."

Harper, a private investigator, was disgusted when Amy told him what she had done. Unlike the other men in whom she confided, he believed her. He knew the ugly truth when he heard it. He was called by the prosecution but was officially considered a hostile witness.

"We were in the bar for about five hours. I was struck by the fact that the entire discussion was about her; she never expressed any emotion about the dead wife. She said she was afraid that the dead woman's father and brother would kill her and she wanted my advice as to how to protect herself.

"She has a very narrow mind; it's not that she's stupid or slow, it's that she is completely selfish, completely narcissistic," Harper noted. "She really does not care about anyone who does not serve her needs in one way or the other and is, obviously, quite ruthless if someone gets in her way. She asked my advice about protecting herself and showed me a card on which she had written the phone numbers and addresses of two of the victim's relatives. The victim's father and one of her brothers.

"I asked her why she was giving these to me and she said if anything happened to her I was to give the information to the police," Harper told the court. "This woman had inflicted a terrible death on her lover's wife and left her to bleed out. And <u>she</u> wanted protection!"

Amy took the witness chair for the second time in two days. As the star witness, she enjoyed giving quick answers. She looked forward to matching wits with Larry's attorney when it was his turn to cross-examine her.

She would flash the jury a bright smile one moment and look downcast and miserable the next.

She seemed to enjoy telling the court about how she turned herself in to the police and how she was responsible for gathering evidence against Larry. She left her seat to demonstrate how she led police to the sporting goods store in the and pointed out what sort of knife Larry bought for her to use.

On impulse, she removed the high-heeled shoes she was wearing in court and walked through the courtroom in her stockings because she was wearing flat shoes that day, Valentine's Day, when they bought the knife that would slice Felicia's heart.

"Now what the hell is she up to?" Brocail whispered to Glanville "She gonna do a little tap dance? Demonstrate the physics of a knuckle curve?"

Glanville said there was nothing she could do that would surprise him even a little bit. "I think she's done what we needed her to do," Glanville said. "I don't think there's anything she can do to hurt the case but with her, you do worry." The detective shook his head at how his life had been consumed by this case for the 15 months since Amy had telephoned him at 3 in the morning that Memorial Day Saturday and summoned him to Manhattan to fetch her.

She was Wistful Amy as Brocail, on cross examination, drew out details of her many affairs, the who, what, why, where and how of random sex, the hurt and abuse she felt at being used by her ex-lover Larry Cusack.

Larry's lawyer just let her roll right along. This was good for his side because she went too far; she was repelling the jurors.

The man for whom she had killed, the man whose babies she wanted to bear, the man she wanted in her life forever looked at her with so much hatred that she shivered and finally averted her gaze.

"I don't deserve to go to jail," Amy insisted, her voice rising and showing tension, "but I'm not testifying to get a reduced sentence. If I hadn't confessed, don't you guys get it? If I hadn't come forward, he would never have been tried for this crime."

That, indeed, was the absolute truth.

Amy held everyone's attention as she told the jury the story that she had told the investigators four months earlier. Her voice has always been childlike, high and tremulous and was more so if she was upset or excited. Her behavior on the witness stand was at the margin of acceptability. Her strange laughing and giggling were not as bad as the behavior during her arraignment, but veterans of that skirmish were expecting the worst. She worked on being demure and then returned to giggling. She beckoned Pascoe to the witness stand and, in a clearly audible stage whisper, said she had to get off the stand and go to the bathroom.

Hey Amy! Be sure to look under all the bathroom doors. Sometimes people hide there.

Up to this point, Amy had dealt with people who were willing to indulge her every whim to keep her as a cooperative witness. But before she could get off the stand, she had to be cross-examined by Robert Schwarz, Larry's lawyer.

"Did you enjoy entrapping my client, Miss Halford?" Schwarz asked.

"Did he enjoy fucking me?"

Linda Ellis

"Heeeeere's Amy!" Brocail *groanedto the insideofhishead.*

"Yessss!" Schwarz highfived inside his head.

"Order, order!" the judicial gavel pounded the bench again.

"Continue, Mr. Schwarz. Miss Halford, don't do that again. And stop crying."

"I enjoy having justice done," Amy told the court. "I did not entrap him; I was playing cop. I like participating and being with cops. Cops make me feel safe."

Entrapment is a legal defense that claims the defendant was induced to commit a crime not contemplated by him. I didn't entrap Larry when I asked to meet with him, she told the jury. I just wanted to see the right thing done and I was the only one who could do it.

"I was there," she said earnestly, being Helpful Amy. "I did the killing, but I only did it for him because he told me he could only marry me if she was dead. " I should not go to jail for this murder," she said, looking annoyed. "It wasn't my fault. If I was the judge, I'd let me go home today,"

Her time was up. The 15 minutes of fame a mere memory, past its sell-by date. As she was excused from the witness box, she was reluctant to take that first step. It was in that moment of stepping down that she faced the truth about herself. She had been Clueless Amy.

The woman she had slaughtered had had a legion of friends and a strong, loving birth family. Felicia had had two children who loved her. Unfortunately, she had also had a husband who degraded her, ignored her and ultimately ordered her death as he would a take-out dinner combo.

Amy figured that the swamp her life had become was a result of sleeping with this truly bad man. He had cost her any hope for happiness. This was all his fault.

Her family and friends for years to come would be fellow inmates in women's prison. She would have to try harder now to make friends. She had not had many friends in grade school or in high school. It was critical that she learn now how to make friends in prison. There were books about that, right? Well, not making friends in prison but just making friends...

She was Puzzled Amy as she left the box, held out her hands for the cuffs and was led away.

She paused near Larry's seat and looked down at him. "You always liked me in handcuffs, Larry."

He nodded.

Chapter 10

The Slam Dunk

Felicia Cusack was the 93rd of 481 murder victims reported to law enforcement agencies in New Jersey in 1982; an 11 percent decrease from the 540 murders reported in 1981.

Firearms were used in 41 percent of the murders where the weapon was known. Knives or cutting instruments accounted for 30 percent, while physical force and blunt objects each accounted for 9 percent of all murders.

In murders where the relationship of the victim and offender is known, 54 percent were friends or acquaintances, 25 percent were relatives, and 21 percent were strangers. The percentage of strangers murdering strangers was rising slowly but surely and that worried law enforcement officials a great deal.

Saturday, the day on which Felicia Cusack was slain, notched the most reported murders, 89, as delineated by day of the week. Sunday was the lowest with 55.

May recorded the highest number of murders, with 58, while November was the lowest with 33.

Males accounted for 86 percent and females 14 percent of those arrested for murder.

The question before the jury would be the following: did Amy Lee Halford (one of the 14 percent) act alone? Or did her lover conspire with her to murder Felicia Cusack and thus become one of the 86 percent?

Would Larry Cusack walk?

The selection of the Cusack jury had been a long and winding road across the surface of the lives of the 300 people called for that particular jury pool.

The lawyer who would argue for the prosecution, Greg Brocail, and Robert Schwarz, Larry Cusack's hired gun, had considered the latest sociological data available on picking a jury. Both were familiar with research that attempts to compartmentalize prospective jurors in ways that can streamline the process.

Here's the way the system works in state criminal courts: waves of groups of potential jurors are brought into the courtroom. After being introduced to the lawyers and the defendant and being given a brief outline of the case, the potential jurors are asked a series of questions. Some are obvious ("How are you employed?"), others less so (What magazines do you read?").

Employment is a key variable. Engineers and scientists are thrown overboard fast by the defense to prevent an outbreak of analytical thinking. The prosecution would say goodbye to anyone who had or was working for a non-profit organization or as a sociologist or social worker. Experience has shown prosecutors that people who choose that kind of work are likely to find excuses for aberrant behavior.

Over time, the jury pool is winnowed as people are excused "for cause" – they might have trouble being evenhanded because, say, they've been victims of crime.

Each lawyer can also excuse a certain number of potential jurors for no stated reason. Those are peremptory challenges. They're limited in number, depending on the case, and the lawyers treasure

253

them. It's with them that most of the hunches get played.

It's because of them that some lawyers hire pollsters to do an attitudinal/demographic study once the jury pool is known. Normally, this can only be done if the client has deep pockets; in this case, Schwarz decided to assume the costs himself, using volunteers where possible.

First we wanted to survey a random sampling of the registered voters in the county, Schwarz explained. We got 15 volunteers to make phone calls, asking for demographic information and we had questionnaires developed to have an understanding of attitudes about this type of case.

"Two weeks before trial, we got the list of 300 prospective jurors on the case. We had the survey information so we knew what to look for when we made the 'drive-by' of all 300 homes," he recalled.

"Four of us drove around the homes and the neighborhoods, looking for signs of rigidity such as chain link fences or American flags. We were looking for people who would be sympathetic and open-minded."

"We learned a hell of a lot from bumper stickers. They're very revealing," Schwarz noted.

The study to set up the ratings was both demographic – age, sex, marital status, political affiliation, education, occupation, religion, nationality – and attitudinal. For the latter, 10 questions were asked of the random sampling of prospective jurors.

For example:

1. If people work hard at their jobs, they will reap the full benefits of our society (1)

strongly agree. (2) Agree. (3) Disagree. (4) Strongly disagree.
2. Under unusual circumstances, a person might be justified in breaking the law
3. If someone breaks his marriage vows he will stop at nothing.

The Cusack defense team put the data together, fed it into a computer and came up with a profile of an "ideal" defense juror. No one even remotely resembling that ideal passed through the box during jury selection, Schwarz recalled ruefully.

"It was a reach, I know. I picked one juror because he wore a bow tie and that showed non-conformity. We don't have a whole lot of non-conformists agreeing to serve on juries in Harbor County."

Cusack's lawyer excused all but two women jurors on the panel. All the jurors not challenged by Schwarz were middle-aged men, several with high-school level educations. He challenged two electrical engineers.

Brocail excused a government employee and a banker.

On the selected panel, which included two alternates who would be eliminated by lottery at the end of the trial, were four people with high school diplomas and five who had not completed high school. Two were college graduates, three had attended but not completed, college and one had a doctorate in elementary education.

According to a sociologist who had drawn up the demographic profile of the "ideal" juror for Schwarz's purposes, the jury was a disaster for the defense. In the sociologist's rating, a male or female Jewish

Linda Ellis

Democrat under 30 years of age holding a professional position was perfect for the defense.

The majority of this jury was Catholic, Republican, blue collar with average age of 45.

Larry was Catholic, blue collar and 45. Somehow, Schwarz told his wife, he didn't think the jurors would feel they had a whole lot in common with Cusack despite statistical overlaps.

On the Cusack case, this jury would sit three weeks listening to opening arguments, evidence and summations. They would be sequestered for two days as they deliberated.

At the end of that time they would deliver their verdict.

The judge would render sentences at some point after the verdict was announced.

"Sometimes," Schwarz concluded, "although you've astutely judged your jury in light of the case, your draw has been bad. Some days, you don't agree with the judge on some issues. Some days, your client is the bug instead of the windshield."

The Bibles were distributed, the jurors were sworn and everybody went to work.

If the jury found that Larry had conspired with Amy, as the state claimed, he would be subject to the same punishment as if he had wielded the knife himself. If the jury found him guilty the verdict would be as if he himself had embraced Felicia and lowered her to the dirt and gravel and stench while continuing to rip her flesh, to spill her blood.

That's what conspiracy is in the eyes of the law.

256

He didn't do that. He was *seen* not doing that. But did he conspire with Amy to do it? Did he draw the dirty pictures?

I'll draw the dirty pictures here, Dad. Mommy don't look. I lov

There were two keys to Larry Cusack's defense. First Robert Schwarz, Larry's attorney, had to discredit Amy. That sounded like a lay-up but you never know, Schwarz' associates said. Then came the tough part. Schwarz had to explain away the statements on the tapes when his idiot client was trying to get laid and Amy was trying to prevent him from discovering the wires draped dangerously near the breasts that he, Larry, had paid for.

"You know, I loaned her $2,500 for the boob job and she still owes me $1,000," Larry had told Schwarz.

lordgive me patiencewith this idiot who will escape thedeathpenalty byabout the lengthof a pubic hair and he's worried aboutgetting paidback for herbreasts Schwarz mumbled tothevoiceinside his head.

"Larry, "Schwarz said patiently, "Amy's breasts are probably great and it must be frustrating that you are not getting the benefit of them or the loan repaid. We really need to focus here, though, on a way to keep your sentence at less than 40 years, by which time your best feature will have fallen off."

Schwarz began his campaign on the first front in mid-July by filing court papers for information about Amy Lee Halford's mental state. Much would rest on her effect on the jury.

Schwarz had asked for a change of venue for the Cusack trial, a pro forma move in any high-profile case. His request to move the trial to neighboring Granville County had been, as expected, denied.

Linda Ellis

The trial was scheduled to begin in mid-October.

"Her (Miss Halford's) mental state at the time of the murder, at the time of the arrest and during incarceration is of key significance in this case," Schwarz said in court papers filed with Superior Court Judge Gillian O'Donnell.

"The case may come down to a test of credibility and truthfulness between the defendants," the court papers said. "The demonstration of Miss Halford's state of mind and behavior during incarceration leads one to believe she is far from being stable at this time.

"As just one example among a plethora of such examples, she repeatedly telephoned, against express orders of the prosecutor, the home of one of the prosecutor's principal investigators assigned to this case. She would call in the morning and even late at night so that she would be likely to find him in. The last time she did this she wanted tranquilizers.

"The time before she wanted cuticle scissors. Of course, the detective is going to get out of bed at 11 at night and bring a prisoner a sharp pair of cuticle scissors. This is not funny, your honor, because Amy Halford really believed that Detective Carlyle would - and should - do that for her.

"She has been told numerous times that any request for anything, anything at all, must go first to her attorney, Mr. Pascoe. She indicates that she understands that and then just goes ahead and calls Det. Bryan Carlyle anyway, at home. She behaves like a willful child, and she is permitted to behave this way because she is the chief witness for the prosecution. But she is not stable. She has diminished capacity and this court should put no credence in her statements."

258

To reinforce an image of Amy as a pathological liar, Schwarz called to the witness stand the woman who replaced Amy in Larry's bed. Julianna Greer was a good-looking blonde, a 22-year-old single mother and she was Larry's biggest fan. She told the jury that Amy was a "sickie" who did nothing but lie. Amy was completely capable of murdering Mrs. Cusack just so she, Amy, could marry Larry.

Julianna and Larry met at a New Year's Eve house party in the Cove, she said. They made love that first night.

"Our relationship was of a steady nature," she testified.

What does that mean? Schwarz asked.

"We slept together regularly and are - were- monogamous. My mother would take the baby (she had a two-year-old daughter) those nights.

Julianna said that she stayed at Larry's home on the average of two nights a week. The relationship lasted until the Friday before Memorial Day Weekend. On the day before Amy confessed to murder, Julianna told Larry that Julianna's mother would no longer keep the toddler for her. My mother doesn't approve of this, she told her lover. I can't stay.

The timing was a complete coincidence, Julianna said. Neither of them had any advance warning or even a hint that Amy was about to destroy everyone's life.

Asked about the death of Felicia Cusack, Julianna said Larry mentioned to her during their relationship that prior to his wife's death he was trying to mend their problems. He was sorry, he said, that she had died before he had the opportunity to do this.

259

Julianna believed him.

"Amy should get the death penalty for what she's done to those kids," Julianna said vehemently. "In jail, they'll take care of her. They don't like people who've hurt kids."

Schwarz presented and discussed psychiatrists' records that were permitted because they derived from jailhouse interviews.

Amy had told several psychiatrists that from an early age she felt a need for sex. The question remained as to whether she liked sex as an act in itself or instead was addicted to the attention it brought her, the head fake of affection, the "let's pretend" love that the sex inspired.

Brocail, for the prosecution, said men anecdotally see sex as straightforward gratification, and sometimes a cigar is just a cigar, Schwarz said. But some men have a built-in radar that hones in on women like Amy who will kneel for kisses and get on their backs for hugs. And then these perceptive men may, if they like, play these women like puppets on a string.

Larry Cusack took the stand in his own defense in mid-November. He denied categorically conspiring with Amy Lee Halford to kill his wife.

"I do not deny that Felicia and I had serious marital problems," Larry said. "But we were working on them. We had decided to stay together at least until the children were away at college. I promised not to philander. I lied about that, OK. But Amy lies about <u>everything</u>."

Amy is a pathological liar, he told the court. For instance, I never told her I would marry her, ever. I did not give her a diamond ring for her birthday. I may have bought her a bottle of perfume, but nothing I can remember, he said.

People who knew Larry, friend or foe, believed him about the ring. "Larry would never spend that kind of money on anyone but himself," Jenny Russo said.

Psychiatrist Stanley Conte testified about his diagnosis of Amy as having a personality disorder. He described her as "pretty sick." However, Conte said, he could not give an opinion on whether Miss Halford could accurately relate the events surrounding the murder.

Dr. Randolph Platt, a forensic pathologist from North Carolina, testified that in his opinion the weapon used to kill Mrs. Cusack was a double-edged blade and therefore the knife Larry Cusack had bought with his credit card could not have been the murder weapon.

Larry said he met Amy on a commuter train.

"She walked up to me and whispered 'Are you a cop?' I said I was," Larry said. "Two days later, I saw her on the train. She started asking me routine kinds of questions, like 'Are you married?' and 'Where do you live', things like that. Sure it was flattering, I was 43 and she was 20, something like that, 21.

"She said most cops are not happily married."

His story of events dovetailed with hers right up until the murder. They did go to motels in Jersey City at least twice a week. His wife did find out and she threw him out of the house for a while. He was sleeping on a bunk bed at the police station. He told Amy about it and she was really happy. She insisted he move into her Hoboken apartment immediately.

261

"She always had dinner on the table for me and had my clothes washed and ironed and ready for me to wear," Larry said. "But I missed my kids and my wife" and he told Amy in mid-January 1982 that he was moving back to Gullwing Cove.

Howdid he noticethe difference? one of the femalejurors said totheinside of herhead. At one place he gets his laundrydone his dinnerserved and he getslaid. At the other place, he gets...same things!

"Then she told me she was pregnant. ' Oh, great', I said, something like that. I was pretty mean about it. I only missed using protection once and that's the one time she gets pregnant. So I got the $425 and took her to the doctor in New York and she had the procedure. I had no good way to explain that to my wife, so I just refused to answer when she asked about the money."

The lawyers watched the jury's reactions to everything Larry said, just as they had analyzed the jury's feelings about Amy.

On the second day of his testimony, Larry Cusack denied plotting with his former lover to kill his wife and said that the vengeful woman made up a story involving him in the crime. He denied that he planned the murder. He denied that he coached her on how to stab Mrs. Cusack. He denied that on March 20, 1982, he led his wife to a location in the South Strip section of Boothbay where Miss Halford waited to kill her.

Earlier that week the jury heard the taped conversations between Cusack and Amy, recorded during the Memorial Day weekend after Miss Halford had turned herself in.

Cusack said his statements admitting involvement in the murder were made as part of a game Amy played with him. Amy was making up a dangerous story and he was afraid it would be taken seriously. He has a job and a family, he stressed to the jury, and he had to placate a woman he calls a "nut" and a "dangerous woman playing a dangerous game."

She didn't have much to lose, he noted, while he had a whole structure in place that was getting shaky while she played this "game".

She got a "glazed, starry look in her eyes" when she related the story Cusack said she fabricated. He said he feared she would continue to harass him and to call his teen-age daughter and frightening her.

"She called Grace one night and told her 'Your father killed your mother'. It was a bad thing Amy did there, that call. But I was older, a lot of it was my fault, the sex, the leaving home, the lies to Felicia, misleading Amy as to whether I would ever marry her.

"On the tapes, when I said, 'We planned it, it was perfect, we did it and it's over,' I was referring to the sex."

He said he was also referring to the extramarital sex when he said the words (here he was read from a transcript):

"We have both made a huge fucking mistake and we're both paying for it now...If we shut our fucking mouths and just say...yeah, I was drunk out of my mind, we both were, we didn't know what we were doing or saying, then we can work out of this."

When questioning him about his behavior at the murder scene, assistant prosecutor Brocail asked Cusack what he did when he heard his wife call his name.

"I was 75 to 100 feet away and started a slow jog back," Cusack said.

"It takes a fast runner 10 seconds to run a 100-yard dash. That's one-third of a 100-yard dash," Brocail said.

"I'm not a fast runner," Cusack said.

Judge O'Donnell explained to the jury what was required in order for them to find Cusack guilty of conspiracy in the murder of his wife. The defendant is guilty of conspiracy with another person to commit a crime if, with the purpose of promoting that murder, he agreed with Miss Halford that she would kill Felicia Cusack based on a plan Halford and Cusack drew up together and executed as a joint plan.

If the jury found there was a conspiracy to commit murder, then Cusack is as guilty of murder as his co-conspirator.

In his defense Schwarz portrayed Larry as the victim of a second crime – the attempt by an embittered girl to trap the man who no longer loved her.

All through the preparations for the trial, Larry maintained his innocence and never changed the story he told Schwarz.

Larry did not want to testify.

His appearance had changed dramatically after four months in county lockup; he was gaunt, seemed to have shrunk in height and focused in on no one. He was perfecting that thousand-yard stare that prisoners need as a survival tool.

Schwarz did not want him to testify.

But to discredit Amy's testimony and give an explanation for what he had said on the tapes, Larry had to testify.

Amy will say anything to get back at me for dropping her, Larry told the jury. Once after he had broken up with Amy and started seeing another woman, he said, he visited Amy. After they were in bed, she told him the story about killing Felicia. He told her he didn't believe it and she started pounding on his chest.

"Amy was hitting me because she said she screamed at Felicia as she was stabbing her, 'You killed my babies,' over and over. Amy blamed Felicia for the abortions and she blamed me and this is how she is getting revenge," Larry testified. "And this whole thing is wrong because at most one of those pregnancies was my fault, one at most. I'm a cop. I know what goes on in the world. I do not have sex without protection. I never trust the woman to protect me; I do the worrying for both of us. One time, once, I was hammered and I had sex with her, with Amy, without a condom."

He was worried she would tell police this wild tale about them both planning to kill Felicia so he played along with her, he said. As a cop, he knew that law enforcement would investigate any claims she made.

When he said on the tape-recorded conversation "We both did it," he meant they had been lovers and on top of that, as Catholics, they had been involved in an abortion. The abortions led to Felicia's death, not a plot by Larry, he said. Because Amy felt guilt she killed Felicia, somehow thinking that if she did that, the worst would be over for her.

He described Amy as a "good bed partner" and began seeing her again about two months after Felicia's death for "physical relief" at the suggestion of his uncle, who made his apartment in Atlantic Beach available for the trysts that Larry called "appointments."

Out on the sidewalk during lunch break, away from anyone connected to the case, Schwarz really blew up.

"If there had been any female jurors favorable to our case there aren't anymore...Appointments? What the hell is wrong with you, Larry? Have you slept through women's lib?

"Yeah, with women" Larry said. Schwarz burst out laughing. It was the first time Larry had cracked a joke in his presence. He had decided that along with other unpleasant traits, this man had no sense of humor. When Schwarz told his wife what Larry had said, she opined that he probably meant it seriously.

Of course he meant it, lard head.

Amy said she would reveal the conspiracy – he the planner, she the executioner - to her favorite detective. Larry knew she meant Kevin Glanville. She would love to get Glanville up to her apartment; she made no secret of her fantasy life with him. She had even told Larry that if Mrs. Glanville were out of the way, she, Amy, would leave Larry alone.

OhshitWillthis nevernevernever end Glanvillesaidto the insideof hishead. .

Thirteen months after the murder, Amy began threatening Larry, telling him she would give them both up. If he would agree to confess with her, she would have sex with him as often as he wanted. He took her up on the sex but told her she was behaving in a crazy way.

There is no way they can get us if you just stay quiet.

I can't live with it anymore.

How would you like to live in women's prison and be owned by a woman named Butch?

*   *   *

The trial ended with impassioned summations by both lawyers. It was scary to see how a good trial lawyer could spin pig shit into plausibility, as Schwarz did that afternoon. He was hoping someone on the jury liked cops enough to give this one a pass. Gotta be in it to win it.

Brocail could have coasted in his closing remarks but he attacked Larry as though he were an adversary to be taken seriously. Juries are funny creatures; he lost a case once because a woman was hot for the opposing lawyer, another woman, and he, Brocail, didn't pick up on the vibes.

Schwarz portrayed Amy as a troubled young girl – cold-blooded, clever and calculating. "Hell hath no fury like a woman scorned," he told the jury.

"Officer Cusack's brain disengages when he wants sex. He is a stupid, selfish man but he is not a killer.

"Amy wanted Larry as a husband and Larry's children as a family and she saw only one obstacle to that: Larry's wife. She decided that with Mrs. Cusack out of the way, she, Amy, could have it all. She admits she killed Felicia Cusack to get these things.

"Once after he had broken up with Amy and started seeing another woman, he said, he visited Amy. And they had sex. And after sex she told him the story about killing Felicia. He told her he didn't believe it and she started pounding on his chest," Schwarz refreshed the jury's memories. As though they were likely to forget these events.

"Sex, ladies and gentlemen, is what has gotten him into this mess. My client has testified that he was primarily interested in one thing from Ms. Halford: sexual relations. He is so focused on sex with her that he had sex with her at the same time she was talking about both of them going to jail for capital murder," Larry's lawyer said.

Then, she and Larry tried living together with the Cusack children and it did not work out. They did not like her and they wanted her out. Had Larry known that it was Amy who stabbed Felicia to death, do you think, ladies and gentlemen of the jury, that he would invite such a monster into the same house with his children? As it was, he didn't think it right for Amy to sleep in the place vacated by their mother.

Their father dated and fell in love with Julianna Greer and she moved into the family home for part of each week. That drove Amy Halford to such fury that she was determined to punish her ex-lover.

Brocail portrayed Larry as "a thoroughly evil man who orchestrated the killing of the mother of his children."

After two days of deliberation, the jury found Cusack guilty on all counts.

Two weeks before New Year's Day, 1984, 22 months after the death of Felicia, Larry Cusack stood before Judge O'Donnell to be sentenced for conspiracy to murder.

He was dressed neatly in a navy blue blazer, blue shirt, red tie with subdued stripe and gray pants. The courtroom was filled with spectators. Sheriffs' officers locked the doors and would only let people in when others left. In the front row of the court sat Larry's mother and father, an uncle, his sister and his daughter Grace. Jake Cusack said he couldn't get off duty to be with his brother.

The fourth and fifth rows on each side of the aisle were solid with Felicia's family. That way, no matter which way Larry looked he would see the people who most loved the woman he had conspired to slaughter.

Larry was brought into the court in handcuffs and sat in the jury box. The handcuffs were taken off when he sat down.

Schwarz moved for a new trial on grounds that were raised during the trial. O'Donnell was polite, even solicitous with Schwarz but rejected all his arguments. Schwarz objected to the probation department's recommendations of 80 years in jail with no parole for 40 years. He said he expected a 25-year sentence, a sentence with some hope of freedom would give Cusack some light at the end of the tunnel while he served his time in prison.

Brocail said O'Donnell ought to give Cusack the maximum the law allows. The aggravating circumstances outweigh the only mitigating circumstance – the lack of a prior record. "I can think of no other defendant who so richly deserves...the maximum. The State of New Jersey, the Girardi family, the victim's children and justice itself is entitled to be angry."

The court must look at the whole picture. Brocail said he remembers going to the scene that night and looking at the pool of blood on the ground. He remembers going to the hospital and seeing Mrs. Cusack's body. He had known her well when she was alive and she was more "alive" in death than many people walking around today – because there was so much love for her and within her.

He, her husband, led her inexorably to her death. He had feigned emotion. If he wanted his freedom so much, all he had to do was walk out the door. Larry was too greedy to lose the things they had acquired during their marriage so he coerced a vulnerable young woman to do the dirty work for him.

If there were any further proof required that Larry was a lowlife, Brocail said, Larry had filed a claim for compensation with the violent crimes compensation board. For his children's sake, he said. Throughout everything, he professed his love for his children. If he had really loved his children, he wouldn't have killed their mother. The court should look at his testimony.

"What he said was patently absurd, it fell of its own weight," Brocail said. "At least Amy Halford can look in the mirror and say she told the truth. Larry can't. Larry is far more dangerous than Amy because of what he did. He is thoroughly rotten and deserves the most severe sanction the court has at its disposal."

Brocail paced the courtroom as he spoke. He occasionally raised his voice for emphasis

Judge O'Donnell said she agreed with the legal rationale of the probation department on sentencing with a long term that can have half set aside for parole ineligibility. O'Donnell said what Cusack did was particularly repulsive.

"He was an instrument who led his wife to her execution by his paramour," the judge said. "The act shows his cunning and deceitful nature. This was an act of a modern day Judas, positioning his wife of 22 years so that his lover could creep up on little cat feet and stab Mrs. Cusack 22 times. The pain must have been unbearable but the very worst aspect of her death would have been that she stayed alive long enough to realize that her husband was not by her side, not touching her, not holding her. She saw him passing her, looking back as we know from that little wave she gave but not coming to her aid.

"There is no compassion in the court's heart for the defendant and we sentence Lawrence A. Cusack to 70 years with no parole for 35 years. Credit is to be given for 200 days served," Judge O'Donnell ruled.

Cusack had not asked to speak to the court before sentence was imposed. He sat stonefaced as he learned he would in all likelihood die in prison. He would be 79 years old if he qualified for parole. He heard a woman shrieking and a young girl weeping; he knew their voices. It was his sister and his daughter.

271

Where was the son he cherished? The one person in this world that he loved absolutely, with no reservations.

Larry, handcuffed and silent, showed no emotion as he was led away. He focused on the row holding the people who had been important in his life. All of them were against him, none for him. Except for Grace, they looked at him with revulsion and disbelief. His daughter Grace looked at him with a hatred so pure and undiluted that it had a force of its own.

Twenty minutes later, Amy was ushered into Judge O'Donnell's courtroom for the settling of her fate. She was dressed in a blue dress with red vertical stripes. Her lawyer, Colin Pascoe, told the judge that this was a particularly sad day for him because Amy used to baby-sit his grandchildren and they had been fond of her.

"I feel her interests and talents lie in the direction of child care and it is so sad that she was coerced into a crime that will put her behind bars for her prime career building years," Pascoe said. "She wore a wire to the meeting with Cusack at personal risk to herself. If he had found it she could have been hurt. In the murder of Mrs. Cusack, Amy was the instrumentality of Larry Cusack,"

Amy looked very nervous, twisting a handkerchief in her hands and looking at her parents, trying to gauge their reaction to all this.

She was told by the county prosecutor that she had been used and abused by Larry, Pascoe reminded the judge and that should be taken into account in her sentencing.

272

Amy's mother wept, her head so far down it nearly touched her lap. Her grief was hope abandoned. Amy's father comforted her mother as best he could, his hand touching her back. The Halfords, heartsick, were seated two rows behind the Girardi family, equally heartsick, furious, desperate for something that would ease their pain.

The Girardis would make it their lives' work to punish Larry and Amy. That went without saying. They felt great sorrow, though, for the Halfords. This was not the parents' fault.

Unlike Larry, Amy decided to speak to the judge on her own behalf. She didn't act like a person who faced a long jail sentence. She seemed to cling to the belief that because she had trapped Larry into the confession that everyone would change his or her mind about the law and just let her go home.

"I was manipulated by an older man who knew I needed to be loved and had control over me," she told the court earnestly. "I am so sorry that Felicia is dead and that her children will have to grow up without her."

Three sisters reached out to keep Joey Girardi from lunging to the witness stand and tearing out Amy's heart.

She had testified for the state in exchange for a plea bargain that limited the amount of time she would serve for the murder to 30 years. Under the agreement, if the judge does not require that she serve a minimum amount of time before becoming eligible for parole, she could serve as little as six years in prison. Amy's voice cracked when she

273

mentioned the possibility of going to jail for 15 years. Her main concern, she said, is about her term.

"I'm not a threat to society. I helped society by going undercover. I did the killing under Larry's control. All the police officers and prosecutors showed me understanding and compassion when I worked with them. They know who the real evil person was in this thing," Amy told the judge.

The judge read from the court-ordered Conte psychiatric report that indicated the prisoner had no remorse about the vicious crime. He may have given her the knife but she is the one who used it, who not only brutally stabbed Felicia Girardi Cusack, but also went on stabbing after the fatal blows had been struck.

"This is the slayer. This is the executioner. Miss Halford showed malice and deliberation."

Amy casts herself in the role of victim but the victim was Felicia Cusack. The judge quoted Aristotle: "What lies in our power to do lies in our power not to do...To be merciful to the cruel is to be indifferent to the good."

This woman showed she was selfish, cruel and brutal. She did what she did to get what she wanted, the judge said, with Amy shaking her head harder and harder so that her bangs flew in one direction and the other.

"Jail – 30 years with 15 to parole. She deserves no compassion from society and will get none."

Amy looked at her lawyer and then looked forward. As she was led from the court she looked toward the back of the court with disbelief and shock.

"They'll get you in jail, you little slut," Felicia's brother Mario hissed as Amy left the courtroom.

"They don't like prisoners who leave children without their mother. We hope they don't get you in there, though, because we are all waiting for you out here. Believe that."

There is a mythology around the kinds of judgments "regular" prisoners make of others, a veteran prison superintendent said. "The people in prison are generally only interested in themselves. Their mission every minute they are in is spent thinking of themselves, their family and when they will get out. They, whoever "they" are, don't give a rat's patoot what Amy Halford did to get herself into trouble, the superintendent concluded.

Her fellow inmates will have the following interests: does she have a drug source with access to the prison cells, does she have regular money coming in for cigarettes and does she like menthol or regular, does she have regular money coming in for candy and soda and does she take a bath every couple of days.

One group will want to know if she brought her Bible and, if not, will see that she gets one. They will ask her whether or not she accepts Jesus Christ as her Lord and savior and pray that she will.

In men's prison, it's pretty much the same except the stories about cops are true. If a prison is a cop, then that prisoner is in for a really bad time.

There was a place for Larry in the downstate men's prison.

He would be occupying it for, at a minimum, 35 years.

Law enforcement officials could not build prisons fast enough to accommodate women.

At the time Amy entered the population the superintendent at that facility said his prison was very near its saturation point.

New mandatory sentencing laws in New Jersey were sending people to jail for longer stretches. Amy would join 350 other women at the women's prison at the northern rim of the state, the highest number of inmates in the prison's history.

The day after sentencing, Amy was uneventfully transported to the Upstate Women's Correctional Institution and Larry to Downstate Correctional Institution for Men.

Amy's first visitor was in the van already when she was escorted in handcuffs to the middle row of seats. Sitting beside her was a young man wearing a credential around his neck.

"Ms. Halford, I'm Paul Shaw, I'm a reporter with *The New York Register* and I have permission from your lawyer to talk to you. But only if you're OK with it. If you don't want to talk to me, that's that. I'm not going to intrude when your whole life has just gone down the Dumpster - I'm sorry, I meant dumper, Freudian slip, whatever.

"At about the time you'll be released, I'll be making a career change from reporting to writing books," Shaw explained. "I plan to go to law school before 2000, so by the time you're free I'll be a lawyer/writer. The Grisham formula for success, it's called." he laughed. "I'd like your story to be my first book."

The van driver revved the engine. The two armed cops accompanying Amy to women's prison looked at the reporter. "Time's up, kid."

He asked Amy to think about cooperating, about giving him material on an exclusive basis, agree to be interviewed only by him. Think about it after you get settled in, OK?

"Here's my card, call me collect anytime, ask me questions, whatever," Shaw concluded.

Amy nodded, distracted by a woman who had come quietly to the side of the prison van.

"I love you, Amy Lee."

"I love you too, Mom."

Part V

The Sequel. 2000

Chapter 11

Las Vegas 2000

Las Vegas is the perfect place for losers to become winners.

Amy Lee Halford (a k a Brielle Benson) knew there was a flip side to that, but she finally held a pair of winning dice. Amy the loser did not exist anymore. Brielle the winner has emerged, holding the hot hand.

Amy/Brielle had paid security and two months' rent on a serviceable one-bedroom apartment near the Strip. She had signed a one-year lease. However, she was sure that she'd soon be living on someone else's dime.

Her life would always be in danger but here she would be much harder to find than if she'd stayed back east.

Three things are within a prisoner's control: her body, mind and soul. A rigorous workout regimen in jail all those years had tightened an already taut body. Reading two or three non-fiction books a week, never less, disciplined her mind. Her soul was on hold despite the prayers of her cellmate, a jailhouse convert whose heart had truly been moved and whose beliefs were seamless.

She'd made it through 17 years behind bars, this new and improved Amy/Brielle.

She should have no trouble landing a job dealing blackjack. She'd be good at it. She'd wear the uniform tailored to flatter her lithe, athletic body, switch on her smile and ask gentlemen in which way they wanted to lose to the house.

Amy was 21 the year she stabbed her way into the spotlight and 22 when she entered the system. She was 39 at her release but a much younger age on paper, backed up by a body that looked about 25. The breast enlargement she'd had at 21 was still, (ha ha!) holding up well.

She bet that she'd have men lining up to take her to their hotel rooms. She'd coax one of them, this time older and richer, to the Elvis Chapel, and then her troubles would be over.

A modest inheritance arriving in the third decade of her life had mushroomed with the soaring stock market. Her mother's aunt, never told of the Cusack affair, had been generous to Amy in her will.

In 1994, Amy had bought a laptop computer that, with supervision, she was allowed to use in prison to track her investments and to exchange e-mail with Paul Shaw, the writer doing the Cusack murder book.

Paying for a new face had not been a problem. Liposuction at the thighs and upper arms reinforced the illusion of youth. Here in Vegas there were plastic surgeons on every corner if she needed a touch-up. Cellulite was the only X-rated substance in town.

Amy/Brielle owned an entirely new identity. The cost of the paperwork far exceeded the bill for the plastic surgery but the Girardis were out there, Felicia's children were out there, and she needed to feel safe.

She was amazed how a life could be erased and a new one put in its place; everything she needed came easily because she had the money.

Amy/Brielle bought a car. In Las Vegas being a pedestrian was considered eccentric and she didn't want to stand out in any way. After 17 years she needed a refresher course in driving.

In a casino coffee shop she met a young man who was amenable to barter: he coached her in driving skills and she coached him in ways to make women scream. Some skills you don't ever forget. Just get back on the bicycle and ride and it all comes back to you - the bad with the good...

Garrison NJ 1983

Larry's appearance changed dramatically after he was arrested. During his trial, when Amy seemed to be regaining baby fat, Larry became pasty-faced but thinner. His chest seemed shrunken, and his face full of hollows and shadows.

After trial, Larry did not fare well at the men's prison downstate. In addition to his having been a cop, the idea of persuading his girlfriend to kill his wife made him a sissy in the other convicts' eyes - and hands.

In just two years of incarceration, Larry seemed to shrink, become shorter, emaciated. He talked to no one, was visited only by his mother and sister and showed no interest in the games men play in prison - even when he was the prize.

In the tenth anniversary year of her sentence, the year she turned 32, Amy learned that Larry had endured death by symbols.

Larry of the talented tongue, of the stroke like a rough blanket, of love in all the wrong places had been found in the

where I left him... Mommy thinks kitchens are for families. One down, one to go in the

kitchen, stuffed headfirst into one of the prison's jumbo sized garbage cans. He had been stabbed once in the heart.

Then his killers (authorities said there had to be more than one) pulled Larry's 28 teeth. The prison doctor said the rictus, the open mouth of horror fixed on Larry's toothless face, left no doubt that he had died screaming. The doctor also said that the loud dying took a long time. Where were the guards?

Send in the clowns, then. No guards, No harm, no foul.

And what, the New York tabloids wanted to know, is the significance of the teeth? And of the pictures cut out of magazines and then left next to Larry's body, paper doll clothes, an outfit with a cranberry-colored jacket, a white blouse with ruffles at the throat and cuffs, a black tie, a plaid skirt and gray shoes?

The hardestpart of the whole operationwas finding pictures of badclothesfrom the '70s.finally at a library booksale there wereold magazines they told the insidesoftheirheads.

The New York *Post* headline the next day read "Jailed Cop Bites the Big One." The subhead told its own story about how Amy had changed: *Knife-wielding Bimbo Keeps Mouth Shut.* You betcha, the knife-wielding bimbo whispered to the *Post.* I am shut down. I don't talk anymore and I don't bite anymore but I know what the teeth thing is. He'd go home to Felicia covered with bite marks. Felicia must have told Julia, she told her friend Julia everything, and then Julia must have told Felicia's brothers.

Amy figured it had been a couple of Felicia's brothers who had tortured and murdered Larry. From what she had heard Larry was probably happy to die. Amy wasn't ready to join him. She drew directions on a mental map from Larry's prison to hers and watched the killers every step of the way. How would they get in? What would be the instrument of choice?

That was seven years ago. If Larry's killers had intended to slay her as well, they had gotten lost along the way. It was odd that she had been allowed to live as it had been her hand that actually held the knife. Hers was the wrist of a killer; Larry had merely choreographed the dance of death. Perhaps she owed her survival to a shortage of men in women's prison. Any man was hard to miss, and a man who didn't belong would be noticed in a New York minute.

But then again, Larry's killer could be a woman. God knows there were enough women out there who would cheerfully rip every tooth out of his lying, dying head. Who was strong enough to stuff him into a garbage can after finishing him off? Felicia had seven surviving sisters in addition to the fraternal tag team of Joey, Mario and Carmen Jr. One of the larger sisters could have done the job. Blood ties are the strongest.

*   *   *

She knew that from personal experience.

Back in 1983, when Amy was marched out of court in handcuffs and into a prison van, two people

285

stood with her and only one really gave a damn. In the end, her mother loved her. Helen Halford and Paul Shaw, the reporter, were there to wave goodbye.

Her mother visited or called her at least three days a week. Helen still worked part-time but on weekends she made the four-hour round trip to Upstate Women's Correctional. She worried constantly about the Girardis, despite Amy's assurances that prison was a safe place.

Amy, who found herself infinitely interesting, had begun a diary at an early age and kept it up through thick, thin and murder. She continued to chronicle her life at UWC. The journals were of great help to Shaw as he tackled the book beyond the outline. His agent had sold the book about the Cusack murder to a publisher on the basis of an outline and two chapters.

Amy was the major player in the narrative. Larry allowed Shaw to visit but barely spoke. He had access to all the documents, the medical and investigation files. Felicia's family was very willing to talk but had secondhand information only. Amy is the story, Shaw's publisher said. Shaw agreed.

Shaw was in frequent contact with Amy. They communicated, on average, twice a week. Amy talked into Shaw's tape recorder frequently and kept the written diary as backup.

*   *   *

Sunday Jan. 15
Dear Diary and Paul,

What'll I do when you are far away and I am blue what'll I do. How about I will write down all the ways I want to torture my lawyer for not getting me a better deal?

First thing is Pascoe's balls come off. His balls for his bills. Hah! With scissors. Dull scissors. Hah! I can see you shuddering at the thought. You gotta be tough if you're gonna hang with me, Paul Shaw. Get it? Hang?

You like Pascoe, though, because you did the deal with him and he sure likes you. You asked him for exclusive rights to me, to my story and when you told him the terms, Pascoe must have been a very happy man. I did the dirty work and he gets paid for not doing his job for me. Oh, well. The way it works, Amy, he said.

Over and out for now.

Bye,
Love, Amy

*   *   *

"I talked with Amy's lawyer, Colin Pascoe, about a deal before the trial even began," Shaw said in an interview. "I would pay the lawyer her remaining legal charges from the first dollar earned by the book, first dollar after my agent gets her 15 percent. What I got in return was exclusive rights to her story, interviews only with me and a way to communicate with her no matter where she was. And I had my

287

lawyer review her lawyer's billable hours and Pascoe and I have come to an agreement on that."

Pascoe leaped at the chance to recoup at least some of the costs of representing her. Pascoe told Amy that she should make the deal with Shaw.

"Why should I?" she asked Pascoe.

"You owe me a lot of money, Amy."

"What do I get?" Amy wanted to know.

"You get to be famous, maybe even a movie, probably a movie for TV and that would be great. Here's why you get none of the money: a guy named Son of Sam. He butchered several women in New York City, remember?

"OK, but then a reporter sold the Son of Sam book proposal to a publisher for huge dollars, and there was outrage that a sadistic murderer could profit from his crime. So before he could, New York passed a law that a convicted felon cannot get a dime from his or her story. Most other states copied it."

"But you can profit, as the lawyer who defended a convicted murderer," she said. "As the lawyer who got me a bad deal, obviously. The law was written that way by...what a surprise! Lawyers!"

"The way it works, Amy," Pascoe said. "Sign here."

Sunday Feb. 13
Dear Diary & Paul,

I hate this place. It is disgusting. I hate being treated like a child, being degraded, being told when to eat, sleep or be sick. I don't trust those officers who strip search us, make us squat and cough and look into our ears and nose. My mother and the nuns taught us modesty and I am not supposed to take my clothes off in front of other people.

I don't want to go on. Now I'm beginning my 3rd year at women's correctional and I don't feel correct yet. Just what are they supposed to correct in here?

There's a whole big world out there and I'm scared of it. Nobody is real. People know other people but nobody can be just one big family. People are so different. How come other people have friends?

I like to watch TV. I can turn it up loud so I just concentrate solely on it and I can block out everything around me. I don't like people around me when I watch TV. They make too much noise. Why don't people like me?"

Bye.

Love, Amy

Most of what Larry and his lawyer had said to the jury had been true, Amy wrote in her diary. She would have to think long and hard about letting Shaw know what she was about to write. She wouldn't use the tape recorder for this yet.

Larry never intended to marry me, she told her diary. I was just in denial about it. He did say he could not marry anyone unless Felicia was dead. That had been enough of a tease for me that I was willing to give it a shot. Or a stab. (Ha Ha).

The reason I couldn't produce the diamond pre-engagement ring at his trial is that there never was a ring. Larry told the truth.

Larry's shock and panic were real, dear diary. This diary has a strong lock

Not strong enough to keep the Mom army out, Amy

289

Linda Ellis

Larry had <u>not</u> bought the knife that I used to stab her. The pathologist who testified for the defense had it right: it was a double-edged knife that I bought in New York. Moore Goodwin was with me. Moore's probably terrified of me. Good.

Larry never told me that Felicia would blackmail him if he asked for a divorce because he never told me about the arson or the Democratic Club money. He was telling the truth about that too. No one believed him, poor pathetic Larry. I found out about those two things from the girls I coached in basketball. Half the town knows.

Larry is pretty simple – he never understood how devious I am and that I am so much smarter than he is. He never saw past his cock. Men usually don't.

Sunday Mar. 20
Dear Diary & Paul,

I'm special. I was put on this earth for one reason but I haven't been told why yet. I'm still waiting. I'm so confused. I want to yell and scream and hit and punch, but I'm holding it back. I don't want to be put by myself here in jail.

Nobody can help me because I don't know who to call. It's Friday night and people are out. Lately my heart has been beating real loud and fast and I have been having trouble breathing. People are punishing me for being different.

Someone should have seen how sick I was. Gary (Prentice) told me to get help but I was too scared...I like Kevin but he's too busy right now. He doesn't come visit me anymore. Bryan came to see me. He couldn't stay too long. I wish he did. I like to talk to

290

Bryan. He listens. He doesn't say what I say is stupid. My dad always did. I wish Kevin or Bryan was here. Why do they have to leave me? I feel safe when I'm with them. The other girls laugh at me 'cuz I love to read.

Love, Amy

Sunday April 7

"Hi Amy. It's Paul. How ya doin'?

"Listen, Amy. I have a question... I know there's static but I'm on my cell phone here and that happens...Listen, Amy, is there anything in particular you wish you had done before you were arrested? Something that might seem insignificant but gnaws at you?"

"I think about it a lot. I'd like to be wired again and then I could fuck Larry's brains out and we could get the noises on the wire. That would show everybody, especially Kevin, how good I am at fucking. It would make Bryan and Kevin want to fuck me. I'd like that. I'm so mad I didn't think of this sooner because I could have had anything I wanted that day.

"Paul?"

"Yeah?"

"How's the book going?"

"It just got a little better, Amy. Thanks. Bye."

Sunday April 14
Dear Diary & Paul,

I don't want to be a big girl anymore. I want to swing and play with toys and sit on Kevin or Bryan or Chief Lou's lap and be held. I like Chief Lou. He likes me. I wish he were my daddy. He'd protect me from the bogeyman.

I like TV. I like cop shows. I wish I were a cop. I always wanted to be a cop. Cops are safe. Nobody is helping to put the puzzle pieces back together that are in my head. I've been trying for a long, long time to do it. But I haven't succeeded and now I'm having trouble finding all the pieces. It's amazing the cops I hung around never figured I needed help.

I always went to the doctor because I was sick – but I was not physically sick. You know I did go to the psychiatrist. I only went once or twice. I feel like I'm going to have a heart attack. I'm tired all the time. I can't think straight. . I slept till 10:30 this morning. Somebody stole a brand-new pair of tube socks from my cell while I was sleeping this morning. Somebody stole my shower slippers one day from the processing room. The jail won't replace any of the stuff that is stolen. I think that stinks!

I'd rather go to a hospital. . I have to get a proper diet. My body is swollen again from the starch turning to sugar. My body is all jittery. I wish Dr. Conte would come to see me today. I don't want to call anybody. I don't want people mad at me.

Why can't I be protected so I can read in peace? Cartoons are on but I can't concentrate on them. Marion Bay and Shelley Winston came to see me today. I can't believe how pretty Shelley is. They both got so big. I haven't gotten any older and one day they are just going to pass me by age-wise.

I told Shelley to tell her dad to keep the Sunday papers coming and the magazines are great too. I begged Marion to get help and quick. She has always been a troubled kid and I've always tried to help her. (!)

They know it's not my fault. Why don't they let me go? I'm not a bad kid but if I stay in here too long I'll probably go bad. Jails are for bad people.

I'd probably move to Texas or some place far from here and then I wouldn't talk or write to anyone back here. Maybe I'll write to Kevin and Bryan and my Mom of course and the Corrigans but that's it. But I can't take a chance to write to anybody because the Girardis would find me so fast!

Love, Amy

May 18
Dear Diary and Paul,

I want to eat a lot of candy but I'm trying not to do that. You asked me about the food in here. Sugar makes me sicker. Food is very important to me because when I do get out the things I ate for seventeen years will show in my body and my mind.

With sugar, I go crazy inside my head. I've had to eat white bread for the past two days because the food was sandwich-type. I don't like to eat sugar. I crave it more and more. I could eat hundreds of candy bars right now. I want sugar so much.

I was a bad girl at dinner. I ate chocolate pudding. Boy will I pay for that. Yuck. But it was real good so I treated my taste buds. We had chicken a la king tonight. It was OK. I hope my body doesn't start to shake. But I'm probably close to a sugar overdose. I hate when that happens. Withdrawal is painful. I crave sugar badly. I'll have to cut out the bread again

293

and go through withdrawal again. Why can't they feed me the right food?

Why can't I get food that doesn't hurt me? Even though I wrote my doctor and asked him to send me a special diet everyone says they won't follow it. I'm hungry. Three days of bread and I'm going nuts. My heart is racing so much. But I'm still sleepy too. Is somebody drugging me?

Love, Amy

"Amy, phone for you. It's that writer."

"Amy, hi. Can we talk some?

"How you feeling?"

"Scared, Paul. I'm afraid in here but I am much more scared of what waits outside for me. People can get to me here, they might hurt me but I don't think I would die in here the way Larry did in his jail. They watch us much more because of the babies. The inmates with babies get to have them in here for visits so there are just always guards around us. If anything happened to those babies people would lose their jobs.

"I'm scared of her brothers, especially Joey. I know he's going to have me hurt. I'm scared of John, of course. He was his mommy's boy. I don't know about Grace as far as being afraid. I've talked to Dottie [Miller, Grace's best friend) and she said Grace would not talk about any of it, that she has not even begun to heal. Please don't let them hurt me."

"The book being out there soon, it'll help keep you safe. Once stuff is out there, people get cautious."

June 28
Dear Diary and Paul:

TV is where the lines get drawn in the sand in jail. It's huge. TV is so important in here. Where you get to watch and who chooses what shows are big deals. Maureen and Delia had their mats on the floor to watch TV. They put them out first thing in the morning. Nobody but Karla can sit on her mat. And I'm not allowed to sit on Tracy's but Maureen is. Luca and Debbie are TV buddies, they share a mat. Maureen and Delia were in arts and crafts. I moved Karla's mat back and put mine in her spot. It's now 9:00 and part. 2 of *Quincy* is on. That's what I wanted to watch, Paul. Is that asking so much?

I guess so. I saw part 1. All I wanted all that day was to see pt 2 of that *Quincy.* Maureen and Delia wanted to watch the movie *Lucky Lady.* Tracy comes back and sides with them. All three are now sitting on <u>my</u> mat. They turn the channel to watch the movie. Now Dianne comes back. Carol tells her to come watch TV and tells me I have to move my towel. The others are on my mat. This place sucks.

I feel I'm destined to be nobody going nowhere. What type of life will I have with a record? I'll never be able to get a good job. Who will marry me? No one will love me.

Thinking about TV makes me wonder about Pete O'Neal. Did he get married? He was a big star in the NFL, running back with the Packers. When I dated him he was at Fordham playing football. It's the only time I was a sports groupie. I wish I could do it over, what happened there.

Linda Ellis

Sunday July 3
Dear Diary & Paul,

I want to break stuff and hit people really fucking hard. Fucking hard. Ok! I'm ready to kick out the window and run. I don't care if they shoot me. No one steals from Diane or anyone else. Death has got to be better than this! When I was a teen my family and I had our worst fights when I couldn't watch what I wanted on TV. We had a few TVs but we could only watch one. I hate it when there is something on TV that I want to watch and I can't.

Someone sent me an audiotape as a gift; it's a bunch of hymns, with no name on the package, no name on the card. Just from a friend. I like this. So of course the guard nearly ruined it by checking the tape to see if I could do harm with it. Right, like I'm going to make a bomb out of it. Well, they will only let me listen under supervision because Wanda explained that an inmate unrolled the tape once and...well I don't want to think about it.

It's *When I Walked In the Garden* and *Stand Up! Stand Up! for Jesus* and one of my favorites *Amazing Grace*. In that movie with Sally Fields, I think it was Sally Fields, where she was fighting to get a union at her work and then someone killed her. Anyway, the song *Amazing Grace* went all through the movie. You don't think Grace, the Grace that's Larry's daughter, sent me the tape do you? Is it going to explode? Well, that would at least not be boring.

There really is a mouse in here. Not the mouse I have with my laptop either. I saw it tonight. They won't put mousetraps in here either. That's bullshit. It's unhealthy to have mice running around.

296

"Hi, Amy. How's it goin?"

"Hey, Paul. OK. Becoming a short-timer in here."

"If you could have had solitary, would you have preferred that all these years?"

"You bet. See, if I could have, I would have lived in the hospital wing. I don't mind keeping to myself and as long as I do I should have my own TV. I'd rather stay locked up alone, even in my cell, with a 19-inch color TV. They could serve my food to me in here and let me out once a day to bathe. I could have all my books in order, lined up with no one to mess them up."

Sunday August 30
Dear Diary & Paul,

If my Mom forgets to bring toothbrushes, I have to buy them from the commissary and they're too soft. My teeth are going to rot. Why can't I go to the hospital where I can have my own things and a place to lock them up...I'd like to have a key to my cell from 6 a.m. to 11 p.m. so I can come and go as I please without having stuff stolen.

Loraine complains because most of the time I'm first on line for lunch and supper and if all I do is complain about the food what am I doing in line. Well, I don't complain anymore and there are some things I'll eat!! Fuck her!!! I can't handle much more.

Linda Ellis

Monday August 31
Dear Diary and Paul,

Those two-faced cops I had loved so much, Kevin and Bryan and Luke, deserted me the minute I testified against Larry. I would not miss them. What bastards. Don't even think about it, about getting back at them. Concentrate on staying alive.

Speaking of staying alive I heard that Carmen Girardi, Felicia's father, is completely disabled by a massive stroke. Two of the surviving nine sisters are no longer surviving: Christine Girardi Potter in a car accident and Sherry Girardi Donato of bone cancer.

However, Maria's husband, the FBI agent? I learned he comes from a very rich family. He could track me down when I get my freedom. He'd have the money and Maria would have the time. I don't think Maria wants to be that closely associated with the Girardis, though. She's above them now.

I have no illusions about the danger I face. The biggest danger is from Joey Girardi. Joey's connected. He belongs to two families, so to speak, and neither family forgets grudges.

Bye for now.
Love, Amy

Sunday October 14
Dear Diary & Paul

I'd like to leave a few men on this earth and then get rid of everybody else. I'd just like somebody to take care of me. My parents said I always wanted to be an only child!

298

I think I should have a hysterectomy. I used to like kids – now I hate them. I used to want a lot of kids, now I'd like to have everything taken out. Gary (ob-gyn) wouldn't do it for me, though. He said it was unnecessary surgery!

Sometimes, tho, I like kids. Sometimes I want them. When Larry loved me, I wanted kids. Now I don't want to be loved by anybody.

Whenever I get really angry I feel as though I get this superhuman strength. It's scary.

I'm glad I have some control over not getting violent.

Love, Amy

In two years, she would be free from this physical space but would also be vulnerable to the Girardis. With her expanding pool of funds, Amy began to think of ways to protect herself.

"Amy. Amy! Wake up now. This is it, your big day. You're going to be released right after breakfast. Your Mom called. She can't get here to take you home but she's sent a friend, a woman whose name is, can't remember, but it's like the name of a country.."

"Noooooo...Not Andorra, not Felicia's sister Andorra..."

"Hello, Amy Lee. You don't know me, but..."

"You're not Andorra," Amy heard herself saying, as though she were in a dream or down at the bottom of a well. "You're not Felicia's sister. Who are you? You must be Andorra's daughter, your mom's the one who moved back to New Jersey so she could be nearer Felicia...My mother wouldn't have sent you. Go away! Guard! Help!"

Linda Ellis

She peered out the bars of the cell and could see no one. The walkways were deserted. There was no one to help her.

"Why, no, Amy. I'm not Andorra although of course I remember her. The family called her Andy. She's not with us anymore.I really am a good friend of Grace's. She asked me to assess your situation, find out your plans, where you'll be dying...I mean *living* now that you're out. It is interesting to see you after all these years, 17 years, my goodness. You've remained quite fit and healthy despite your....incarceration. Of course, I've only seen pictures of you. John has a lot of pictures of you.

"Please excuse my bad manners. I didn't even introduce myself. "I'm Erin. I'm John's wife."

"Oh no Amy screamed to the inside of her head. Oh sweet Jesus, she must have some kind of concealed weapon. John was Felicia's favorite. He hates me so much. This woman is here to kill me and I was sure it would be Joey Girardi."

"Hey Amy!" She heard Loraine's voice in the distance.

"Wake up and quit yelling you've got us all awake here you stupid bitch!"

She woke up. Still in jail. Still safe.

Dear Diary & Paul

In nursery school, we got picked up in a van. We had to take naps. Nobody liked me. Nobody liked me in kindergarten or 1st grade either.

In 5th grade I got in trouble for pulling at the front of the boys' pants.

300

High school was awful. 9th grade everybody found out I wasn't a virgin anymore. Guys wanted to date me just for a piece of ass. If I gave it to them they never called back. If I didn't they still never called back. You figure it out. I've stopped trying.

I hope the diabetics get peanut butter and jelly sandwiches tonight because I get Carol's. I only eat the peanut butter'd piece and I give the jelly part to Tracy.

I wish I could have dental floss. Why can't I have my things? The only thing I would hurt myself with would be a gun. I have always wanted to shoot my tummy – just to see what it feels like. I fell on my head a couple of years ago. I was doing a round-off back handspring and I did a round-off ½ semi. The reasons I had all those car and other accidents are because I was mad and wanted to get really hurt or even die.

Snacks should be up soon. It's 11 o'clock. They usually come up around 10:30. Only pregnant people and diabetics get snacks. Oh, I forgot to tell you. Tracy mops my cell for a bag of 25-cent potato chips. I have a maid. Hee hee hee.

It was salami and cheese. Carole gave me ½ of hers. She usually eats everything but pb & jelly. Why she gave me ½ I don't know. But I ate it anyway.

Good morning Diary & Paul,

I told her [the guard) to lock my cell this morning so nothing was stolen. It's my last day here, one more night, so I swept and mopped my floor today and dusted. I gave the maid the day off.

I'm going to read all day today. When I leave tomorrow I'll have to start supporting myself again and won't have all this time to read.

You know I was thinking about joining the Army but they'd find out my real age and I'd be too old. Of course, there would be a few stipulations like I could go see Gary (her ob-gyn) whenever I deemed necessary. The proper diet. Then I'll join. Or maybe I'll become a porno star. That might be fun. But again, it would have to be on my terms.

I think the Army would have been a better choice as far as having a future.

We had a good dinner. Ziti and peaches. Believe it or not the ziti was good. Maybe because it's my last dinner here.

Bye for now,
Bye forever,

Love, Amy

       *   *   *

She'd made it.

She was Brielle Benson.

Tomorrow she had a job interview at the SilverLode Casino. She had financial independence and she had her looks. Not a soul on earth knew where she was.

Her mother, thanks to e-mail, would know her daughter had made it to anonymity alive. Amy hoped that when she had children she would be a good mother and stick by her kids no matter what. Her mother had been there for her nearly every day of the past 17 years, by phone if not in person. So she was here. Free to live but also free to die.

Felicia's family and the private detective they had hired would hurt Helen Halford if they thought she knew Amy's whereabouts. That would be unthinkable. Amy didn't dare contact her in any way other than on-line.

* * *

Las Vegas got a bad rap, she decided, after doing months of research on the best places in America to be someone else.

Yeah, it looked honky tonk on the main thoroughfares but away from the casinos it was fine. It was safe. She had never seen so many cops and the casinos had armies of private security.

What Amy didn't comprehend, the prison psychologist said later, was the force of the hatred that had festered while she was behind prison walls, a force that was sending out exploratory tentacles, twitching its way toward knowledge.

She took the job at SilverLode, dealing blackjack, enjoying the atmosphere of money and risk. The patrons were well dressed and well behaved and the work itself was easy. She just had to bide her time until the right man came along.

"Brielle, hey, dinner time...
"What's there, Jason, anything good?"
"Yeah, there's a hot corned beef and Swiss on rye, that deli on the corner that makes New York style corned beef, they sent over some sandwiches. I know you like that. Here, take it in the cafeteria and relax for a while. You look a little tired."

* * *

How did Pete find her? Judge Kevin Glanville, Superior Court, Harbor County, NJ asked John and Erin Cusack, who were visiting from London. John Cusack was an investment banker on a two-year assignment abroad.

Glanville, who owed his judgeship to a 3 a.m. phone call 18 years ago from Amy Halford, had followed Amy's life. She had made him a star. She had also made him a man who feared he might have put his family in harm's way.

A movie called *Fatal Attraction* a few years back had made many former friends of Amy Lee Halford more than a little nervous.

"Through her e-mail address, which Pete learned purely by accident. Paul Shaw's wife, Pamela, and Pete's wife, June, e-mail each other via a chat room for women who like to do crewel embroidery, which is especially ironic because that was my mother's hobby," John said. "Sometimes there are general information e-mails and they get forwarded to a long list of e-mail addresses, of people who are in the chat rooms.

"Pete's wife June answered a question that Shaw's wife, Pamela, posted to the group. So June wrote a personal note to Pamela's e-mail address. They became on-line chatters about embroidery, sewing. When e-mails are sent around, when things are forwarded to a list of that person's personal addresses, the addresses are out there.

Three months ago, John continued, Pete saw an e-mail address on one of the forwards that nagged at him for days. He knew Shaw had done a book on the Cusack murder. He focused on this strange e-mail address. He told me that when he got it, his skin actually got cold and clammy and he had goosebumps. He saw this (John wrote it down for Glanville and the others) and then Paul got it all: biteback@delist.net.

*　　*　　*

If you bite me I'll bite you back, she would say in foreplay.

She had an addiction to deli sandwiches when he knew her and she liked the corned beef at the deli on River Street in Hoboken. biteback@delist.net [deli st.] Clever Amy. Not clever enough. Screwed so many of us you forgot which inside joke went with which guy, didn't you?

Well Amy/brielle/deli st/ you'll never see river streetagain, Pete O'Neal said to the inside of his head.

Got her, got her at last the evil bitch. She killed my baby.

Mutual friends had set them up back in the early 80s. He was sowing wild oats at Fordham and she was living in Hoboken and just wanted to have fun. They'd seen a lot of each other. She would come to the games. Then there'd be games after the games where she knew the playbook better than he did.

He paid the full charge for the abortion. She had found it strange that a football player, such a big guy, would cry like that when he gave her the cash. He said now they both had blood on their hands.

He had begged her to have the baby. He would take care of an adoption. He would pay for all the hospital costs. He would find her another job when she was ready.

Please, Amy. Don't kill my baby.

She said she had to stay in school and then get a good secretarial job. She couldn't do that if she had to carry the baby to full term and then give birth. She would have to skip a lot of classes and tell the school why. Besides she was involved now with another man, a married man.

O'Neal found a computer expert and gave him the e-mail address. The expert, using internet-protocol numbers, tracked Amy's physical location, or rather the computer's location, in five hours. By using her computer from home instead of at a more remote location, Amy had made it easier for Pete to find her and begin to plan their reunion. The private detective got him all the information he needed.

*   *   *

Amy/Brielle was feeling better but the gastroenterologist here at All Saints Hospital in downtown Las Vegas had said she had had a wicked bout with food poisoning and she'd be in the hospital overnight. Like everything else in Vegas, the hospital was luxurious. She had a single room and a view of the mountains in the distance.

He had been fairly certain that it was only food poisoning but thought he would run some tests tomorrow.

There were even a few nuns here, nursing sisters they were called when she was a little girl. That's something you didn't see a lot anymore. I guess everyone wants to live in Vegas, Amy Brielle mused. Even nuns like it here.

306

Priests around to give last rites. Good place to die if you're Catholic. Here's a priest coming in the room; I didn't think I was **that** sick.

"Hi, father. Am I that sick?" she smiled.

He's drawing the curtain around my bed. Am I supposed to do a confession here? That would make his day! I've never done it with a priest.

"Hello, Amy – or Brielle as you call yourself now. You're sicker than you would ever imagine. You may not remember me but you killed my baby. I'm putting duct tape over your mouth because I don't want to be interrupted here. Duct tape is amazing stuff, you know? When we're done here I'll just peel it off and no one will be the wiser.

"I told the very nice nurse out there that we would not want to be disturbed for awhile," he said, wrapping her hands and feet in restraints.

"I hope you enjoyed the corned beef sandwich the other night - I remembered how much you liked that deli on River Street in Hoboken and especially the corned beef so I made sure that sandwich got to you all the way from Hoboken, New Jersey, birthplace of Frank Sinatra. I told the kid at the SilverLode it was a surprise [*foodpoisoning*) from an old friend and slipped him $100 to keep the secret.

Amy, are you feeling pain now?Does it feel like "stabs" of pain?

"Now, Amy, pay attention. The pain that's coming will make it even harder for you to sort out which baby was mine," O'Neal said, "but I know. I know his soul is in heaven and yours is about to go to hell."

307

Recognition dawned in Amy's eyes, widened in terror.

"I see you remember. Pete O'Neal. That's right. Fordham. Blind date. You were asking for it and even though I was a good Catholic boy, I was ready to give it to you. You were damned good, yes you were. So good that I didn't want to interrupt the flow with something as tacky as a rubber."

A hypodermic needle was prickling her arm before she could move. She could only scream to the inside of her head because the duct tape covered her mouth. The pain hit her like a jackhammer and was a gift that just kept on giving.

"I see your pupils are contracting and the first spasms will be along any minute. They'll last a good while. They'll blindside you. Labor pains are different, *I NEVERHAD THOSE she screamed to the insideofherhead* you know they're coming. These won't be as predictable," Pete explained to her wide eyes and writhing body.

"I had a great career in the NFL; you know about that because you've bragged that you'd been fucked by a Pro Bowl wide receiver. I've followed your career as well. I would have had a great family too, Amy, but you took care of that. All these years, a great wife, all the money in the world to raise great kids, big house for the kids to grow up in, big property, big Lab named Amazing Grace, a kid kind of dog

Amazing Grace please save a wretch like me she screamed behind the tapeand to the insideofherhead

but I can't produce kids, Amy. I've been shooting blanks all these years. My wife, God bless her, had stuck with me through it all. Tried to talk me into adoption but that's like coming in second in your division, you know? So I'm losing her, losing my wife because she wants children before her clock stops ticking. Who can blame her? I've lost my faith too, Amy. All the Hail Marys and fertility specialists that money can buy have not produced kids for me. God fumbled. All I have left is my dog, my Amazing Grace, *how sweet the sound.*

"There is more than one victim from your days of fun in the sun, Amy. How you feelin' there, girl? *Flesh and heart, please fail, please* It won't be too long now. My son was a victim just as much as Felicia Cusack, God rest her soul too. My soon-to-be-ex-wife is a victim.

"I begged you to carry little Pete to term and give him to me or give him up for adoption. Do you remember? *I REMEMBER I REMEMBER SWEETBLEEDINGJESUS PLEASE STOP WAS BLIND BUTNOW I SEE she screamedinside the tape.duct tape, has1001 uses.*

"My folks would have cared for him until I was married. You were nearly six months pregnant; it would have been only three more months out of your pathetic excuse for a life and *he* would have had life. I committed a mortal sin by getting you pregnant and I confessed it many times but your sin, Amy, was cosmic.

"I only wish you could die the way my son died: scraped, vacuumed, your skull collapsed and your brains sucked out. We have to settle for something less grotesque but as you can tell, I am drawing out your pain as long as possible. I've talked to a lot of sports docs over the years about pain. Pain facts are filed away in my Amy file. Some things make pain last longer than others. As you now know."

Foam bubbled around the edges of the tape on her mouth. Her body arched in agony.

In about the time it used to take O'Neal to snap on his helmet, target his brain to the right page in the playbook, catch the spiral coming down right into his arms from the cold and cloudless Green Bay sky, run a broken field for six, and then leap into those Lambeau arms, Amy Lee Halford died.

R.I.P Amy. "P" for purgatory . Don't leave the light on for me..Two down, none to go.

Characters

Leading roles
21-year-old girlfriend	Amy Lee Halford
43-year-old philanderer	Lawrence Andrew "Larry" Cusack Jr.

Victim and her family
Wife/mother/victim	Felicia Girardi Cusack
Son	John Lawrence Cusack
Daughter	Grace Marilyn Cusack
Father	Carmen Girardi
Brothers	Carmen Girardi Jr., Mario Girardi, Joseph "Joey" Girardi
Sisters	Andorra "Andy" Slayton, Victoria "Vicki" Quatraro
Sisters	Sherry Donato, Deborah Ferraro, Maria Holley
Sisters	Geraldine "Gerry" Bucci, Josephine Cooper
Sisters	Christine Potter, Elizabeth Girardi

Husband and his family
Husband	Lawrence Andrew "Larry" Cusack Jr.
Mother	Gladys Cusack
Sister	Dolores Cunningham
Brother	John "Jake" Cusack

Cusack family friends/associates
Dottie Miller	Jeff & Jenny Russo	Simon Brossell
Cindy Glenn	Joe Maloney	Evan Marshall
Julia Miller	Dania Sher	Denyce Buckley
Eddie Cicotte	Stu Vosberg	Brian Downing

Mark Buckley   Andrea Downing   Steve Gagne
Julian Buckley   Joe Pulaski   Tony Giglio
Cal Winters   Martha Fullerton   Julianna Greer
Ted Cruise   Megan Tolliver
Phyllis Emmerman
               Gloria Loomis

Hospital/Medical
Joseph Simmons M.D.
Rouchdi Rifai M.D.
Bonita Nelson, switchboard operator
Jennifer Chapman, switchboard operator
Earl Averill, security guard
Gary Prentice M.D.
Kevin C. Pearson M.D.
Matthew R. Donohue M.D.
Stanley Conte M.D.
John Morrill M. D.
John Lando M.D.
Michael Burling M.D.
Mark Hawkins M.D.

Law Enforcement
Prosecutor's Office (PO):
Glenn Beatty, county prosecutor
Greg Brocail, 1st assistant PO
Steve Balterri, chief trial lawyer PO
Leland Halliday, chief of detectives PO
Bryan Carlyle, detective, PO
Kevin Glanville, detective, PO
Omar Rodriguez, detective, PO
Bonnie Boudreau, investigator, PO
Carl Hayden, photographer, PO
Cy Blandon, surveillance, PO

David Manning, Gullwing Cove patrolman
Mike Morland, Barrington PD
Carl Lazerie, Hoboken PD
Gillian O'Donnell, judge, NJ Superior Court
Peter Johns, Boothbay Police Department
Luke Weathers Boothbay PD
Tim Hudson, Boothbay PD
Larry Dolan, Boothbay PD
Neal Siegel, Boothbay PD
John Marzano, Boothbay PD
Jim Whitney, Boothbay PD
Fred Tenney, Boothbay PD
Peter Agnostelli, Boothbay PD
John Fargo, PO staff

At Dublin (restaurant)

Ann Padgett	Jeff Padgett
Dan Padgett	Patricia Cirrino
Juan Gonzalez	Phil DeVito

At Atlantic City

Andrew Kepler
Barbara Kepler
Nancy Hackman & Constance Ramy
Hakim Hassan Abdul
Mike Ferraro

Publications

The Coastal Call   The Weekly Times   The Register

Arson-related

James G. Kobritz
Andy Newlin

Church
Fr. Ed Nitkowski/St Mary's parish
Fr. James Doyle/St. Genevieve's parish

Witnesses
Reggie Cleveland
Nate Cromwell
Rhonda Malone
Grace Brown

Amy's roommates in Manhattan
Mimi Goldberg
Alice Chilton

Amy's male friends of significance
Moore Goodwin
Peter O'Neal
Frank DiMarco
Paul Shaw

Suspects
Dennis Bottalico
Chris Rolf
Eugene Brower
Tom Rolf, suspect's father
John Tallant
Rob Steinem
Perry Clayton
Tony Castillo

If you found Linda Ellis' **Death at a Dumpster** absorbing, you won't want to miss her next look at the seamy side of life – only this time the seam is on a fastball thrown by Randy Johnson and the theme is the abiding love of Jesus Christ.

Turn the page for an intriguing preview of

Passion Play: The Rising Fastball of Christianity in Baseball

By Linda Ellis

"Therefore since we are surrounded by such a great cloud of witnesses, let us throw off everything that hinders and the sin that so easily entangles, and let us run with perseverance the race marked out for us." Hebrews 12: 1,2. (New International Version)

Chapter 1

Covenant
Throw the Ball, Hit the Ball, Catch the Ball

John Smoltz, Andy Pettitte, John Wetteland, Kevin Seitzer, Gary Gaetti, Walt Weiss, Terry Pendleton, Todd Hollandsworth, Greg Gagne and a cast of hundreds in major league baseball believe that Jesus Christ died for their sins.

They want you to believe that as well.

They have, in many cases, lived their own gutter-to-glory stories.

Some were really bad boys before faith transformed their lives.

They carry testimonial cards describing how they came to Christ and when asked for an autograph, the card is handed over as well. They are walking the walk, not just taking the talk.

Cy Young award-winner Randy Johnson of the scary sinking fastball stares down the long barrel of an opposing bat and remembers promises made and kept.

"He promised He would come into our lives in, *Revelations 3:20*," Johnson said. "Our Lord said, 'I will stand at the door, and knock: if any man hear my voice, and open the door, I will come in to him and will sup with him and he with me'."

Before Johnson makes that first pitch, his eyes burning, hair flying, unfolding a body that appears to have the wingspan of a 747, he says this to himself:

"Lord Jesus, I need You. Thank You for dying on the cross for my sins. I open the door of my life and receive You as my Savior and Lord. Thank You for forgiving my sins and giving me eternal life. Take control of my life. Make me the kind of person You want me to be."

Johnson visits prisoners during the off-season, a witness that he feels is the most effective use of his celebrity status in the matter of bringing souls to Christ, in shrinking the number of souls who will be left behind at Armageddon.

"They will not be left behind," declares the fireballer, "and I don't want you to be left behind." Where do you want to spend eternity?"

"The film *Star Wars* says you have the Force, you have the power and you can win over evil," said John Wood, who teaches a course in Christianity in Film at Baylor University in Waco TX. "That's the message celebrities can bring especially well."

Anthony Telford distributed several translations of the Holy Bible at scripture study class at the home of coach Jerry Narron in early August 1992. Telford's own Bible is well thumbed and well marked and very well used. He begins each day with biblical passages; he ends the day with prayer.

In the 2001 season, he is still joyfully following his Lord and his baseball career wherever they take him and his family.

Telford is a middle reliever in the bullpen of the Montreal Expos.

Thirteen years before, the righthander was facing an uncertain future. His life was moving on a straight line into oblivion, his throwing arm damaged, his anger overwhelming.

"Girl, you would not have wanted to know me then," Telford declared. "I threw Gatorade tubs in the dugout. I had a vicious temper, punched walls, trashed clubhouses, cussed, went with women. There's nothing I haven't done.

"He knew that," Telford said, pointing skyward. "He died for those sins. He died for me. I didn't know that then."

It was at that low point that converging forces set him on the path to eternal salvation. Now he walks with Jesus Christ every moment, every pitch, every victory and every defeat.

From a pitching standpoint, 1988 was easily the worst of Telford's career. He was in the Baltimore Orioles' system and made only one appearance, winning the season opener for Class-A Hagerstown. He was felled that night by a shoulder problem and was out for the season.

"It was a test of faith I didn't have yet. It was rough. I had surgery and went back to work, to pitching but I was running on empty."

Something was missing. Something was wrong.

"Then late in the '89 season I was in Frederick (MD) and I went along to baseball chapel with Pat Kelly)the former Baltimore outfielder). And it was there in baseball chapel that I was saved. Then everything fell into place, blessing after blessing. I married an angel, literally, in Christine. We walk with the Lord together and forever. Jesus died on the cross to pay for my sins and he loves you so much He died for you too."

There is the dark side.

When athletes who have professed their faith fall from grace, the fall hard and they fall in living color. The press mimics a pack of wolves, ripping the flesh off the fallen hero. Ask Darryl Strawberry, so riddled with cancer that he wants to die but at the same time terrified that he is damned to spend eternity in hell.

Darryl needed to grab onto first principles, his hometown pastor in Tampa said. Darryl knows we are saved not by deeds but by grace. Darryl will not be left behind, the pastor said.

"Once a week we have baseball chapel and we thank God for that time together," said Andy Pettitte, a pitcher in the Yankees' starting rotations. "We ask Him to bless us and permit us to glorify Him on the ballfield."

"Believers give us people we can count on emotionally and mentally," Yankees manager Joe Torre told ESPN in 1998. "We know they're going to be there for us, for the team, and we know that they're going to be responsible. There are so many challenges off the field for players at all levels that it is such a relief for a manager knowing that the guys who come to chapel are not going to be problems on the field or off."

Printed in the United States
5164